NO MATTER HOW IMPROBABLE

FIERCE
INK
BOOKS

NO MATTER HOW IMPROBABLE

ANGELA MISRI

A PORTIA ADAMS ADVENTURE

CANADA | est. 2012

No Matter How Improbable
Copyright © 2016 by Angela Miisri
All rights reserved

Published by Fierce Ink Books Co-Op Ltd.
www.fierceinkbooks.com

First edition, 2016

Library and Archives Canada Cataloguing in Publication information is available upon request.

ISBN 978-1-927746-72-1 (paperback)
Also available in electronic format

Edited by Allister Thompson
Cover design by Emma Dolan

The text type was set in Baskerville Old Face.

For Jaya

CASEBOOK SEVEN PRINCIPESSA

CHAPTER ONE

LONDON, SUMMER 1931

The knock at my front door made me flinch. Nerissa reacted as well, her keen bloodhound ears twitching, but her other senses must have given her more information, because by the time I had risen to answer the knock, she had returned to the scraps of leather that previously held her attention.

I peeked through the spyhole and relaxed as well, recognizing Annie Coleson's bright blonde halo of hair.

"Annie," I said, opening the door to my friend. "Sorry for the hesitation. I thought it might have been one of your more persistent peers."

She laughed prettily, peeling off her gloves as she came in. Her entire ensemble was in shades of yellow, from the buttery color of her skirt to the light tan of her gloves. Nothing was from this season and all looked well worn, but somehow Annie always managed to look perfect. "Not another fearsome reporter in sight! Did I not tell you, Portia? I knew they would drop off after a few weeks."

"Well, they haven't 'dropped off' quite as quickly as that ... I still had Mr. Bill Rull knocking incessantly at my door as recently as two days ago," I answered, gesturing with annoyance at my ajar door. "And those two photographers from the *South London Press* follow me all over the city, snapping photos with anyone I stop and speak to, from homeless truant to tailor."

The kettle beckoned with its shrill whistle, so I turned that way, continuing my complaint. "And that is not even accounting for the random Londoners who seem compelled to stop by and satisfy their curiosity about a woman 'acting' like a detective. Most pretend to have a case for me, but not a few have come in with no purpose at all except to stare at the oddity I have become. I would be thankful for the return to quiet, my tea notwithstanding."

"I'm sorry, Portia, but at least most of the attention has been positive," she replied as she dropped into one of the comfortable wingback chairs in front of the unlit fireplace. "Only a few of the papers have written negative comments. Most are quite taken with the idea of a female detective."

"*The Post* called me a freak of nature," I reminded her, replacing the teapot's lid over its steeping contents.

"They *compared* you with a freak of nature," Annie corrected with a scrunch of her button nose, as she often did when she was arguing. "I believe they compared you with a sheep who has learned to walk on its hind paws, did they not?"

I grimaced, and she said, "Everyone else wrote the predictable background story about Dr. John Watson and his passing of this townhouse to you, his previously unknown granddaughter. And nearly everyone remarked on the fact that you were a great beauty and an up-and-coming socialite. Well, everyone except me, of course."

I couldn't help but smile at her cheeky grin. Her story about the various cases I'd had a hand in graced page A2 of *The Sunday Times* and had brought her considerable attention from both her editors and the paper's owner. Of course, she had the advantage of being the best friend of the main subject of the piece, but regardless, I did not resent her acclaim.

"And then there were a pair of interviews with your schoolmates in the ladies' society section of *The Free Press*," she continued, her grin widening as she crossed her ankles, the heels of her pumps looking very worn at the edges. These were used shoes, I would guess, worn by a much heavier woman before my friend had come into possession of them.

"How did I come off?" I asked, only mildly curious as I carried the tea and cups over to where she sat.

"Not well," she replied as I set the tray down. "Did you not read them?"

I shook my head. "Yours was the only article of interest to me. The others were brought to my attention by Mr. Jenkins and Mrs. Jones; otherwise, I wouldn't know of them either. Besides, I well know my reputation amongst the student body at my college."

I took my seat just as another knock sounded at my door.

"Come in, Brian," I called, having recognized his step.

The tall constable did as I bade. "Afternoon, ladies. May I join you?"

"Of course," I replied, already up and headed to the kitchen for a third cup. "Are you just returning from the Jameson Factory, then?"

Brian looked nonplussed for a few seconds and then looked down at the cuffs of his uniform trousers. "The ceramic dust?"

"And evidence that you were recently wearing a face mask," I affirmed. "How bad was the explosion?"

Brian Dawes was my downstairs tenant at 221 Baker Street, along with his parents. He was also a constable at Scotland Yard and one of my closest friends, next to his girlfriend, Annie. There was a time when I had hoped he and I might become more than friends, but glancing at his perfect, petite girlfriend, I knew I had missed my chance to make my interest known. The fact bothered me like a repetitive pinprick whenever I saw these two friends of mine together.

"Bad enough," he replied, pulling a stool up to my small coffee table and somehow arranging his lean, six-foot frame on it. "Looks to me like a case of negligence on the part of the chief foreman. The man was warned several times of leakages by his men; he chose to ignore them."

"Lucky, then, that the explosion happened at night when nobody was working," Annie offered.

Brian nodded as he took a sip of his tea. "That it was, Annie, and the insurance company was out this morning declaring that they wouldn't be paying a thing if the foreman was the cause."

"And what about this foreman?" asked Annie, tucking a short blonde curl behind her ear and looking curiously my way.

"We found him half in his cups at ten o'clock in the morning," answered her boyfriend. "Claims he didn't even hear the explosion, though the pub we found him in was but two miles from the factory, and the barman said he'd been there since eleven the previous night. The barman left him snoring in his booth rather than attempt to wrestle him to the door and found him still asleep this morning when he came down."

I took another sip as the two of them shared a look that amused and annoyed me at the same time.

Finally, and predictably, Annie broke the silence. "Seems odd, doesn't it, Portia?"

I smiled, settling back in my chair as I met her light blue eyes levelly. "Odd? No, it sounds like the constabulary has the culprit in hand. And negligence, though a weak motive and a pathetic excuse, is still a motive."

The couple looked at each other again in that way that made my stomach clench, and I put down my cup with a clatter. The longer these two were together, the more they seemed to share each other's thoughts and opinions. They seemed to be becoming one person, and that irritated me to no end for reasons I chose not to dwell on.

"I know what you're about, my friends," I said, reaching for the teapot and refreshing each of our cups. "And I assure you, it is unnecessary. I am well."

"A month since your last case ... a month till college starts up again," Brian said, holding out his cup, his brown eyes on mine. "A few cases might make the time pass more easily."

Annie nodded encouragingly. "And the Jameson explosion is only one example — surely you have been following the case of the missing MP?"

"He's in the south of France with the ex-nanny," I said dismissively. "Which is morally questionable but not actually against the law. The problem is that to the media he has broken faith with the English public..."

"Wait ... the south of what?" Annie said, her eyes wide. "How do you know?"

I waved my hand. "Oh, something I read in *L'Humanité* a few weeks ago regarding some recently purchased real estate and a vineyard that corks his favorite wine." I ignored Annie's frenzied retrieval of her notebook and her quick scribbles. "It's really not that important. The man is incredibly bad at covering his tracks. If he had actually committed a crime, which he has not, I am confident Constable Dawes and his able-bodied associates would locate him as quickly as I."

"Able-bodied, yes. Able-minded — sometimes," Brian said with a smile, earning an annoyed look from his girlfriend.

Annie was obviously torn between this line of argument and her desire to know more about the moonlighting MP. She proved her friendship for me once again when she said, "And what about your own able mind? We have been warned that if your puzzles run out..."

"Oh, come now, Annie, you see for yourself that she is in good spirits!" Brian interrupted. "And I told you and my good mum that she would see through any ploys to provide her with stimulation."

Annie's raspberry-tinged lips compressed into a pout at his treacherous retreat, and he lowered his gaze, finding his tea suddenly very interesting.

"Are we still going shopping this Saturday?" she fired at me, pointing a finger.

"Yes. For shoes, I believe, though what I will do with a fourth pair, I know not," I answered, glancing again at her pumps and deciding to buy her a pair instead. My financial situation was quite a bit better than hers, the combination of very low expenses, the rent from the Dawes, and a wealthy benefactor in the form of my grandmother, Irene Adler. Annie, on the other hand, took care of her twin thirteen-year-old brothers while her father sent money back to his family from his work in my hometown of Toronto. Annie had lost her mother when she was very young and had been working since she was sixteen, when her father lost his job in London and was forced to go overseas to find work.

"And you're still having dinner with Dr. Whitaker on Monday evening?" she threw out as her second volley, bring my attention back to the present conversation.

"Tuesday, in actual fact, Annie," I replied, unable to keep from smirking. "But thank you for a public reading of my social schedule. You should add to it that I am attending Dr. Ridley's thirtieth birthday party tonight, that I plan to take another sweep through my messy attic, that I have another lesson this week with Jenkins, and oh, I plan to walk Nerissa at least twice a day and bathe every single day."

Her eyes narrowed at my sarcastic joke while Brian choked on his tea.

Annie gave up her glare with a sigh, clapping him on the back. "We have good reason to be worried, you know, Portia. Mrs. Jones told us we needed to watch out for you whilst she was away."

My eyes met Brian's over our teacups. Mrs. Jones was in fact Irene Adler, infamous criminal and also my grandmother. Though Annie, like the rest of London, knew of my late maternal grandparents, Dr. John Watson and Constance Adams, she knew nothing of my very alive paternal grandparents: Sherlock Holmes and Irene Adler. Brian knew all, though, and while happy for the former connection, he was not happy about the latter and since learning the truth had been on the lookout for any evidence of wrongdoing by my grandmother.

It was yet another thing for me to worry about, because to be honest, I couldn't be positive Adler wasn't still dipping her toe into the wrong side of the law.

"I know. For a while there she was stopping in every day to check on me. I believe she would have delayed her trip to New York had she observed any return of my depression," I said, annoyed but unable to stop my grandmother from doing anything — including recruiting my friends. "But she left, Annie, obviously satisfied with my emotional state."

Annie collected up our cups, placing them back on the tray that held my plain white teapot, and then stood up to take it all back over to the kitchen. She returned and leaned in to give me a hug. "All right, then. I am not convinced, but I suppose that will have to be good enough for now."

She stepped back, her small hands still on my arms. "But if anything changes, if you start feeling sad or bored..."

"Yours shall be the first name I call," I assured her, looking over her shoulder at her boyfriend as he gazed at the two of us and feeling that familiar swoop in my stomach.

CHAPTER TWO

On the way home from walking Nerissa, I stopped at the cleaner's and picked up my dress for the evening. I had borrowed it from my grandmother: a black chiffon ensemble that ended just below the knee in a lace fringe. I paired that with a tulle headpiece set with black beads and a pair of black pumps.

A knock at the door signaled my date, and with a final check of my outfit, I answered it.

"Portia, you are a vision tonight," Gavin Whitaker said, his eyes appreciatively running the length of my body. "Truly lovely."

"Thank you, Gavin," I replied with a smile, taking in the new black suit, evidence of a fresh shave — professionally done, a light gray pocket handkerchief in his front suit pocket that also had a small piece of paper sticking out of it, and shiny, newly polished shoes. He looked very smart.

I motioned for him to come in. "I just need to dig out a suitable purse, and I promise we will be on our way. Did you want something to drink before we leave, Gavin?" I called from my bedroom, opening the closet and digging around at the bottom.

"No, thank you, Portia. Can I prepare something for you, though?"

"No, thank you! Oh, here it is," I said, finding a black clutch wrapped in a scarf and pulling it out. Popping in my lipstick and powder, I picked up my shawl from the bed and rejoined him in the living room, where I found him staring out the window.

"Are you ready, then?" I asked.

"Actually, I'd ... I'd like to tell you something, if you don't mind risking being a few minutes late," Gavin said, turning toward me. "Really, I should wait till tomorrow, when it is announced officially, but I had to share my good news with someone."

"Well, then," I said, my eyes running over him for a clue and catching on the creases at the knees. Hours of sitting in a new suit, looking your best, meant an interview of some kind. But it was the small piece of paper peeking out of his coat jacket where I could read a part of an address, '18 Bel,' that told me who he had been meeting with, before he even opened his mouth.

"Last semester I was told by an old acquaintance that a highly reputable university was looking for a visiting professor to come and speak on the subject of poisonings. You know of my interest in the subject. You know also that I have asked to be assigned any cases from the Yard where poison is suspected to be involved," he said as I came to stand beside him.

"Indeed," said I, "never more evident than in that case of mercury poisoning with that poor child and his mother. None of us made the connection between that form of poisoning and the perpetrator, and you saw it within moments of arriving at the scene, as I recall."

"Yes, well, that is true." He glanced down, showing a modesty that wasn't common with him.

I smiled at his graciousness, remembering the opposing emotions I had felt at the time: incredulity, jealousy and finally acceptance at being shown up by Gavin's superior knowledge of the subject. I was, after all, accustomed to being the person who astounded others with my inductive skills. It was difficult to be one of the astounded crowd, and I can't say I handled it gracefully.

"Well, I do hope the Austrians were vocal with their praise tonight," I said, moving past the unpleasant memory and adjusting the tulle headpiece so that it didn't press so on my ear, "and that you received their offer with less deprecation."

It wasn't until I lowered my arms that I saw the look of anger Gavin tried to hide.

I quickly replayed my last words in my head and realized my mistake as he again dropped his eyes from mine with a flush in his high cheekbones.

"Oh dear," I said, reaching out to gently touch his hand, "I've gone and ruined your surprise. Gavin, I am dreadfully sorry!"

He looked down at his pocket and pushed the small piece of paper further in so that it was no longer visible. "I know that you must have known my news from the moment I came in the door, Miss Adams. And I appreciate that it is a reflex for you to 'solve' every mystery — even the ones that are not actually crimes, but I do wish you would once in a while let me surprise you."

I nodded. "Please do go on. You were talking about your field work in cases involving poisoning."

He forced a smile. "Well, it seems that the University of Saxburg is impressed by my work — especially the paper I co-authored last year on Scottish Highland plants and their poisonous traits, and I have been asked to speak as a visiting professor this fall."

I clapped my hands, overacting a bit to make up for my earlier blunder, but my guest didn't seem to suspect my enthusiasm at all, preening under my applause.

"How marvelous Gavin, truly," I said, and this I meant wholeheartedly. I headed to my icebox. "This calls for a celebration." I brought out a champagne bottle wrapped in a yellow bow.

Gavin Whitaker burst out laughing for the first time in our acquaintance, surprising me with the pleasing sound. "Now, surely your detective skills did not prepare you well enough for this bit of news that you bought that for this very occasion?"

I grinned at him conspiratorially, gathering the only two fluted glasses in my apartment before returning to his side.

"I will do the honors if you tell me where the bottle came from," he said, reaching for the bottle, mirth still dancing in his dark eyes.

"If you would," I agreed, "and it was a gift from the fine gentlemen at Lloyd's of London for the 'Insurance by Post' case — you recall?"

My handsome guest frowned. "I don't believe you told me of that one, Portia," he replied as he popped the cork free and hastily tipped its dripping contents over a glass.

"Eh, it was a short case, and I was only involved for an hour or so," I said, accepting a glass of the bubbly drink. "Sergeant Michaels brought me in right at the end to determine where the bank notes had been mailed."

"Which of course you did," Gavin said, raising his glass.

"Resulting in this very fortuitous gift," I answered, raising my glass as well, "and allowing me to properly congratulate you on this appointment!"

We clinked glasses and took a sip.

"Mm, very fine," he said, sitting back down.

I agreed, pushing Nerissa's curious nose out of the few drops that had hit the wooden floor. "So you were at the Austrian consulate on Belgrave — who did you meet?"

He patted the address in his pocket. "The dean of the university and his wife, but tomorrow I am invited to take tea with the British ambassador to Austria and some visiting nobles."

"Brilliant," I said, fighting the urge to correct him (Austria no longer had a nobility, it having been abolished more than ten years ago). "Honestly, I couldn't be happier for you, Gavin. Or more proud."

"Actually, that was not the only piece of news that I want to share with you, Portia," Gavin said, putting his glass down on the windowsill and reaching for mine. I gave it to him and allowed him to take both my hands.

"I will be in Austria for a month, you see, starting in September, doing a speaking tour of three universities and a few constabularies as well," he explained.

I said nothing.

When he didn't speak again, and I felt my impatience bubbling up quicker than the drinks at our side, I said, "A month is not long. You'll be back in time to celebrate your birthday amongst friends."

"I could be back, yes."

"Or?" I asked, honestly not sure where he was headed with this.

"Or you could join me for my birthday in Austria," he said, the words falling out of his mouth in a rush of uncharacteristic nervousness.

I was taken aback, which must have reflected on my face because he said, "This is a turning point in my life, you see. No more struggling to be taken seriously amongst the elite. I will finally and rightfully be seen as an equal."

"Gavin, I know I've said this before, but anyone who looks down on you..." I started to say, but he shook his head, interrupting a speech I had made many times before.

"The gates of Pellam Orphanage are always just over my shoulder," he said, standing and pacing in front of me. "The boys I grew up with, the things we had to do survive ... they are still stark in my memory, and every step I take forward should be a step away, but sometimes it just seems like I'm walking in place."

"What do you mean, Gavin?" I asked.

But he seemed lost in his thoughts, speaking not in conversation but in a long-buried soliloquy. "So many of those boys. Boys I knew from birth, almost. In prison, or dead, or starving on the streets. So few of us made it out and into real lives. Is it any wonder we stayed close? Is it truly a fault that we cleave to what we know?"

I had never heard Gavin speak so fervently about his mates at the orphanage, so I didn't interrupt, sensing this was something he just needed to say.

He rubbed at his forehead. "We did what we had to do to shake off Pellam. No one will ever convince me we were wrong. No one else lived through what we did. Unclaimed. Unloved. Forgotten."

I had to stand. His voice had dropped low and into a melancholy tone that scared me. "Gavin. No one judges you, I least of all. You have risen above all expectations, and you have done it alone."

I took his shoulders and gently turned him toward me. "You have done remarkable things," I said, and I cupped his chin to force his wounded eyes to meet mine. "And this is just the beginning."

He pulled me into his arms and held me like that for a few beats, his embrace tense and his shoulders tight. I laid my head against his shoulder and waited for him to regain his calm, as I knew he would.

"I want to celebrate this moment and never look back," he said finally, pulling back but keeping me within the circle of his arms. "And you're the only person I want to celebrate with. Don't answer right away, Portia. Think on it and give me your answer next week."

"Of course I will, and thank you for the invitation," I replied, giving him a broad smile while in my head I found myself again wishing for my mother's counsel. She would know the proper time in a relationship to go away with one's boyfriend. I never paid attention to such cultural mores, but I resolved to act like the adult everyone believed me to be and make a logical decision.

"Very good, then," he said. He released me, rolled his shoulders back and extended his elbow to me. "Shall we make our way to the Ridleys'?"

CHAPTER THREE

L ast year, I had been hired by Elaine's brother, who was a classmate of mine. The casebook I had titled "A Case of Darkness" had almost ended in tragedy. In the end, I only managed to prevent half of his crime — James Barclay's attempt to frame his sister, Elaine, for murder. I was not able to stop the murder itself. Their father, the right honorable Justice Barclay, had succumbed to James's murderous plan, a thought that still gnawed at me.

At the very last moment of the case, I had realized that James was the true murderer, and Elaine was absolved of the horrific crime.

She and I had stayed relatively close since, I attending her wedding earlier this year, for example. And she always invited me to any society party she threw, of which there seemed to be many. Her late father's dramatic murder, her inheritance of all his considerable wealth and the family's connections to royalty and government made her a society darling. My grandmother approved of this and encouraged it. Irene Adler was determined to push me to the heights of London society, whether I wanted to be there or not.

I almost always declined these invitations, except when my boyfriend expressed an interest in attending. What memories was he so determined to leave behind? What things had he done that so haunted him?

Thinking about his tall, brooding presence always brought comparisons to the other men in my life. He was most like Sherlock Holmes, my grandfather, sharing an incredible intelligence, a somber attitude and an antisocial turn when it came to facts and situations that were beneath his regard. Gavin was handsome and would be considered quite a catch were he not so indifferent. He challenged something in me that was not easy to define. Not competition per se but an intellectual swordplay that was almost addictive.

Looking over at him on the cab ride over, his chin on his knuckles as he looked out the window of the back seat, I considered that my attraction to Gavin was almost unemotional, but I had come to believe that was the type of romance my personality was destined to enjoy. I, too, could be taciturn and cold, and most men found me either intimidating or unfeminine once I spoke my mind, which I did often and without preamble. Looking at the relationships I had actually studied up close, I thought ours the most well conceived.

Take my mother's second marriage to the disastrous drunkard Jameson, for example. That had been a nightmare to witness, even with her trying her best to shield me from the worst of his vices. And then there were Sherlock Holmes and Irene Adler. Passionately attracted to each other from their first meeting, they had been on-and-off lovers and enemies for decades. The best thing to come out of their trysts was my father, the worst, years of hatred and resentment after his death. They knew they were ill-suited to one another and yet were unable to fight that attraction.

I reached into my pocket to pull out the silver pocket watch Gavin had given me, rubbing my thumb over the raised edges of its engraving. What good did it do to pursue emotional romantic ideas of a relationship? Surely, I would find the amorous looks and touches between a couple like Brian and Annie distracting and vexing. The way she worked so hard to make herself pretty every day, for example. A waste of any measure of the practicality of time. No, better that I be in a relationship that could be put aside when I had more important things to focus on and that I could enjoy in a practical fashion when time allowed for it.

An abrupt halt called my full attention back to the event of the evening: a party to celebrate Elaine's husband's thirtieth birthday. Gavin exited first, paying the driver through the window and then walking around to open my door. I stepped out with a smile for him as he took my hand. We made our way up the stairs to the Ridley home, arriving at the same time as the Lord Mayor of London, Maurice Jenks, much to my date's delight.

We were ushered in through the lobby and into the grand ballroom, and I felt a little overwhelmed by the colors and smells and sounds. In such situations I found it hard to focus, with clues and secrets dying to be identified in every new person I met.

"Alfred Duff Cooper," said a mustached man standing near the entrance, extending a hand to me. "I make it a point to always introduce myself to the comeliest women in my vicinity."

I gave him a polite smile, introducing Gavin as my date, and would have moved away, but the two men seemed to have more to say to each other. Cooper was the financial secretary to the War Office, which I couldn't believe Gavin was interested in, but I was wrong.

"I really must say hello to Mrs. Ridley. Gentlemen, please do excuse me," I said, eliciting a genial nod from my date and another ogling from Cooper.

I spied Elaine Ridley with her husband across the room and hastened over.

"Portia Adams," said her husband, extending his hand and introducing me to the gentlemen they were speaking with. Both wore military garb. "So very glad to see you here."

"Happy birthday, Mr. Ridley," I replied, accepting a chaste kiss on my cheek.

"Portia, my dear, you look stunning. You really must tell me where you found that dress," Elaine said, steering me away from the three men. "Do excuse us, gentlemen. You will not find this conversation compelling, I promise you."

I was already doubting the reasons for this maneuver, since Elaine was well aware of my lack of interest when it came to fashion when she pulled me out the doors that faced the gardens, left open to allow for better airflow.

Once outside in the dim light of the electric lanterns, she pressed an envelope into my hand.

"What is this, Elaine?" I asked curiously, turning it over in my hand to study her name and address printed neatly by a right-handed woman.

"An oddity that gives me worry," she replied in a hushed tone, taking my hand and leading me further out to the magnificent gardens surrounding her estate. The roses on either side of the cobbled pathway ranged in color from white to bright red, but it was the smell that was intoxicating, surrounding us in a cloud of scent. She glanced around us, her long, dark hair flowing in curls down her back as she turned toward me again.

We were alike in height and coloring, though her eyes were green, and she was resplendent in a sequined cream sheath dress with shoes that tied around her slender ankles with matching cream ribbons.

"I believe that my friend, Frannie," she explained, pointing at the letter in my hand, "has written this letter. I believe that she may be in trouble."

I made to open the letter, but she reached out to stop me. "Please ... this is hard to explain, Portia, but due to recent events in my friend's life, this must stay between the two of us."

I frowned, thinking of the secrets I already had to keep in my life. I was in no hurry to add to them. "Apologies, Elaine, but your words make me nervous — is there some illegal affair revealed in this letter? Because if so, I would prefer not to read it at all." I held the unopened letter back out to her. I was, after all, headed into my third year of law. I didn't need to further complicate my life with more criminal activities than I already had during the one and a half years I had lived in London.

She nervously twisted the large diamond on her hand and then pushed the letter back toward me.

"It is not a criminal matter — at least, I don't think it is. Actually, I don't know what to think of it ... it could just be me being paranoid again." She pressed her finger against the bridge of her nose and then opened her eyes. "I swear to you, my hesitancy stems from the fact that it comes from a seventeen-year-old girl I love dearly, like a little sister, but who has shown ... questionable judgment in the past. Not criminal intent ... just immature judgment. It may come to nothing at all — in fact, I hope it does. But I know that as a detective you will look at it and be able to tell me in an instant if I am worried for naught."

My curiosity was fully aroused by now, so I nodded. "I will take you at your word, then. Shall I read it now?"

"Oh no," she said. "This is hardly a suitable venue for intrigues — at least of the non-romantic kind."

She giggled nervously, linking her arm with mine as I dutifully tucked the letter into my purse. "Read it when you get home, Portia, and if you are amenable, I will visit you in a few days so that we might discuss it."

CHAPTER FOUR

That was all we said that night, except to pass on the dance floor in the arms of our respective dates, but as promised, a note had arrived yesterday inviting me to a late supper at Restaurant Boulestin in Covent Garden.

Opening the letter now, I reread it for a third time as I dressed for my dinner with Elaine Ridley.

Dear Elaine:

If it please you, remember to send some wedding photos to help me imagine attending and being with you.

Did Rose Black attend? She had earlier mailed that she intended to; don't think you told me?

Know that I miss you by the way, for who else would put up with my ridiculous banter?

Don't stay away long, Elaine, tell Mr. Ridley that my parents request your presence here.

Love, Frannie

I gave Nerissa a pat on the head as she lapped up water, and then I tucked the letter into a beaded purse.

I stopped in front of my mirror to pull my brown suede jacket over the white silk blouse and suede skirt I had chosen for the night. It wasn't my preferred manner of dress, but since 'coming out' to the public, I had made the decision that my public persona was going to be memorable so that my private persona could be all the more forgettable when I needed to be just that.

This latest outfit had been chosen by my grandmother, who had been thrilled when I described my public versus private plan of dress. Brown boots and lace gloves completed the outfit I had come to think of as a disguise and, with a quick dash of peachy lipstick, I was out the door. A few Londoners who saw me exit 221 Baker Street started whispering amongst themselves and pointing. But by hailing a cab I managed to evade their questions handily.

We pulled up to Boulestin's in about twenty minutes, and though Elaine had not yet arrived, the host was more than pleased to escort me to the table my friend had reserved in our names.

She arrived moments later, wearing a fur-lined ensemble and trailed by a photographer, who was quickly dispatched by the staff. The photographer managed to get three shots off before he was removed, making me doubly happy for my disguise.

"Portia, I am so glad you could meet me," she said, leaning down to kiss me on the cheek.

"Not at all. I have never had the chance to sample Chef Boulestin's cuisine," I answered with a smile.

"I hope you don't mind, but I ordered for us already," she said, pulling her chair close. "Consider it an apology from me for exciting your curiosity for something so trivial."

"Trivial?" I repeated with surprise.

"The more I thought about it, the more I am convinced that my recent ... troubles," she said, looking around to see if anyone was listening in too intently, "have made me overly paranoid — looking for ghosts where there are none. More likely than not, my Frannie is just acting out, as teenagers do, and I am taking that attitude expressed in her letter and attributing complex meaning where there is none."

I took the envelope out my purse, sliding it across the table toward her. "Why don't you tell me about your relationship with Princess Maria Francesca?"

She jerked back slightly, only her natural poise keeping her from knocking over our water glasses. "I don't know why I am surprised, since I have been the beneficiary of your skills before, but I have to ask, how did you know that the Frannie in my letter is also the Princess Francesca?"

I turned over the letter and held it in front of the candle on our table, which revealed a pale watermark: "The seal of the House of Savoy, unless I am mistaken, or at least according to my library book on European gentry," said I. "And you already told me your friend was seventeen, which made the only possibility the Princess Francesca, the youngest child of the Italian royal family."

"You are right, of course, and Frannie and I have been close since childhood," she confirmed, taking back the letter as a waiter delivered a bottle of chilled water and our *salades de pommes de terre aux piments*.

He stepped away with a smart bow and she continued. "Our parents both had summer homes in the Porto Ercole, near Tuscany. We correspond a half-dozen times a year by letter, but I have not seen her in person since her eleventh birthday party five years ago, and I was very sad when she could not attend my wedding."

She hesitated, dropping her eyes from mine to take a sip of water, so I contented myself with enjoying the delicious potato salad.

"Frannie made some youthful mistakes," Elaine finally said. "I heard about them discreetly through her sister, who is closer in age to me, and at first I thought that was why she did not come to my wedding — because her parents were punishing her by keeping her close and under their watchful eyes."

She tapped the letter that now lay face down on the table between us. "That is ... until I received this letter."

We chewed in silence for a few minutes as a couple was escorted past us, the lady of the pair nodding imperiously at Elaine and looking curiously my way. Elaine nodded back, watching them take their seats in a dimly lit corner of the restaurant before turning her attention to me.

I frowned. "There is no Rose Black, is there? Is that some sort of code between you?"

"Yes ... and no," she replied, matching my frown as our salad plates were silently replaced with our *entrées: foie de veau.*

"There is no Rose Black — at least, no person of my acquaintance, but the name has no significance between Frannie and me. It's the first time I have heard it," she explained. "In addition to the letter being much shorter than her usual correspondence, there was a reference to a person I have never heard of who was supposed to have attended my wedding? It was very confusing."

She shrugged slightly, picking up a new fork to start her second course. "We used to play all sorts of games over the summer months, Frannie, Yolanda, Mafalda and myself. Word games, number games, pretending to be spies and soldiers, all kinds of ridiculous hours were spent making up codes and code names and such." She smiled at the memory.

Then she tapped the letter again. "At first, when I read this, I thought it was a code too, but when I didn't understand it right away, it set off alarms in my head. Reading it again now, I see no code we ever used; I must assume I am seeing things that aren't there. She is being short with me because she is in a rebellious teenage phase of some kind. Perhaps the reference to Rose Black is just a joke that I don't understand."

I opened my mouth to disagree, but she spoke again, pointing her fork at me, her eyes alight. "Except she asks for photos from my wedding ... which I sent her family months and months ago — so what can that mean? Is she not receiving my letters? Or is that a joke as well?"

"Out of interest, what was the content of your last letter to the princess?"

"Well, actually, it was about you," she admitted. "I wrote to her about your brave move to step out from the shadows and embrace your God-given talents."

I blushed. "Brave is hardly what I would call it, since I fought the idea tooth and nail."

She waved dismissively. "Miss Coleson was right to encourage you, and your fame is well-deserved. Anyway, two weeks after I wrote to Frannie about your public debut, I received this confusing missive from her. I phoned her several times, you know," Elaine said, poking at her food, her eyes downcast. "I spoke to her staff every time. She has not returned my calls once. I do not know what is going on."

I put down my glass and said, "Elaine, I believe your original intuition to be correct. There is a very different message hidden in this letter."

She pressed her hand to her chest, her eyes widening. "What? What is it you saw?"

I pointed at the letter, hovering a finger over every fifth word in turn, reading only those words aloud: "Please send help. Being blackmailed. Don't know by whom. Don't tell parents."

As soon as I finished the last word, Elaine snatched at the letter, turning very pale and rereading the words under her breath. "Oh, my poor Frannie, it was a code. I am so blind! I looked but did not see it!"

She looked up at me worriedly. "But who would dare to blackmail a member of the royal family?"

I raised my hand as a waiter picked up our plates, replacing them with bowls of fruit compote, and I maintained the silence until he had stepped out of earshot. "I have to ask before we jump to conclusions: is Frannie the type of girl to seek attention by frightening you? Is she overly dramatic that way?"

She shook her head in adamant denial. "No, never. She may be young, but she would not try to frighten me like this. The message you have decoded cannot be misconstrued as a joke. It is real. And it makes sense. Her letters have been so odd, shorter and shorter for the past few months. If she asks that we not go to her parents, we must respect that."

I thoughtfully took a bite of the dessert then said, "There is no further data to be acquired from this letter, so I would merely be speculating as to why someone would blackmail the youngest and least powerful member of the royal family."

Elaine poked at her fruit, her cheeks still very pale. "She begs for my help, Portia. I must do something."

"Oh, indubitably," I agreed. "But heed her words, Elaine, she asks you to 'send help.'"

"Of course!" Elaine dropped her spoon with a clatter, causing two waiters to sprint to our table, one picking up the dropped item, the other offering a replacement.

She thanked them absently. "She asks for *your* help. I had just written to her about your exploits, and it can be no coincidence that her very next correspondence asks for me to 'send help.'"

I had of course already come to that conclusion, so I simply nodded, finishing my meal with a grim smile.

"Then you will go?" she pressed, color coming back into her cheeks. "With me, I mean? Immediately?"

"As soon as we can come up with a plausible reason, yes, I think that would be best. We must remember that Princess Francesca does not want her parents involved, and she even coded her letter to you, which means that she feels watched in her own home. We will want to keep the real reasons for our impromptu visit to ourselves. So, how will I gain access to the Royal Princess of the House of Savoy?"

CHAPTER FIVE

I taly? On such short notice?" Gavin asked as we strode in step behind Annie and Brian.

He looked a little worse for wear since our last meeting, his trousers creased and a patch of stubble apparent under his chin where he must have missed it. He being so careful and attentive to detail, I noticed these things as quite out of character. I wasn't sure how to broach the subject with Annie and Brian at our side. I wondered if his follow-up meeting at the Austrian embassy had gone badly.

"It was very kind of Mrs. Ridley to invite me as her traveling companion," I replied, the lie rehearsed and delivered on cue. "Mr. Ridley is very busy at work, and I have a few weeks till college starts up again. It seemed an ideal plan."

"I think it's a smashing idea," Annie called over her shoulder, her arm linked through Brian's. "I only wish I had thought of it myself. A break is exactly what the doctor ordered, Portia Adams."

My name caused a passing couple to stare as they passed and then whisper furiously to each other.

My arm must have tensed in reaction because Gavin said, "Doctor's orders indeed — it wouldn't be so bad to get out of the spotlight, eh, Portia? Even for a couple of weeks? I think it a brilliantly timed idea." His shrewd, dark eyes gazed down at me.

I beamed up at him. "Indeed, sir, I confess it was half the attraction."

Annie sighed dramatically. "Traveling the Italian countryside in first class. What a difficult life you lead, Portia."

I smiled at her sarcasm.

"Isn't that Constable Simmons?" asked Annie, tugging on her boy-friend's arm. "He seems to be trying to get your attention."

Turning my head to where Annie pointed, I felt Gavin's arm tense in mine. If Simmons were looking to speak to Brian, why was he skulking in the shadows? Brian gave a diffident glance at the alley as Gavin said, "Are your tickets bought, then, or can we walk you that way?"

I couldn't see Simmons at all, so I turned to answer.

"All is arranged; we leave Monday morning, and I will therefore have to reschedule our dinner. I do apologize."

He looked away for a moment to say, "We do what we must, after all."

I turned quizzical eyes his way. "Gavin?"

"I meant that I must accept that you have been made a better offer," he explained, patting my hand. "It is my loss, to be sure, but I will expect to be recompensed with a double feature in return for my gentlemanly acceptance."

I smiled, glancing again to the alleyway and wondering at Constable Simmons' strange exit, if it had indeed been him.

"Come, Dr. Whitaker." Annie interrupted my thoughts, tugging on Gavin's arm. "I must show you the fine hat Brian refused to buy. I need your opinion to back up my superior fashion sense."

She dragged the handsome man off my arm and into the store, leaving Brian and me standing bemusedly on the sidewalk.

I glanced at the tall profile of my friend, aware of the reasons for his quietness and worried about breaking that silence with another lie.

He glanced at me, opening his mouth, and then obviously thought better of it and closed it with a snap.

I pretended to take great interest in the fur stole the mannequin in the store's window was modeling, while stealing looks at Brian through the re-flection.

"Italy?" he asked finally.

I bit my lip when he raised his hand.

"Is it dangerous?" he asked, his brown eyes showing a combination of concern and anger.

I hesitated, because the answer was not a clear one, and that must have been answer enough.

"Two women traveling by themselves in a foreign country on a case — no, please do not insult me by denying that you are on a case, I well know the signs — that could be dangerous." He crossed his arms. "This is foolish, Portia Adams. Just foolish."

I was offended, even though most of what he said was true. "You over-step, Constable. I no longer have a guardian, and if I did, they surely would not be someone but a few years my senior."

His eyes narrowed, and I thought for a moment I had pushed my friend too far, but my ego wouldn't let me back down, so I stared back at him defiantly. What right did he have to tell me what to do, after all? I wasn't his girlfriend, and the man who had chosen me for that role was nothing but supportive of this trip.

"All right! I surrender. Dr. Whitaker agrees with you, Brian — he..." Annie came tumbling out of the store, giggling, but stopped short, seeing us glaring at each other.

Gavin followed her exit in his usual calm and graceful manner, extend-ing his elbow as if nothing were amiss. "As I said to Miss Coleson, fashion must be classic to be pursued. Shall we continue?"

I slipped my arm through his, appreciating the way he led us on, never pressing me for details despite the scene he had witnessed or my tense-ness.

"By the way, I have thought about it, and I would be most pleased to join you in Austria for your birthday," I said, making the decision on the spot, my anger at Brian making my voice louder than usual.

I couldn't help the satisfaction I got from Brian's expression at my words but was more surprised at Gavin's reaction. His mouth tightened, and he gave me a terse nod. Perhaps he didn't like that I had exposed our personal discussion?

CHAPTER SIX

W ell, I suppose that is everything, then, little miss," Mrs. Dawes said as she rechecked our shared front hall for anything I might have forgotten.

The hackney idled with my luggage as I lingered, trying not to glance too obviously at the inner door that led to 221A.

"And ... you're sure that Nerissa will be no trouble, Mrs. Dawes?" I asked, hesitating as I made to step out the front door.

"Oh, pish tosh, girl," Mrs. Dawes answered, waving her hands and all but pushing me out the door and onto the walkway. "That bloodhound of yours is no trouble at all — especially since Bess died."

I nodded as I opened the cab door. She was referring to the recent (and entirely un-mysterious) death of her oldest beagle. My eyes wandered unbidden to the curtained front window, but there was no movement behind its translucence.

"Have a good trip, dear," Mrs. Dawes called out, closing the door to my townhouse behind her.

I closed the cab door and said to the driver, "Victoria Station, please, sir."

"Right-o," the man answered, pulling away from my townhouse.

I flipped open my satchel out of habit, making sure I hadn't forgotten anything, and found my eyes drawn to the seat next to me, where a folded newspaper had been left behind. Even that quick glance revealed that it wasn't an English newspaper, and I reached for it, opening it to read *La Stampa* in bold letters across the top. The date read *11 aprile 1931*, which was close enough to English for me to translate, and I scanned it curiously, aware that I would understand little else of the Italian printed therein. An image had been circled in pencil, and reading its caption, I gleaned that the people in the photo were members of the Savoy royal family.

"Excuse me, sir," I said, my senses humming, "who left this newspaper here?"

"Eh?" replied my cabbie, glancing over his shoulder. "Dunno who he was, miss. The older gent I dropped off on your block. He asked me if I'd throw it out for him but sat back there reading it till you hailed me from across the street."

I sat back, opening the pages of the newspaper until I arrived at the expected sheet of paper with written copy on both sides of the page, the penmanship small and tight. Another quick scan told me it held the same code as the one I had recognized in Frannie's letter to Elaine, and with a grin, I pulled out a pencil, circling every fifth word.

My dear girl:

I hope you forgive this method of communication and the straightfor-wardness of the language, but I continue to be of two minds. On the one hand, I want you in my life as much as you will allow, and on the other hand, I worry that my half century of criminal investigation has made me a target and may make you one as well. It is why I have avoided actually coming up to my old apartments, despite walking by at least twice a month since January.

If you are anything like me, though (and by all accounts you do seem to have a bit of the Holmes touch for this), you run toward trouble rather than away, and therefore the second point is moot.

Your upcoming case in Italy is a perfect example, as royal scandals (the worst kind, by the by) are rife with dangers both political and physical. Watson and Mycroft would have counseled you against accepting it, even as your curiosity (and mine) require that you pursue it.

It is a vast understatement to say that I am not your grandmother, who will impose herself on you regardless of your preferences, nor am I as so-cially adept as Constance or as emotionally grounded as Watson. There-fore, this is my request: I would like to become better acquainted with you, and I'd like you to know me. Could you give some thought to allowing me access to your brilliant young life? My mailing address is below, so please do send me a note when you have decided.

As cold as my reputation is, I find that with great age comes a wistfulness for that which I may have missed while sprinting through the first decades of life. I would regret not at least trying to be part of your life. If you choose to say "no," I will never reproach you for it. I will, more than anyone else, I believe, understand and respect your wishes as I did your mother's.

Your grandfather

PS: I do hope that Nerissa is actually aiding your work and not causing you too much trouble.

PPS: The young constable seemed quite put out this morning, leaving Baker St. before you at a quick march. Perhaps I should speak with him about respecting your superior judgment and intelligence?

I closed this remarkable letter with shaking hands, fighting the urge to order my cabbie to take me to the address included within.

My grandfather, Sherlock Holmes, had finally reached out to me. After months of silence, he was ready to talk. Since Christmas, my focus had been on rebuilding my relationship with my grandmother, and between that, the cases I took on, my studies and coming out to the people of London as the newest detective at Baker Street, it had not been hard to push Sherlock Holmes to the bottom of my list. I'll admit to feeling a trifle hurt at how quickly he had left Edinburgh, allowing my grandmother's resentments to feed my insecurities about my newly discovered family.

"How did he know about Elaine and Italy?" I wondered aloud, thinking of any clues I might have left behind to indicate my true reasons for this · trip. He must have dug my translations out of the rubbish bin, or perhaps he had been sitting within hearing distance of my dinner date with Elaine.

"Eh?" said the driver.

"Oh, nothing," I mumbled, carefully folding the coded letter and sliding it into my satchel.

"We're 'ere, miss," the driver said, pulling up to the corner. He climbed out of the hackney to pull my bags from the boot. I joined him at the front of the cab.

A porter raced up to look at my tickets and take possession of my bags as I followed, my mind a thousand miles away and my heart too full to allow me to speak.

CHAPTER SEVEN

The porter led the way to the first-class cabin I would be sharing with Elaine Barclay. She was already sitting, nervously awaiting my arrival.

We talked for a while about the arrangement but soon ran out of steam, and Elaine headed off to the dinner cabin for a distraction as much as to sate her appetite.

I stayed behind to write a long letter to my grandfather. I am not a sentimental woman; in fact, some in my college had gone as far as to call me cold when pressed by reporters. It was a description my mother had heard again and again over the years, poor woman, one that she defended me against till her dying breath. She wouldn't have been surprised at the spark of excitement that burned in my chest as I answered his overture.

I did want to spend more time with him. A year ago, when I had first arrived in London and was being assailed with revelation after revelation, the time was wrong to be hit with the added complexity of getting to know Sherlock Holmes.

But now I was happily ensconced in my new home at Baker Street and a quarter of the way through a degree in law. I was ready to know more about my father's side of the family.

My mother's decision to close herself off from anyone related to my father was her choice. I didn't fully understand it, and my heart ached at how lonely she must have been in that resolve, but I simply did not share her view. I wanted to know everything about both sides of my extended family: the Watsons and the Holmeses.

I had brought no photos of my dear, departed parents, but since the casebook I had titled "Truth Be Told," I had taken to wearing my mother's silver cross again. I had forgiven her for hiding the truth from me, perhaps understanding more about her motivations as my life got more complicated and I was forced to hide truths from people I loved. I thought of Brian Dawes and shook my head. He knew enough. He didn't need to know everything about me. He had chosen to share his heart with someone else, and I had done the same.

I thought about Gavin Whitaker and realized that I never felt guilty hiding truths from him. He had never asked about Watson, Holmes or Mrs. Jones, or even about my late mother. He seemed content to know about my present and was entirely unconcerned about my past. I believed if I told him everything — that Irene Jones was Irene Adler and that she was my grandmother, he would be unfazed by the knowledge or the fact that I had kept it from him. Maybe that was why he had never mentioned the boys he had grown up with at Pellam Orphanage — and I had surely never asked.

It was the opposite of Brian's reaction, which was hurt and angry at my obfuscation.

I was terrible at relationships, I thought with a shake of my head, and the irony of lying to the people closest to me was that I had no one to talk to about the strategy.

So I wrote to my grandfather about my wish to spend more time with him and some of my burning questions about his life with my other grandfather, Dr. Watson. I asked about any correspondence he might have had with my mother after my father's death, and whether he had followed my early development, as my grandmother had. The discovery of a hidden scrapbook, and of course access to all the diaries both men had kept, had painted a tantalizing picture with vague watercolor edges. When I returned to London, I vowed, I would work at filling in the blurry strokes on that canvas.

Traveling as Elaine Ridley's maidservant might have annoyed others (Elaine herself was quite apologetic about it), but I was more than happy to be left behind in our private cabin rather than be forced to socialize as she supped in the dining car.

I had scarce been allowed a moment alone since the press conference a month ago, so this was a welcome respite.

We had decided to apply our disguises on the train, just in case. This meant that Elaine needed to behave as though she were simply a wealthy traveler and I her humble servant.

My clothing was already far less expensive or showy than hers, so I used our time together outside the cabin to practice my British accent, trying to emulate my friend Bruiser Jenkins' Cockney, because I felt I knew it best. When we were alone, we mapped out our plans in more detail, and Elaine started a list of preliminary suspects.

"The truth is that Frannie is quite alone in that house," she explained as we walked the length of the train for a bit of exercise. "Her older siblings are married, and the king and queen travel constantly. She is left at various family homes, surrounded by servants."

"And what of her friends?"

"Few, sadly," she answered, stepping aside as a couple stepped between us, headed the other way. "Being royal limits the sorts of friends you are permitted to make."

I stopped at the window for a moment to watch the countryside fly by. "But you and your family grew close to them."

She nodded, joining me. "Fortunately, yes, due to the similarities in our fathers' choices in real estate. But while I would come home to school and friends, the princesses would go home to servants and tutors."

The sleeping cots in first class were lovely, and we got into a bit of a rhythm, me rising early to sit in the lounge area with a book, listening closely to the accents around me and practicing when I could.

I would spend hours looking out the window, enjoying the trip and the anonymity of our travel.

Elaine would join me at some point, and I would escort her to the dining hall, where we would eat at a table alone and speak sparingly in order to maintain the servant-mistress cover we were honing.

"I wish we were there already. Who knows what could be happening to Frannie while we travel," she said as we walked back to our cabin.

"Tomorrow we take the boat to Calais, Mrs. Ridley," I replied, applying my accent liberally as a porter passed us, "and then it's one more train ride to Turin."

Stars spun by us through the windows of the train, and I realized we had stayed later than I thought in the dining car.

Elaine waited until the porter was well out of earshot before saying, "I think it is a good thing that you will be employing your accent amongst Italians, Portia. It really is dreadful."

She opened the door to our cabin with the first smile I'd seen on her lips in days.

"We could switch, you know," I suggested with an answering grin. "How about for the rest of this trip we play Canadians traveling through Europe?"

This boat trip was much shorter and less fraught with anxiety than my previous one, when I had traveled from New York to Britain in the care of a stranger toward a future that was entirely unplanned.

Elaine and I stayed up top for the two-hour trip, enjoying the sunshine and sea spray of the channel, watching for the dolphins and whales the captain promised.

"And remember, at the first sign that she is in danger, we gather her up and take her to the king and queen. Blackmailer be damned," Elaine said, her hair whipping around her face.

"I would never put a woman at risk for the sake of solving a case, Elaine," I assured her.

The entire trip by train, then boat, then train again, took a little over three days in total, and before I knew it, the conductor was announcing our arrival in Turin.

Elaine had sent word to the Savoy household of our arrival, so as I disembarked, I looked around for someone who had been sent to pick us up.

Casting my eyes about as Elaine waited in the cabin, I listened to the excited calls from family members finding each other on the crowded platform and allowed myself a daydream of doing the same with my grandfather when I returned to London.

Spying a letterbox, I wove through the crowd of people exiting the train and deposited my letters — one for my grandfather and another for my grandmother, sent to her hotel in New York.

"Possibly they will send their old manservant, Mr. Salvatore," Elaine had told me. I saw no one fitting his description as I pulled a few coins out of my string purse for the porter who stacked our bags at my feet. I did see a young man in a waistcoat speaking to one of the conductors in rapid Italian and watched the conductor nod and point to the window of the carriage I had just left.

Sure enough, the conductor nodded at me, and the young man hastened to my side.

"*Buongiorno*, Signora Ridley," he said in a deep voice, bowing slightly. He had what you might call classic Roman features, with a thin nose and clear skin, full lips and dark hair that curled over his thick eyebrows. His build was lean and athletic except for a slight thickening at the waist — no doubt a hereditary trait. I was surprised to feel a twinge of attraction toward the man, physical beauty not being something that normally affected me.

"Oh no, I'm just Lizzie, Mrs. Ridley's maid," I replied, hoping my accent was not noticeably pronounced and making sure to relax my speech, forcing it to be less formal, as my disguise required it to be. "You must be from the Savoy estates? I'll fetch milady from the train."

He seemed to understand enough of my words, because he replied, "*Si.* I mean yes, Signora Lizzie, I am called Lorenzo," and he stooped to pick up our luggage, the scent of soil and something more fragrant wafting up from his thick black hair. "The car is very close. Is this all the bags?"

"Yes," I answered, turning to step back onto the train to fetch Elaine. "Maybe we should call a porter?"

But by the time I had turned back to face him, he had all four bags balanced in his arms.

I shrugged (despite being impressed by this show of strength) and did as I had promised, quickly leading Elaine out to the platform. She was wearing a navy skirt and top that was tailored to perfectly fit her trim, tall figure. She had pulled on tiny white gloves, a silk scarf and a white hat while I had been looking for our contact and looked every bit the part of a wealthy heiress.

The young man's dark eyes widened, and he tried to bob a bow at her, but the bags in his arms precluded it. Instead, he led the way off the platform and toward a waiting convertible with its top down.

The driver was an older gentleman who, upon sighting us, pulled open the back door and stood there till we took our seats. His back was obviously bothering him, because he took a few minutes to adjust himself more comfortably in the driver's seat with a small tubular pillow.

Though noticeably well trained, the two men kept sneaking curious glances back at the two of us. Lorenzo, whom I surmised was also the gardener by the added information of a slightly sunburned neck, seemed more fascinated by me than Elaine. I logged that away while we sped along through incredible landscapes of green and yellow.

But all the Italian fields in the country were nothing when compared with the sight that greeted us as we pulled into the long driveway that ended at Racconigi Palace. To say it was magnificent would have been a ferocious understatement, and even Elaine seemed moved as we drew closer, reaching out to grasp my hand.

We pulled up to the front steps, where another man hastened down the stairs to open the car door for Elaine. I opened my own door, but Lorenzo hopped out to hold it open as I exited and then ran around to get our bags.

Elaine, meanwhile, followed the butler up the front steps, so I picked a small piece of hand luggage out of the boot and followed.

"Signora, we welcome you at Racconigi," the butler was saying to Elaine in stilted English, opening the door wide and ushering us in. Despite carrying four times more than me, Lorenzo and one of his peers sprang past me with our bags, so I entered the palace last. Perhaps that was best, as the sounds of their exertion masked my gasp as I took in the marble stairs and gilt staircases.

"Would Signora care to ... take to the rooms?" the butler carefully said in English, gesturing at the stairs. "Or ... Signora would prefer *la biblioteca* while I let *la famiglia* know of your arrival?"

She inclined her head. "The library, my good man. Though, my maid, Lizzie," she gestured to me, and I curtsied, "can accompany my bags to our rooms."

He nodded, and with a clap and a few words in Italian, he directed the staff to do just that. I followed them up the stairs, still carrying the little piece of hand luggage.

"I can take that, Signora," Lorenzo said to me as I followed him into a beautiful room at the end of the hallway, "if you are restless to get back to your *padrona*."

"*Padrona?*" I asked, not recognizing the word.

"Ah *si* ... I mean ... your Signora Ridley," he answered, his smile beatific.

I smiled back, because it was impossible not to — his charm was hard to resist — and then he gathered up his peers and with not a little elbowing and chatter pushed them out of the room. He turned to give me a cheeky wink, and then he left.

His forwardness gave me pause, though the investigator in me knew it could be useful to encourage his attentions, making him a source of information in this situation. Nonetheless, I waited a few moments before leaving the room as well, making my way down the stairs and in the direction of the library, where Elaine had been led.

The doors were open, and the thousands of books that were stacked floor-to-ceiling were almost as breathtaking to me as my first sight of Racconigi Castle. There were wrought-iron ladders on wheels along the bookshelves, a fireplace, no fewer than six couches and a huge Turkish rug on the floor. Standing in front of one of the bookshelves was my friend, her back to me. I glanced around and seeing no one quickly came to her side.

I had opened my mouth to ask her about the people we had met already when a voice sounded to the right of us, surprising us both.

"You were ever an avid reader."

We turned in unison to see a lean woman in her fifties, framed by the sunlight streaming through the window-paned door, through which she had obviously just entered the room.

I mentally flipped through my list of descriptions, taking in the tightly bound hair, perfect English, starched collar and carefully cared-for watch fob, identifying the speaker before Elaine responded.

"Nanny Pina, how are you?" she replied as the woman's bottle-green eyes ran curiously over me.

"I am well, child," the older woman answered, inclining her head slightly, "but look at you, my dear ... so changed from the young girl who would play at my knee."

Elaine pushed her hair over her ear in a characteristic gesture. "Do you really think so?"

The nanny's eyes were drawn to the large diamond wedding ring on Elaine's finger. "Yes, though the child I can still see in your eyes, of course." She stepped back. "We were most surprised by your letter and the quickness of your visit."

Elaine shrugged lightly, playing her part well. "Frannie's letters made me miss her so, and Mr. Ridley is writing an important paper for a journal. It was a perfect time for a visit. Are the king and queen in residence?"

"No, they are traveling in the capital at present," Nanny Pina answered thoughtfully, swinging her gaze back toward me. "And this young lady is your ... maidservant, then?"

I lowered my eyes, hoping that wasn't suspicion I heard in her voice, but any answer my friend was going to make was interrupted by the sound of another female voice, speaking in rapid Italian and headed our way.

"Elaine? Is it really you?" asked a young girl who came into view at a run. She stopped suddenly, seeing that there were three of us in the library.

Princess Francesca's dark eyes widened above dark circles as I smiled hesitantly at her, trying to fade into the background as a good servant would.

Elaine strode straight up to the young girl and drew her into a tight embrace — one that was returned with equal passion.

"Ah, Frannie, it is so good to see you," Elaine said, stepping back to hold her friend's face in her hands.

Pina gave the two women a few moments before once again turning her eyes curiously to me.

"Ma'am, if that's all, I should go and unpack your bags," I said, my eyes lowered and dipping a quick bow to the princess.

"Yes, Lizzie, that will be fine," Elaine said, not looking my way. "Nanny Pina, Lizzie is, as you surmised, my body servant. I hope you don't mind my bringing her along to help me?"

Pina's eyebrows rose questioningly, but she nodded. "Of course, I will advise the chief steward. Will she be staying in the maid's quarters?"

I tried not to stiffen at being talked about in the third person and to ignore the princess's staring eyes, hoping the nanny was less observant than I.

"If you could send a cot up to my room, I would prefer that she be by my side should I need her," Elaine answered, taking her friend's hand and leading her to a sofa, effectively dismissing both the nanny and me.

I bowed again and stepped out of the room, noting that Pina hesitated for a few moments but then followed me out, leaving the library doors open and directing me to follow her toward the kitchen.

"I have never known Mrs. Ridley to travel with a maidservant," she said over her shoulder.

I shrugged, offering no answer, watching the woman's body language as she looked back and frowned.

I heard her whisper something under her breath in Italian, and then we arrived in the huge kitchen. My attendance of Mrs. Ridley was announced to the mostly disinterested staff, and then without a second glance from Pina, I was released to make ready the signora's room.

I took my time heading back to the bedroom, purposely taking two wrong turns in order to acquaint myself with the mansion a bit better.

Many of the rooms were designed with a specific cultural motif, like the silk-wallpapered Chinese room. The Greek-themed rooms boasted marble statues and elaborately painted ceilings. I would have liked to spend more time in each but didn't want to draw attention to myself. Most of the furniture in these rooms was covered with cotton sheets to battle the dust of disuse. Obviously, these rooms were for family and guests.

No one questioned my exploration, though the staff I passed did look curiously at me. I finally made my way back to the front stairs and back down the long hallway that led to our bedroom and was taken aback to find Elaine waiting for me, alone.

"Lizzie — at last," she exclaimed.

"Mrs. Ridley, what are you doing up here already?" I asked, closing our door securely behind me.

She waved her hands agitatedly. "Moments after you left us, the steward came in to announce that Frannie's tutor had arrived, and she was whisked away before I had a chance to find out anything at all."

I nodded, deciding we would do well to work while we talked, and set about unpacking the luggage.

"Not surprising, really. The life of a princess is, I am sure, scheduled to within a moment of her day."

Elaine paced back and forth while I worked. "But did you see her, Portia? How ill she looks?"

I glanced up at her as I closed a dresser drawer now packed with blouses. "I did. The girl has lost some weight too quickly to be healthy, and she has make-up over the dark circles under her eyes ... so either she or someone else is trying to disguise her misery."

A knock at the door made Elaine jump, so I answered it, and two men brought in the cot she had ordered for me. I smiled at them, again recognizing Lorenzo and wondering how many jobs he worked at this estate.

"Do not worry, Mrs. Ridley," I said, pulling out a dress that would be suitable for tonight's dinner. "At supper you will have the opportunity to get the story straight from the horse's mouth."

She sighed, finally turning to unpack her shoes. "You are right, 'Lizzie,' and while I do that, what will you be investigating?"

"Everyone else," I answered grimly.

CHAPTER EIGHT

D inner was a learning experience. I headed to the kitchen ahead of
Elaine to advise the staff of her preferences, doing my best to
communicate in an exaggerated Cockney accent to the Italian-
speaking kitchen staff. I helped serve the first course in the large dining
room, noting that the princess had not yet joined the table, and then
Elaine quickly dismissed me to find my own vittles, so I returned to the
noisy kitchen.

It held a large oak table where various household staff would eat in
shifts throughout the day, depending on who was on duty. Most of the
staff looked at me curiously, and very few spoke English, so I simply mimicked their routine, following a couple of giggling maids as they got
cracked bowls out of a cupboard and dished themselves soup straight out
of a huge pot.

Lorenzo appeared out of nowhere, causing more giggling, and he
stopped beside me with half a loaf of bread in hand. "Signora Lizzie, you
must try Mama Rosa's fresh bread. It is to die and come back to life for..."

I again found myself smiling at his handsome face and took a sniff of
the bread. Rosemary and sage assaulted my sense of smell, and my stomach growled loudly in response.

I blushed, but the kitchen staff found it hilarious, the rail-thin cook
slapping her floury hand on my shoulder and lecturing me in Italian.

"She says, 'Wait until you actually taste it'," Lorenzo said with a wink,
pulling me to sit at the table with ten others.

The food was distractingly tasty, and though I did my best to catalogue the people in uniform around me, Lorenzo kept trying to engage me in conversation.

"Your English is very good," I said.

"I have family in Roma," he explained between bites. "There it is much easier to learn the English because so many of the people can speak it. I was visiting them only a few months ago."

I nodded. As I ate, I looked round the room, noting the similarities between members of the staff and surmising that many were members of the same family. A woman was delivering freshly laundered uniforms and clothes, walking from person to person, handing them small bundles. At our long table, she handed a small, pleasant-smelling package to everyone sitting there but Lorenzo and me.

"How long have you been with Signora Ridley, Lizzie?" he asked, ignoring the woman and already well into his second bowl of soup.

"I've known Mrs. Ridley for nigh on two years now," I answered honestly, looking around the table for any suspicious interest and finding none. One of the young maidservants kept scratching at her elbow, making me wonder if the faint bulge under her cream blouse hid a bandage over a healing wound. Two of the stewards sat apart from the rest, playing cards over their meal, and one of them had a lump from goiter.

"That is not long all," Lorenzo said, calling my attention back to him. He had finished eating and now sat with his face propped up on his hands, elbows on the table.

"No," I agreed, taking another sip of soup, "I warrant you have been 'ere much longer?"

He frowned. "'Warrant?' *Dispache...?*"

"Ah, I was just asking how long you 'ave worked for the royal family?"

"Since birth almost," he replied with a radiant smile. "My father was gardener before me, my mother still cooks here." He pointed at the skinny older lady who had clapped me on the back. She glanced over at his words and gave a smile not unlike the one on her son's face.

"Most of us have been serving this family for generations," he said, waving his hand around the room. He quickly repeated his statement in

Italian, prompting a mirthful response from the assemblage.

"Most?" I asked, picking up his bowl and mine and taking them over to a large stone sink.

Lorenzo followed as he answered. "Yes ... most ... is that not the right word, Signora Lizzie?"

"Of course it is. I was only surprised that no new staff come through — quite the opposite in London," I explained, pivoting to give one of Annie Colson's patented smiles to soften the question. "I thought we might 'ave something in common — being new myself..."

"Ah, but no, you need not worry," he replied, taking the wet dishes from my soapy hands as I quickly and efficiently scrubbed them clean, "we are all *amice* here."

I fought down my impatience and instead tilted my head at a young couple that had just entered the kitchen and were casually picking through a fruit basket. "They, for example, don't seem to 'ave been 'ere long..."

"It is true what you say, but they are *famiglia* still." He pointed at another of the cooks standing near his mother, who glared suspiciously at us when she saw us looking at her. "Carlo and Lia are nephew and niece to Signora Martina you see there. They were away studying in Roma and recently returned. They are not very friendly yet. You need not speak to them."

I catalogued that information for later, noting how the two stood off to the side and greeted no one as they quietly whispered to each other. Their cream-and-navy uniforms were obviously newer, and they hunted through two cabinets before locating the one with the mugs. Lia wore a very intricate Catholic cross around her neck and rosary beads at her waist. I glanced around at the other uniformed people and saw no one else wearing beads, though I knew the Catholic religion was very popular this close to the pope and the Vatican.

"Why do you worry about how long the staff have been with us, Lizzie?" Lorenzo asked, leaning against the wall and crossing his arms, his smile wide. "Are you to stay with us a long time? Need we find a room for you in the servants' quarters?"

I blushed at the way he was appraising me and shook my head. "I don't know, but I can't stay 'ere chin-wagging much longer, or else my lady will hear about it ... 'scuse me."

I did what I could to help out around the kitchen, taking the opportunity to speak to as many of the staff members as I could, despite the language barrier. Pina came in and out of the room, seeming to take responsibility for more than her position but commanding quick responses from the staff. Lia seemed curious about me but did not return my smile, and Carlos did his best to stick to her side as she walked around the kitchen. They, too, each retrieved a package of clean clothing from the woman who was obviously the laundress.

Not having Annie's naturally social personality, I don't think I would have been as successful had Lorenzo not followed me around, seemingly interested in all I had to say and therefore at my elbow to translate my words.

The fact that I didn't understand Italian turned out to be as much of a detriment as it was a benefit to my work. The downside was obvious and anticipated — that I didn't understand most of their conversations. But the upside was that it gave me a chance to follow their body language without the distraction of the words they were saying. In addition, because they knew I didn't understand them, I believe it allowed them to relax around me in a way they couldn't have if I had been a stranger who spoke their language fluently.

This meant that by the time I headed back up to the room, it was past eleven o'clock, and I was bone-weary from a day of traveling and socializing. I was surprised to find two large men standing at attention at the bottom of the staircase. As I passed, they whispered at each other in quick Italian, and I could see that neither of them was armed, not even with a nightstick.

Trying not to seem too curious, I curtsied as I passed and headed up the staircase and down the hallway, knocking on the door before I entered.

I stopped suddenly at the sight in front of me: Elaine in her night-clothes bent double over our tiny balcony, her head and shoulders invisible as she hung over the metal banister.

"What in the...?" I whispered and thankfully had the presence of mind to close the bedroom door behind me before dashing toward her.

Five steps into the bedroom, the true situation became clear, and I threw my efforts into grasping the arm of the person silently struggling to get onto our balcony. With my added strength, we managed to pull the princess to the safety of our room.

We collapsed onto the floor, all of us shaking and staring at each other before the young princess threw herself into Elaine's arms, her sobs as silent as her precarious ascent into our room.

I shook my head and got up to get some towels out of our private bath. Rolling them up, I tucked them securely under our door and then walked out to the balcony to look down. I scanned the grounds and thought I saw movement, but in the full dark of the countryside, it was hard to be sure.

I closed the windows securely and turned back to the two women kneeling on the floor.

"What were you thinking, Frannie?" Elaine was saying, her hands still linked with the princess's.

"I had to ... *dio mio!*" the princess whispered back, taking gratefully the hanky I passed to her. "They never give me a moment alone, and they could send you back before we have time..."

Her eyes met mine. "You are the lady detective Elaine wrote to me about. You are Portia Adams?"

I nodded and lifted the princess off the floor by her elbows, leading her to a pair of chairs in our little sitting area.

"Indeed, Princess, in disguise as Mrs. Ridley's maid until we had ascertained the level of danger you were in — which, from your daring arrival, I can see you hold quite high."

"Please, call me Frannie, all my friends do," she said, and then more hesitantly, "at least they did when I ... had friends. Oh, Elaine, I fear you are my only friend left in this world..."

"Princess," I interrupted before the tears could start anew, "you must tell us why you feel this is the only way to speak to us alone. I noticed that there are guards posted downstairs. Is that normal when the rest of your family is traveling?"

She shook her head and then nodded, her face drawn. "It was not, as you say, normal, until a few months ago, when I..."

She hesitated, looking shamefacedly at Elaine, who gave her hand an encouraging squeeze.

She dropped her eyes to her lap and fussed with the hanky. "You must understand, I know what I did was foolish ... and immature, and that my father was right not to trust me after that."

She glanced up at me, so I nodded, even offering, "You ran away from home?"

"Yes, twice..." she admitted, looking sadly back at her lap.

"Twice?" Elaine repeated, but I held up a hand.

"So the guards are there to keep you from leaving, as opposed to for your protection," I said, determined to keep the princess talking while we had her to ourselves. "That is a convenient time for a blackmailer to ply their trade..."

"Indeed," she mumbled, pressing the hanky to her eyes. "I felt very angry at my parents for their control of my life, I felt ... I don't know how to describe it ... it is so hard for me to remember that I was so selfish and self-involved. When the first letter arrived, it was like someone understood exactly what I was feeling. For the first time, I had someone on my side."

"Just so I can rule it out as useful to this case, the first time you ran away from home, it was out of sheer pique?" I asked.

"Portia..." Elaine said, her eyes darting back and forth between her friend and me.

"No, she is right, Elaine," the young girl admitted, nodding sadly. "I was bored and angry, and I just wanted to be ... well ... free of all of these rules..." She waved at the finery around us. "I had no concept of what I would do, where I would go ... I just wanted to be away. And they caught me within two miles of the house. It was a pathetic escape on a selfish impulse, but I have paid for my foolishness, I swear to you. I have paid."

She pulled out a bundle of letters and handed me one. It was of course written in Italian, but Elaine leaned over my shoulder anyway, scanning down to the bottom.

"*Tio amico* Marco?" she read, "that means 'your friend, Marco' doesn't it, Frannie?"

She nodded, a rueful smile drifting to her lips for a second, like the sparkle of a snowflake before it dissolves into nothingness. "Would that he was."

"So you ran away, your parents punished you, and then this first letter arrives, and...? Did you write back?" demanded Elaine.

"To where?" I said, holding the page up to the light and finding no discernable watermark. "I cannot believe it came with an address, Elaine. How many more of these did you receive before your second attempt to run away from home?"

"Three," she admitted with a sigh. "The first two were so encouraging, so understanding..."

"With no hint of demands or blackmail, correct?" I prompted, reaching out for the second and third letters the princess extended to me.

She shook her head. "None at all, just empathizing with my situation as the youngest daughter of an important family and promising to help me, and to help my father."

I opened up the letters, scanning for clues as Elaine asked, "Help your father how, Frannie?"

"With his work, Elaine," the young princess replied, punctuating her words with gestures. "Il Duce is so ... popular, and his pull with the Holy See grows stronger every day, which only makes him more popular with the people of Italy. Oh, if you read some of the newspapers, what they say about my father and mother." She shook her head, tears sparkling in her eyes.

"And what did Marco promise you in terms of help with your father's political issues?" I asked, setting aside one letter and reaching for another.

"I did not know," she whispered, hanging her head. "I was to meet him and find out, but I was caught trying to slip away while shopping with my mother in Torino."

I nodded, looking down at the letters in my hands. "So then you decided to forgo meeting in person..."

"It was impossible after the second time I was caught," she answered, shaking her head. "Nothing I said could convince my parents that this second attempt was for a totally opposite reason — my motivations were so different now. But Marco, he said it mattered not. In his next letter, he described what he had wanted to tell me in person." She flipped through two more letters before handing me a new one. "He told me who it was that was speaking against my parents — he told me everything."

I looked over the three-page letter she had handed me. "I will need an English translation of this letter then, Princess. For now, all I can tell you is that they were written by a right-handed woman with a confident hand," I said. "And who was it Marco identified?"

A knock at the door made us all spring up.

"Signora Ridley?" a woman's voice called through the closed door.

"They must not find me here!" whispered the princess, color dramatically falling from her face as she sprang to the window, pulling it open and starting over the balcony again.

"Slowly, I beg you, Princess," I whispered, signaling Elaine to get into the bathroom, hurriedly pointing her in that direction, and then I called out toward the door in a loud voice, "One moment, ma'am, we are readying for bed!"

I held the princess's arms as she deftly climbed around the banister and then repeated the action twice more, finally reaching her own room.

As soon as the young girl had swung herself safely into her room, I turned, grabbed a dressing gown and ran to the door.

"Yes?" I said, shoving aside the towels under the door with my foot and sliding our bedroom door open a crack, trying not to sound out of breath.

"Ah, Signora, you took a long time to answer," said Nanny Pina, who stood behind a young maid who held stack of towels.

"Apologies, ma'am," I answered, opening the door a bit wider so that they could see in. "I was not dressed for company."

The nanny swept her gaze quickly round the room. "As I see, and where is your mistress?"

"Washing up for bed, ma'am," I answered. "Shall I take these towels for her?"

"Not at all," the nanny answered, pushing the maid in front of her and coming into the bedroom.

"Lupe was supposed to ready your room. She has failed and is correcting her mistake."

The maid obviously did not speak English and only looked stupidly at the two of us until Nanny Pina barked at her in Italian. The girl jumped and scampered over to the bathroom door, knocking uncertainly.

Elaine swung open the door commandingly, her skin a pasty green from the masque she had hastily donned.

She glared at the young maid, who mumbled apologies in Italian, obviously more frightened of Nanny Pina than of this stranger, because though she tiptoed around Elaine, she followed through on her assignment, hastily dropping off the towels on the appropriate shelves.

"Really, this was not necessary, Nanny Pina," said Elaine, walking casually over to the chairs we had so recently occupied. "Lizzie checked the rooms earlier, and she is more than capable of seeing to my needs."

By now the maid had bobbed two more curtsies, and under a new barrage of angry Italian from her superior, she made herself scarce as quickly as possible.

"Of course, Signora Ridley," the older woman answered. "We are unused to your," she slid her eyes toward me, "upgraded travel style."

Elaine smiled frostily, made all the more menacing by the mud masque on her face as the woman bowed slightly and followed the maid, closing the door with a click.

"Well, *get* used to it," Elaine hissed to the closed door.

CHAPTER NINE

Despite having much fodder to discuss, we were both so tired from the drama of the evening that we fell asleep a little after midnight.

My sleep was uneasy, filled with visions of incomprehensible suspects in a vast marble palace with a maze of corridors. For some reason the phantom images of my friends flitted in and out of the dreamland of this palace, Brian appearing angry or dour behind one door, Annie worried as she passed me silently on the staircase, and Gavin always walking away from me, his broad shoulders too far away to reach out to. My escape from London and its emotional pull on me seemed to extend to the recesses of my mind.

Elaine did not seem to have fared any better, and we opened our eyes almost simultaneously as the sun came up over the horizon.

I hauled myself out of bed, sure that "Lizzie" had chores that must be done, and made quick work of my bath and dress.

When I came out of the bathroom, Elaine was pacing back and forth, a small folded note in her hand.

"No, Elaine," I said, anticipating her plan.

"Portia, I want you to deliver this note to Frannie in secret," she replied, ignoring my refusal and pressing the note into my hand, reminding me of the way she had handed me a letter a few weeks ago, starting this whole adventure. "Tonight, we run away, but together! We will cause a distraction and make an escape — to Calais or maybe to Lisbon. I have connections in both who would be ready to help us."

I shook my head. "No, Elaine, I am afraid it will not do. Even if we succeed in getting the princess out of here, the blackmailer will simply follow through with their threat — and we do not even know what that threat is — so we cannot logically measure the risks. It is too soon."

"But ... Portia, you saw her," she said, wringing my hand. "How desperate she is."

"Desperate, yes. In physical danger? I don't think so," I replied, aware of how cold I sounded. "Her parents have installed guards because they care for her safety, and unless they are part of this plot, she is safe at least on that front. No, I believe the threat is against her father; it is the only power she holds. Not to her person."

Elaine's mouth thinned to a hard line.

"I need time, Elaine," I said, decisively handing the note back to her and reaching for my apron. "Time to figure out who has a motive for blackmail, and that has to start with the threat. Now, I am going downstairs to prepare your breakfast. Shall I suggest to the cook that you intend to take it in the garden with the princess?"

Elaine brightened at my suggestion. "Yes, yes, a good idea. And I will make it my mission to find out what this blackguard wants from my poor Frannie."

I nodded and walked out the door. No guards stood at the top or bottom of the staircase, so I headed unchecked straight into the noisy kitchen. I received smiles from a few of the staff, and I returned them in kind. The breakfast for Elaine and the royal family was still being prepared, so I followed the lineup to the big pot, which today was filled with some kind of porridge. I spooned myself a small amount, poured a coffee, and headed to a table where the two of the guards I passed last night sat in conversation. They looked slightly surprised as I sat down, but they resumed their conversation in Italian. Their uniforms were slightly different than those of the kitchen staff, with small jackets over their cream tunics, but both outfits bore obvious signs of repair from years of wear.

When I finally sighted the person I had been waiting for, the maid who had come into our chambers last night with the towels, I waved her over. At first she looked shocked at being singled out, but as several of her peers elbowed her smilingly, she shyly brought her coffee and biscuits over to the table I shared with the guards. One of the men sat up a little straighter as the petite brunette took her seat across from me, a blush rising on her flawless skin.

"My name is Lizzie," I said, pointing at myself and then offering my hand. The girl wavered, actually glancing up at one of the guards for encouragement before extending her own hand. "*Mio* — Lupe, Signora."

"Lupe, what a lovely name," I said, turning to the guard to my left. "And you are?"

Haltingly, in a combination of English and Italian, introductions were made, with not a few trace glances between the guard named Enrique and the maid, Lupe.

I smiled to myself, and my eyes met the other guard's. It was obvious we were thinking the same thing, because he raised his mug, pointing toward the carafe to our left.

I quietly joined him, hoping not to disturb the other two as they shyly exchanged pleasantries.

"*Amore,*" sighed Matteo as I tipped the carafe toward his mug.

I nodded, understanding one of the few Italian words in my repertoire. "So good to see her smiling after last night's ... fuss."

Carlo entered the room, stopping to say hello to a very young boy in a servant's vest. I observed that he seemed quite relaxed with the child and noted the patience with which Carlo listened to his questions.

"Fuss?" repeated Matteo, drawing my attention back to him. "*Dispache*, Signora, what means this 'fuss?'"

"Oh, nothing, really," I said, taking a sip of coffee. "Just a bit 'a trouble betwixt that nanny and Lupe. Do you not 'ave a word for fuss in Italian?"

"Ah yes, Signora, even in Italia, we have fuss," said Lorenzo, appearing once again out of nowhere and deftly inserting himself into our conversation. He smelled like fertilizer, but even that did little to detract from his appeal as he wiped at his glistening forehead with the vest in his hands before putting it back on. Matteo gave him a laughing elbow to the chest and followed with some rapid-fire Italian between the two friends.

Matteo nodded his understanding. "Ah yes, *capisce*, what is this fuss of last night, Signora?"

Lorenzo slipped between us to get at the coffee as I spoke. "Last night that poor girl Lupe got quite a scolding from that Pina about something ... well, tiny ... that was the fuss I was talking about."

Before my words were even translated, I noted how Matteo's shoulders straightened and his nose flared at the mention of Pina's name. Hearkening back to my training at the hands of renowned lawyer Ian Myers, a man known for his abilities to read body language, I took a mental note as Lorenzo quickly translated my words for the guard.

His words caused a great deal of gesticulation on Matteo's part and finally a waving of both hands to end the conversation.

"*Dispache*, Signora, I go now. Work," Matteo said abruptly, bowing out of the conversation with a displeased air.

"*Dispache*, Signora Lizzie, Matteo ... he sometimes ... he takes his job ... too far," explained Lorenzo.

"I think you mean he takes his job 'too seriously,' but seeing as he's a guard in the royal household, I suspect he takes the job just seriously enough," I replied, then realized I had slipped into more formal speech than was called for, gave a tiny smile and shrugged, glancing over at Carlo and realizing that his good mood had fallen from him. His anger was palpable, even from across the room, and it was not directed at me. It was clear that his glare was for my handsome companion, which Lorenzo seemed to notice, drawing me aside by the elbow before he spoke again.

"What happened to Lupe, well, it is not uncommon," Lorenzo explained, his back to Carlo now. "The last few months, I feel, Pina has become difficult."

"Really? Why?" I asked, my eyes moving between Lorenzo and Carlo. Carlo's mouth had compressed into a hard line when Lorenzo had touched my arm, and he seemed to be vacillating between leaving and coming over to us.

Lorenzo took his time doing up the buttons on his form-fitting vest before he spoke, and then said, "No one knows, but she has talked about retiring soon, and we think perhaps she does not know where she will go, or what she will do after she leaves."

"Doesn't she 'ave family?" I asked, already knowing the answer, having asked Elaine that very question the day before.

"*Famiglia?* Ah, no," Lorenzo answered as Carlo came to a decision and walked back out the way he had come.

"What about you, Signora?" Lorenzo said, drawing my attention back to him. "Do you have *famiglia?* A husband waiting for you back home in England?"

He was smiling at me in a way that made me suspect he knew the answer.

"No, it's just me, I'm afraid," I answered.

"Just you is quite enough, I would guess," he replied, crossing his arms in what I was coming to recognize as a characteristic stance for his flirtations, because it emphasized the size of his biceps, "but surely you have someone — a pet maybe? A dog?"

I frowned, wondering if Nerissa's hair had made an appearance of some of my clothing, sparking the astute question.

"No, no dog, no cat," I replied instead, making a mental note to check all of our clothing for pet hair. "Really, I've enough trouble caring for meself, let alone pets ... and working for the Ridleys takes up most of me time anyway, so..."

"I see," he answered, smiling, his eyes speculative and simmering with unasked questions.

"Excuse me, ma'am," I said, taking the opportunity to speak to one of the cooks as she bustled by with an arm full of breads, "my mistress wishes to take her breakfast outside in the gardens — may I do so, please?" I articulated my message by pointing out the back door toward the gardens.

She answered with a *harrumph* and a string of Italian belted out at top volume. She was answered by two or three other voices, Lorenzo's included, to which her answer seemed to be another grunt, followed by a nod.

She pulled out an old wooden tray from a cupboard and started plunking utensils, a plate and a cup on it.

"Actually, for two please, ma'am," I said, holding up two fingers to clarify. "My mistress wishes to take her meal with the princess."

Despite my English, the kitchen quieted at these words, the cook's eyes widening as she looked around at the rest of the staff. Then she shook her head slowly and started speaking to Lorenzo, who came back to our side, his hands out as he replied.

"*Si, si,*" he finally answered, turning my way. "Lizzie, the *principessa,* she takes her meals in her room, you see ... so it is not possible for her to eat in the gardens with your Signora Ridley..."

"Oh, by whose authority?" I asked, and then added, "My mistress will of course ask me that when I tell her."

Lorenzo looked at the cook, who looked back at him. "It is the ... how do you say ... Pina's rule."

"Very well," I replied, sensing this was not the time to push and lifting the tray carefully, hoping my lack of practice was not obvious. "I shall let my mistress know."

I need not have worried. My partner in this endeavor was neither shy of conflict nor intimidated by rules. Within ten minutes of hearing that she could not possibly have breakfast with the princess, Elaine had placed a guard at each end of the garden, had two place settings out in the gazebo at the rear of the estate, and had Lupe and me serving a light breakfast to her and a very wan-looking princess.

"Elaine, what did you do to get all of this arranged?" whispered the princess as I pulled out a chair for her.

"I simply mentioned that my next stop on this sojourn in Italy was a visit to see your parents in Rome," Elaine answered with a steely glance toward the house. "The head steward couldn't accommodate me quickly enough after hearing that."

"Princess, are we quite sure of this young maid's understanding of English?" I said, smiling toward Lupe.

The princess spoke in Italian to the young maid, who blushed and returned my smile.

"Yes, her English is limited to one or two words. She did not have any schooling at all, you see, unlike some of the staff, who took time away from this place to pursue training. Aldo, who works in our stables, apprenticed in Siena with his family before coming back here to work, and Lia just returned from Rome, where she was to have taken vows, but she changed her mind," she answered. "I just told Lupe that you were very happy to have made a friend here in Racconigi."

"Ah," I remarked approvingly, because it aided me in gaining trust with the staff. "Best, I think, if I stay quiet now, so I will step behind Mrs. Ridley's chair here while you two talk."

Elaine meanwhile, murmured over her water glass, "And don't look, but there is someone watching us very intently from one of the third-floor windows, so let us use our time efficiently."

She smiled broadly at the princess as I surreptitiously bent over the table to rearrange the cutlery and peeked up through my lashes at the window.

"Now, start where you left off, Frannie," she said encouragingly, her tone purposefully light, though her words were serious.

Frannie nodded. "The letter you wanted me to fully translate is in my pocket. When we leave, Lizzie, I will leave it under my napkin for you," she said, her words directed at me though her eyes were on Elaine. "In it, the writer pointed to ... to the vicar general of Roma as a very vocal source of ill will toward my parents..."

"Who?" asked Elaine, confused, looking to me despite the people watching us.

I glanced around at two gardeners working with their tunics undone about ten feet away, the sweat marking their clothes under the direct sun.

I stepped forward to cover the mistake, refilling her cup of coffee from the carafe. "The vicar general is a high position in the Vatican, if I am not mistaken. He speaks for the pope, does he not, Princess?"

"Yes, and I would say his name but for our audience. But what you say is true, Lizzie."

"And then what happened, Frannie? After you got this letter identifying this man as a problem?" Elaine prompted.

I stepped back again, smiling at Lupe, who smiled back.

"I wrote some letters," Frannie said, her voice shaking. "I wrote some horrible letters, Elaine, to this very powerful man. I am such a fool."

There was no way to disguise her upset. Lupe stepped forward with a frown, asking something in Italian.

They had a brief conversation, during which time Elaine and I busied ourselves in banal chatter about her meal. The person who had been hovering at the window was no longer visible, and the two men gardening, who I did not recognize, had moved back toward the shed.

Finally, Lupe stepped back, scampering off toward the kitchen.

"I told her I bit my tongue," the princess explained, "and asked for a bit of ice to soothe my mouth."

"Quick thinking, Princess," I declared, "but perhaps we should expedite this interview while we are relatively alone? So you wrote letters to the vicar general. Go on."

"At first, I swear to you, my writings were polite and simply asked for his support, but as his responses became increasingly hostile, so too, I admit, did mine."

"He wrote directly back to you, Frannie?" Elaine asked incredulously, glancing up at me for my reaction.

I waved my hand for the princess to continue.

"I couldn't believe how defensive and then offensive the letters were," the princess said, twisting her napkin as she remembered the correspondence. "I should have told my parents right then. I should not have allowed myself to be angered so."

"Did you continue to get letters from Marco, Princess?" I asked, stepping forward to replace her untouched fruit plate with a plate of pastries, noticing that Lorenzo had strolled into the gardens and with a friendly wave to me headed to the shed to join his peers.

"Only one at that time, warning me that I had a direct conduit to the Holy See and that I must not endanger that by involving my family or friends."

"Of course," Elaine said, patting her friend's hand as Lupe came back into view.

"Perhaps now is a good time to bring out your wedding photos, Mrs. Ridley?" I suggested, stepping back as my counterpart arrived, breathless.

Lupe apologized profusely, handing the linen she had filled with ice to the princess.

Elaine, meanwhile, had wordlessly done as I suggested and spread a half dozen wedding photos on the table between them.

"When did you realize that those letters you were receiving were not actually from the vicar general?" I asked, stepping between Lupe and Elaine.

Elaine gasped but then quickly coughed to mask her surprise, taking the water glass I extended to her.

"When my father called me into his study about a month ago," the princess answered, obediently flipping through the photos, though her eyes were unfocused and her voice wooden with sadness. "It seems that only one of my letters, the third, had actually made it to the offices of the vicar general, and he was at a loss as to the level of accusation and anger expressed within it. He of course had not seen the first two I wrote, nor the ones I thought were coming back in response from the vicar general. He only saw this third angry letter written in my hand."

"Oh dear," Elaine said, taking another sip of water. "What happened then?"

"My father was irate, to say the least," the princess admitted sadly. "I have never seen him so angry."

"But then..." Elaine frowned, automatically collecting her photos back up as she spoke. "Surely you did not continue to write to the vicar after that, Frannie?" ·

When the princess did not immediately answer the question, I nudged Lupe, who quickly stepped forward with more ice. My maneuver was in part because I had sighted the end to our conversation striding up the garden path with great haste.

"*Principessa,*" exclaimed Nanny Pina, followed closely by the head steward, "what in *il nome di Dio* are you doing outside?"

She glared all around, and I followed Lupe's lead, meekly lowering my gaze.

"Apologies, Nanny Pina," answered Elaine, sounding anything but. "I thought breakfast in the fair sunlight would do my friend a world of good."

The older woman seemed to be biting her cheek, but instead of snapping at Elaine, she directed her ire at her charge. "Not at all, Signora Ridley, for you could not have known that the princess's violin teacher has been waiting for her for nearly an hour. But Lupe and the princess surely knew."

Her glare returned, this time followed by some harsh words in Italian for the unfortunate Lupe, who flushed deeply before leaping forward to pull out the princess's chair.

Stoically, the princess turned and thanked Elaine for her company and then silently followed the nanny and the head steward back toward the house. Elaine waited a few beats and then, throwing me a look of frustration, stalked off down a garden pathway.

Poor Lupe was frantically trying to collect up the dishes while sniffing away her tears, so I did my best to help her, loading up a tray and following her into the kitchen.

We got as far as the back door before the nervous maid dropped a few items of cutlery on the stones and promptly burst into tears. Leaving my tray on the table beside hers, and eager to escape the wave of female support headed to Lupe's aid, I returned to the gardens, where I found Elaine still fuming.

I fell into step behind her, lacing my fingers behind my back.

"Violin teacher indeed," she hissed under her breath.

"Indeed, Mrs. Ridley, the princess has neither the neck nor upper-arm soreness associated with playing that instrument. This is either a very new hobby or an excuse made up by the nanny."

"Oh, pish tosh, I don't care if she were bent over double with the pain of practicing, Portia," declared Elaine, forgetting our covers in her frustration. "That woman is determined to keep us from helping poor Frannie."

"Again, agreed, Mrs. Ridley," I replied, emphasizing my usage of her formal name. "Only her absence from the house this morning could have facilitated your breakfast with the princess."

Elaine stopped pacing in surprise. "Nanny Pina was away this morning?"

"Yes, early enough that the hem of her dress had been wet with dew. You could still see a faint line where it had dried. And I don't think you would have been as successful with your breakfast plan had she been there to be consulted on it."

"When you looked at those letters, you said you believe them to have been written by a right-handed woman — which I am sure you have noticed Pina is. But you have not pointed to her as Marco, so that means to me that there are parts of this story I know you must understand more than I do, Portia," Elaine admitted. "Tell me what you know."

I took a deep breath and then launched into my understanding of the problem. "Here is what happened: Princess Francesca was identified by this Marco character as the weak link in the royal family — someone who could be manipulated, and someone who was relatively isolated from the rest of the family, physically because she lives here and they travel so much, and emotionally because she is in a phase of her life when rebellion and immaturity are common."

Elaine nodded, so I continued. "So Marco writes to her, becomes her friend, gains her trust and starts talking to her about the things she is worried about, including her fears for her father and his political stance in the country. She gains the princess's trust and then gives the girl a mission that makes her feel important. Marco then points her straight at the person who is causing the problem — the pope — and encourages her to fix the problem on her own."

"And Frannie writes to the Holy See, naïvely trying to fix the relationship between her father, her family and the pope," Elaine offered.

"Yes, the princess writes to the vicar general directly, but her letters never get there," I answered. "In fact, I would guess that they never left this house at all. So she writes letters, Marco writes back pretending to be the vicar general and a dialogue is started."

"And as you discovered yesterday, it is Nanny Pina who deals with the posting of letters," Elaine pointed out.

"In that one case, yes, but to return to the letters, the princess writes to the vicar general, the letters are never delivered, and instead Marco writes back..."

"With Frannie thinking she is conversing directly with the vicar general, when all the while she is writing to this blackmailer, arming them with the weapons they will then use against her," Elaine said, her eyes growing angry.

"Yes, and remember, all the while Marco has possession of her letters, which as she writes pretending to be the vicar in an angrier voice, the princess is responding in an angrier voice," I continued, playing it out in my head. "To the point that the last of her letters to the vicar general were probably incendiary in nature and should never be seen by the Holy See, since they would cause a massive rift between the royal family and the pope, swinging public opinion away from the royal family should they ever be published.

"And then when Marco has all they need to cause the damage they want to, they take one of the letters, an aggressive letter but by no means the worst in the collection they have amassed, and actually *do* send that one to the vicar general."

"Who responds directly to the king, demanding to know what is going on," Elaine said, shaking her head. "The man never saw the first letters, never wrote the answering letters that were angry and therefore came fresh into a conversation that was already boiling over."

"Exactly," I replied, rubbing my hands together. "Proving Marco's threat before he or she made it — that the relationship was precarious and that the king would be desperate to rectify the mistake his daughter had made."

"So imagine what would happen if the other letters got to the vicar general, those ones even more angry in nature..." whispered Elaine, understanding now coming hard and fast.

"Oh, I am sure that is what Marco wants us to imagine, Mrs. Ridley," I agreed. "That is the threat. The question is, what does Marco want? If they want to ruin the relationship between the pope and the royal family, they have the ammunition they need already ... why not just use it?"

"Poor Frannie," Elaine murmured, her eyes brimming with tears.

"Perhaps we should stop wandering so far from the house, Mrs. Ridley. You might enjoy the fauna in the gardens to the scrubs out here?" I suggested.

We walked in silence for a few moments until we were under the window of our shared bedroom. There, we could make out a pair of footprints pressed deep into the earth.

"Are we always watched, then?" whispered Elaine when I subtly pointed out the prints to her.

"Actually, I am not sure it is we who were being watched," I replied in a matching whisper, using a little branch to point out corresponding prints to the left of the first. Elaine followed me as I trailed the back of the house and then pointed to a grove of olive trees.

"What does it mean, Portia?"

"The footsteps are from one pair of rather large — I would guess male — shoes and have very little foliage pressed into them, indicating they are recent," I answered under my breath. "And they are side-by-side, as if someone moved sideways from our window to the princess's."

I could not see her frown, but I could hear it in Elaine's next question. "To what end?"

I thought about it. "Someone was standing under our balconies while the princess climbed from one room to the other. Probably following her progress from below, stepping side to side as she climbed."

Elaine turned back toward me, her eyes wide.

"Yes," I confirmed. "We have an ally in Italy, Mrs. Ridley. Someone who did not want to expose her escape but was there to catch her if she fell."

CHAPTER TEN

To keep up appearances, I soon returned to the kitchens to see what work needed to be done. At first it was obvious that the older ladies of the staff blamed me for Lupe's sad state, but I worked alongside them nonetheless, folding countless napkins and towels until they forgot I was an outsider and returned to their noisy, bustling routines. I noted the pairs of rubber boots by the back door, comparing them with the footprints we had looked at moments ago and deciding the prints did not come from any there.

Once I was dismissed from the kitchen, I made a pretense of looking around for my mistress with two true objectives in mind: find a way to gain access to Nanny Pina's rooms and, hopefully, run into Carlo, whom I had not seen all day. I needed to talk to him about his obvious hatred of Lorenzo, so I walked outside into the gardens, finding the laundress and her assistant hanging uniforms on a long wire. Neither spoke English, so I wandered around the garden and then back in without finding Carlo.

I found the nanny in the library, much to her displeasure.

"Ah, Lizzie, is it not?" she said, barely looking up from the newspaper. "Your mistress sought you earlier. She has retired to her room and requires your attention."

"Yes, ma'am," I answered meekly and headed up the stairs.

Taking them a few at a time, I purposely headed in the opposite direction of our own rooms and instead walked down the east hallway. My earlier exploration of this floor had shown that the nanny and the head steward were the only members of the staff who slept on this floor — probably

more for their service requirements than for their comfort. The rest of the
maids and servants slept on the main floor behind the kitchen. Because
the princess was with her English tutor, no guards were on this level. I tested
the first door after the princess's own rooms and found a sumptuously decorated suite that had to be that of another of the siblings.

I kept going down the hallway, my heart racing, opening door after
door, looking for the right one. At the end of the hallway was a corner, and
around that corner was another door. Opening it quietly, I peeked in and
found what I was looking for: a discreet bedroom with simple furnishings
and a dress that seemed to be of the style that Pina wore, lying across a
high-backed chair.

I stepped in silently and headed straight to the desk, where several letters lay in various states of readiness; I shuffled through them quickly and
efficiently. Nothing caught my eye, so I pulled open drawers, turning over
papers, opening books and shaking them out — all to no avail. With a sigh,
I calculated that I could risk no more time here and stepped away from
the desk, catching a glimpse of my discouraged face in the mirror above
the clutter.

I tilted my head, sure I needed to leave but oddly drawn to the mirror.
I stepped forward and touched the frame, tilting it back so that it was
straight. As soon as I released it, though, it slipped again into the same position, half an inch to the left. My heart speeding up again, I carefully slid
my finger behind the frame of the mirror and after a few seconds found
what I guessed might be there. I pulled out a letter that had been folded
into a small square and tucked into the wooden frame. Once I had it
loose, the mirror swung to its natural position, straight on the wall. Glancing
at the door, I decided I had to take a chance and unfolded the paper, taking a quick scan of its contents, all in Italian and signed "Marco."

Outside the door I heard voices and nearly crumpled the letter in surprise. A few seconds later, the letter was refolded and I had tucked it back
behind the mirror, my eyes on the doorknob to the bedroom I was now
trapped in. I stepped back from the desk, looking to the bed and deciding
it was my only option, as the doorknob started to turn. Throwing myself to
the floor, I slid under it and lay still.

From the floor, the bed skirts only gave me a view a half-inch high, but I recognized the well-worn leather slippers of the nanny as she walked into the room, grumbling under her breath. She stopped at the desk and stood for a few minutes before sighing and walking around to the bed. She sat and kicked off her slippers, and I could hear her moving things around on the bed — God forbid she should decide to take a nap and I be trapped under here for hours.

But it turned out that she was readying for her bath, because a few minutes later, she rose and went into the bathroom, turning on the taps. I waited until I actually heard her slosh into the tub, and then I carefully slunk out from under the bed and fled the room.

CHAPTER ELEVEN

W hy, whatever are you up to, Lizzie?" asked Elaine as she came out of our bathroom to find me tucking a towel under the door to our bedroom.

I was still slightly out of breath from my sprint from the east wing of the house to the west, but I quickly explained what had just transpired.

"You found a letter? Hidden away?" Elaine whispered excitedly, pulling me to the bed. "What did it say? Was it one of the letters Frannie is so worried about?"

"No, it was not written in the princess's hand, but the important part of this discovery is the signature," I answered, pulling off my shoes and massaging my aching feet. "It was signed *tio amico* Marco."

Elaine opened her mouth, trying to put together the clues laid before her. "But then obviously Nanny Pina is Marco — she is the one who is blackmailing Frannie?"

"I don't think so," I said, wishing I could read Italian or that I could have brought the letter back with me. I still felt like we only had part of the picture as I wandered toward our windowed balcony. "Why would she keep a letter written by her own hand hidden that way? Maybe she intercepted one of the earlier Marco letters and is now keeping a much closer eye on the princess? It would certainly explain the tightness of the leash around her charge."

Standing there looking down, I could see Lorenzo working side by side with another gardener. Both were wearing rubber boots, and I wondered just how far Lorenzo's helpful nature extended. Was he the person who had been standing under the window in case the princess lost her footing in her daring climb between our rooms? And why did he not make use of the laundress's services? Twice I had seen her delivering uniforms to the staff, and both times she seemed to have nothing for Lorenzo.

"Damn," I muttered and leapt back to the bed, pulling on my shoes again despite the aches, and stepping to the dresser to pull out a wrap. I needed to get a look at his boots.

"Portia, where are you going, and what shall I do?" Elaine demanded, grasping my hand as I made to leave.

I turned back to my friend and squeezed her hand. "We are getting closer, Elaine, I promise, but I need a bit more time. My advice is to go have a nice long bath. We have much to talk about tonight, especially if the princess visits again."

This time my service was required throughout dinner, Nanny Pina barking orders at me and the other two maids. Her constant demands at one point made me suspect that she had somehow discovered my intrusion into her bedroom, but I shook off the feeling; surely she would have accused me directly of such a thing. More likely this time she was just taking out her frustrations on me instead of Lupe.

On my third trip into the kitchen, this time for a pat of butter that "does not look like a flattened pancake," I happened to bump into Carlo as he carried a small basket of coals for the oven. I had been trying to speak to the sallow-looking man all day.

"Oh, so sorry, sir," I stammered, stepping left and right to get in his way.

He scowled, finally putting his hands on my shoulders, moving me out of his path and then heading to the hearth, scooping fresh coals onto the already hot embers.

"Do not mind Carlo," advised Matteo as I frowned and headed to the icebox for the butter. "He is in ... a bad mood since Lia went away."

"Oh, Lia went away? Where? When?" I asked, trying not to seem too curious while at the same time attempting to shape this new piece of butter into an appealing form.

Matteo shrugged. "A sick relative, it must be. She took with her a big bag of herbs and soups and said she could not work for a few months."

I tilted my head and then walked over to Martina with the butter dish in hand. "Signora, a little 'elp, please?"

With not a little effort and some help from Matteo and one of the other maids, I explained the demands on the butter. The older woman snorted and then snatched the dish from my hands, taking a knife and expertly crafting the butter into the shape of a rose.

"Signora, who is it that is sick? I hear that Lia is tending to them?" I asked while she worked, looking to Matteo to translate. "Me mum taught me a brilliant recipe for chicken soup, if you think it would help."

But after Matteo had translated my words, the woman got angrier and just shook her head at me, pushing the butter dish back into my hands with a stream of harsh Italian that I didn't need anyone to explain.

"Right then," I said to no one in particular. Carlo was watching me intently, unloading the coal in his arms and stooping at the hearth. I took special note of his shoes, comparing them mentally with the footprints outside between the bushes as he brushed his dirty hands on his uniform. So Lia had left almost as soon as we appeared in this palace — coincidence, or had we spooked her?

Elaine had left the table two hours before I was finally released from the kitchen, where suddenly it was vitally important that two bags of potatoes be skinned and five chickens plucked. Pina did not seem to respect the division between kitchen maid and lady's maid and seemed to take pleasure in making sure my every moment was filled with work. While I labored, I formulated plans to avenge my sore digits and found myself missing my sweet bloodhound, hoping she was not bored out of her head by the herd of middle-aged dogs with whom she was now spending her time. Thoughts of Baker Street of course led to remembering how I had deceived my best friends about where I was right now, and the way Brian Dawes had glared at me the last time I had seen him.

Carlo reentered the kitchen, and I assumed he would ignore me as usual, but instead he determinedly walked up to where I sat.

"Signora," he said, his voice deep, his eyes earnest, "you must be careful."

I lowered my aching arms, leaning toward him. "What do you mean, Carlo?"

He licked his lips before answering. "You must pick your friends more carefully. There are those in this household who cannot be trusted. Especially..."

Two giggling young maids entered the kitchen from the back door, interrupting him. They set to gathering up some towels, ignoring us entirely.

I rose, determined to know what he was trying to tell me, and he leaned in to whisper in my ear, "Especially with impressionable young women."

One of the maids called over to him and motioned him to her side.

He nodded at me, and I watched him follow the maids out of the room as I sank back into my chair, trying to decide if I had just been warned or threatened.

All of this meant that by the time I finally took to the stairs to my bedroom, my mood was as foul as it had ever been.

I passed the guards, barely acknowledging them, and opened my bedroom door to find the room empty. Frowning at the balcony curtains, which were rippling with the breeze, I stepped over to the open window, my weariness falling from me like snow melts off a warming automobile engine.

I looked left and right and seeing nothing surmised that the visitation roles had been reversed today, and that was when a knock sounded at the door. I closed the window, hastily ran to the bathroom, opened the tap, and then closed that door, answering the bedroom door.

"Ah, Lizzie," said Nanny Pina. "I trust you and your mistress are comfortable for the night?"

She looked around me at the closed bathroom door, making me glad for my efforts.

"Yes, ma'am, my mistress is just washing up, and she has plenty of towels, don't you worry," I replied, holding the door fast in case she made to gain entry again.

But she made no such move, seemingly satisfied with the sounds coming from the bathroom. "You finished with the assignment in the kitchen, I hope?"

I fought down an angry retort and simply nodded, and she smiled grimly and bid me good night.

I watched her go down the hall and knock similarly on the princess's door. After a few moments, she too answered, they had a brief conversation and then her door was closed. The nanny stopped to talk to the guards and then proceeded down the east hallway and around the corner.

I closed my door quietly, shut off the tap in the bathroom and returned to the open window, climbing over the cast-iron bars and reaching for the next balcony as I stepped out into the dark. Below me I could hear our unnamed ally, though this wasn't the time to expose him, so I said nothing. I was relatively sure I knew who he was, but I felt no need to test his support with my falling body.

Thankfully, his support was not necessary, and I swung myself onto the princess's balcony within moments of leaving my own. Neither of the two women sitting on the floor was surprised when I tapped gently at the window, and the princess leapt up to let me in.

"Miss Adams, you have finally come," she said as she helped me into her room. "Elaine thought it best that she hide here rather than risk the discovery of my absence."

"A good plan, and it seems to have worked so far. Pina has stopped at both our rooms for the night and found us exactly where she wants us," I agreed, nodding at Elaine, who was sitting on the floor holding an unopened letter. "Do not tell me you have retrieved your letters, Princess?"

"No, sadly not," the princess replied. "This was delivered today." Her eyes lingered on the envelope. "We were just getting up the courage to open it when you tapped on the window."

Elaine nodded and opened the letter, and the three of us scanned it, though only one of us could actually read the language.

This letter was singular. Though signed by Marco, it was written in a different hand than the others I had been privy to. And a different hand than the one I had seen for a brief instant in Nanny Pina's room.

"What does the blackguard say, Frannie?" Elaine prompted impatiently.

The contents were very short, a mere paragraph, but we watched the princess's pale cheeks go even paler as she mouthed the words. Finally, she took a gulp of air and answered.

"She or he demands a payment of 50,000 lire, or else they will send the rest of the letters to the newspapers in Rome ... and they want it by the end of the week!"

"Fifty thousand lire?" repeated Elaine, turning to me. "But how can they expect Frannie to come up with that kind of money that quickly?"

"Please don't think me insensitive, Princess, but that is not a ridiculous sum of money for you, is it?" I answered, taking the letter from her hands, noting the smudge in the lower corner and turning over the sheet to assess the writing.

"It is not impossible," she admitted. "My parents have left me access to an adequate allowance, and I do not spend it rashly..."

"It is interesting that Marco seems to have asked for what you can afford," I said, musing at the speed with which the writer had scrawled this note and comparing it with the other notes the princess had provided, "and that she has asked for an amount that you could actually deliver in the time she has allotted."

"I must leave it in Marco's name at a bank. She has detailed the address here." The princess read aloud.

"Portia?" murmured Elaine. "Is this a good thing? Does it mean that Nanny Pina is this Marco? I mean, the woman has done everything in her power to keep us from Frannie. She has filled her days with new lessons and new tutors. She has access to the princess, and her correspondence, · you found a letter from Marco in her possession, hidden away..."

I shook my head. "The letter I found in Pina's room and the ones before this one were written by the same person. I cannot say the same for this latest letter. It is clear there is a connection between Marco and Pina. What I am struggling with is what Pina would gain. She has worked for the royal family her entire life. To cause them pain would seem to cause *her* pain. And for her charge to be so exposed in the press, I don't see how she would not be blamed — she is, after all, the princess's nanny."

The princess was nodding. "It is true. As terrible as Nanny Pina can be, she has been loyal to my family for decades."

"Anyone can be bought, given the right price, Portia," Elaine warned. "I don't care how loyal they are. And 50,000 lire is a lot of money for a woman of Pina's age and income."

I took a deep breath, because of course that was true; it was one of my grandfather's main tenets. In fact, in many of his personal writings, Sherlock Holmes had lamented how little actual gain people had thieved for, or even killed for.

"I think we should get the money together, Frannie. I can help you with it if gathering the funds causes you trouble with your parents. I have some monies with me as well," Elaine spoke up when I stayed silent, "and hopefully we can end this madness as soon as possible."

CHAPTER TWELVE

B ack in our own beds in our room, Elaine fell asleep almost immediately, having worked out a viable plan of action with the princess.
I, on the other hand, tossed and turned on the hard cot until finally
giving up entirely around two o'clock in the morning.

I felt like Elaine was too ready to jump to conclusions, too driven by
her emotions and by assumptions to help me in this case. Glancing at her
peaceful slumber, I fought against the resentment I felt bubbling up inside
me and admitted the truth of the situation: I missed Brian's cool head and
gut instincts. Where I was focused on the technical and physical data, he
invariably provided the wider perspective I was too close to see. Where I
could make leaps of logic from one clue to the next, he was the one I trusted
to deconstruct my assumptions or agree with them — depending on his
own detective skills.

Where I got caught up in details, Brian was able to step back and see
the whole story. And as a sounding board, I had never found a better,
more patient resource.

Silently pulling on my wrap, I snuck out of our room, surprising the
guards at the stairs. They jumped up at my approach. I explained as best I
could that I couldn't sleep and offered to bring them up some tea if they
wished it, but they declined, sitting back down at their posts.

For the first time since my arrival at Racconigi, the kitchens were silent,
though in the corners, the youngest staff snored quietly on cots near the
still-warm hearths.

I carefully heated up some water for tea and then steeped myself a large carafe. Carrying it and a mug, I stepped out into the stillness of the backyard, heading past the gazebo where I had served breakfast to Elaine and Frannie. About a hundred yards away was another gazebo, overrun by vines and flowers, so I chose that as my thinking spot.

The darkness should have been absolute at this time of night, but the gardens had electric lanterns that gave the yard a surreal atmosphere with a dim, flickering light. That, in addition to the multitude of fireflies that circled the gazebo, would have put anyone into a relaxed state. Anyone but me, that is.

Sipping my tea, I allowed my brain to attack the problem without distraction, fighting my way through each unanswered question as though I were cutting through a field of opponents one clue at a time.

The complexity of this crime seemed to warrant a much bigger payoff; that was one of those questions that I just hadn't managed to wrestle to the ground. Brian would see it, I was sure. He had that way of forcing me to sound out my assumptions that often led to a moment of clarity.

And then there was the knowledge of the victim — of her pliability and access to the monies. I leaned back as I mentally circled that clue. The politics, too, the knowledge that this was exactly the right screw to turn in Italian politics, that was ... well — inspired.

The two sets of writing seemed to point more than one blackmailer, but even if it were a team, why now switch the person who actually wrote the letters?

"Intelligent and patient — that is how this crime started," I whispered to the sparkling stars, "and now that Marco has the princess exactly where she wants her ... suddenly she is impatient for it to be over, so what has changed? Is it our arrival? And who wrote this new letter? If there are two people in on this blackmail, it could explain the change in tactics. One simply got sick of waiting and took over the blackmail schedule."

I sipped some more tea, putting my still-aching feet up on the bench. From somewhere behind me I heard movement, and I stilled, listening intently. What was that sound? I concentrated, closing my eyes. Someone was crying ... the princess? No, more than crying, retching, it sounded like. I carefully placed my mug down on the table and looked around into the darkness. There, at the end of the yard, far away from the palace, where the bushes covered a small sewer grate, a petite figure hunched over and coughed.

I slid down in my seat so that only the top of my head and eyes could be seen over the hedges between the gazebo and the person making the sound.

The unfortunate woman finally stood up on shaky legs, obvious even in the darkness, and made her way slowly around the garden to a fountain, washing her hands and drinking and spitting a couple of times. But it wasn't until she tiptoed around the only lantern between her and the house that I could identify her — it was Lia.

I sat up straight in realization and then quickly ducked back down, remembering why I was hiding. I waited until she had left the yard, noting that she did not go back into the palace but instead walked down a long path into a wooded area. Her silhouette in the lantern light had been decidedly rounded. She wasn't visiting a sick relative — she was hiding her pregnancy from the household. It explained why her aunt had reacted so defensively when I had inquired after her absence. But why was she still here? Would it not be better to hide her condition, far, far away from those who knew her?

I suddenly remembered Carlo's words about trust "and impressionable young women." He had been trying to warn me, after all!

"But Elaine, what makes you think that when you hand over the money to this Marco, you will actually get the letters?" I said to my friend as she paced back and forth, picking up items and stuffing them into her bags.

"Obviously, Portia, I will not give over the money until I have all the letters in my hands," she answered, pulling on her gloves. "Now are you coming with me to town or not?"

"I think my time is better spent here, to be honest, but if you could post these for me, please?" I asked, extending some envelopes.

"Fine then," she said, barely looking up at me as she slipped my letters into her bag. "I will be back with the remainder of the money by lunchtime. We shall make this deadline with time to spare, I warrant."

With that, she breezed out the door, her flowered silk scarf flowing behind her, her displeasure clear at my lack of support.

I sighed, heading over to our window to look down at the gardens, where Lorenzo and one of the other gardeners were lifting a large statue and moving it to another location using a trolley. The men moved it two more times before they were satisfied, and as they stepped back I watched a young boy run out of the palace and speak to them. Lorenzo nodded and wiped his forehead again, making his way to a fountain further in the garden, stripping off the top half of his uniform as he walked. At the fountain, he splashed himself three times before vigorously shaking the water from his head.

I frowned, looking back out the window, where he was pulling his tunic back on, and something struck me as odd. He answered a question directed at him from somewhere out of my sight and then headed quickly down the side of the house, buttoning his vest as he walked.

He was out of sight for a few minutes before I realized what had bothered me about the sight of his naked torso.

"It would not be the first time," I hissed under my breath, my heart beating rapidly as I felt an idea falling into place.

Pulling on my shoes, I decided I had no choice but to move on the clues I had uncovered, so I headed out the door and straight down to the library. The deadline was set — as soon as the princess gave in to the demands of her blackmailer, my case would be over, and not in a good way.

I had assumed I would find Pina there, since it seemed to be her routine to read the morning paper while the princess took her morning lessons with the tutor in the room next door. I was not disappointed, finding her sitting at one of the desks near the window and staring out into the gardens, distractedly folding and unfolding the newspaper.

Glancing out the window, I could see the remaining gardener working away on the hedges. I looked back into the anteroom, seeing the princess looking bored and pale in front of her tutor, and so, doing a slow circuit of the library, I closed the open doors and windows until I arrived at the nanny's side.

She noticed nothing until I was practically at her elbow, at which point she jumped and pressed a hand to her chest.

"*Dio*, Lizzie, you gave me a start," she said, looking up at me, her eyes wide.

"I apologize for that, Pina, but it was necessary, I am afraid," I replied, leaning over her newspaper and pulling out the letter I had spied beneath it. I had said those words without the benefit of my exaggerated English accent, which seemed to shock her long enough for me to pull the letter from its hiding spot.

Her mouth opened and shut and she started to stand up, but I pressed her back down into her seat and sat down across from her. "Pina, I know this will seem shocking, but if you can give me a moment to explain, I believe we can actually be of help to each other and the people we represent."

"What ... who...?" she managed to stammer, only now noticing that the letter she had been hiding was in my hands. She reached for it with a shaking hand.

I pulled the letter back and unfolded it. "This is a letter from Marco, isn't it?" I asked, scanning down to the bottom and finding the familiar signature. I flipped the letter over and found the same pressured evidence of a new writer.

"Yes ... it is ... but how do you know of it?" she replied, her hand still extended.

I nodded and handed it back to her. "Because Marco has been equally unfriendly to your charge, the princess, and it is time you and I exposed them before they can do real damage."

"No," she whispered, standing, the letter crumpling in her fist, "he promised that if I did as he bade, she would be safe. That he would leave her alone!"

"You must tell me everything, Pina," I said, remaining seated but leaning forward in my seat, fixing my adamant gaze to hers. "What he wants, what you did and what you know about his identity. And you must tell me now, before we are interrupted."

CHAPTER THIRTEEN

E laine did not actually get back to the palace until suppertime. I helped to serve dinner to a much smaller table of diners, Pina having excused herself with a headache.

My friend looked grim but calm and made the minimal amount of small talk with the head steward, a nervous, sweaty man with a limited grasp of English.

I made my way into the kitchens to gather up the dessert, nodding at Lupe, who was avoiding the dining room since her latest talking-to by the nanny the morning before. Lorenzo stood off to the side, and upon seeing me, he broke into a huge smile.

"Signora Lizzie, it is so very good to see you again, I feel it has been too long," he said, coming to my side and helping me arrange the apple beignets onto the tray I carried.

"'Tis true," I agreed, stepping around a bucket of water and sending a smile back at him. "I did not see you all day. 'Ave you been very busy in the gardens?"

"Ah, no, I was called to escort your mistress on her errands in town," he answered, bowing slightly at the waist. "I understand that she is soon to return to her home, in fact, which saddens me *molto*. But I am sure you will be happy to return to your home."

"Really?" I answered, nodding at Carlo as he offered a lit match. I used it to light the alcohol in the dessert, making it a flambé, and as carefully as possible hoisted the tray onto my shoulder. "Did she say that?"

"Why yes, Signora," Lorenzo started to say, and then was interrupted by a female scream from behind us.

Whirling, Lorenzo realized that his clothes were on fire, and with a cry of shock, he pulled off his vest, buttons flying everywhere, throwing the smoking item to the ground.

I quickly replaced the tray on the table beside me, and I stooped to pick up the still-burning vest by a corner and pushed it into the bucket of water beside the table.

Lorenzo's shock was quickly being replaced by anger, his usually beautiful features now dark as he whirled on Carlo, his Italian coming fast and angry in the adrenaline of the moment.

"Whatever has happened?" demanded Elaine Ridley as she entered the kitchen. Pina too had rushed into the room from the opposite direction, catching my eye and shaking her head at me.

Lorenzo was standing face-to-face with Carlo, and two other staff were trying to convince them to stand down when the head steward stepped between them.

Whatever he said calmed them down enough that Lorenzo turned with disgust still on his face, stepped over to the bucket of water and dragged out his vest before stalking off outside. Carlo brushed off the concerned people still surrounding him, and with an anxious look on his face, he came to stand beside Pina.

"Lizzie?" said Elaine, still looking confused.

"Please, Elaine," I answered, pulling a bundle of sodden papers out of my apron with a sly smile, "call me Portia."

CHAPTER FOURTEEN

It was two days later when we sat at the station awaiting the first train on our long trip home, and the atmosphere could not have been more different.

The princess was laughing gaily at something Pina said, her transformation the most marked.

I glanced her way, and she grinned from ear to ear, moving closer to us and flagged by Carlo and one other man from the palace.

"I know that I have already thanked you for everything you have done, but surely I must thank you again, Miss Adams," she said, wrapping her arms around me for another hug.

I returned the hug with a smile. "And I have already told you several times that it was my pleasure to be of any aid, Princess."

"And we cannot convince you to stay but a bit longer?" Pina asked us both, her hands extended to us. "The happy time you spent with us seems so much less than the horrible time before. Surely you will allow us to treat you to the true Italian experience?"

The train whistle answered the question before we could, and we all turned to watch its slow arrival into the station.

"Soon, I promise, we shall return soon," Elaine said, throwing her arms wide for her friend. Princess Francesca didn't disappoint and hurled herself into Mrs. Ridley's arms.

"Then I will look forward to your return, Miss Portia Adams," said Pina, reaching out to shake my hand with a broad smile. "And though my thanks are less important than that of our *principessa*, I do humbly thank you for all you have done."

She bowed slightly, and Carlo did the same, his tiny smile regretful but sincere.

"You are very welcome," I replied with a slight bow of my own.

"If ever you need anything," the princess said, turning my way and pressing a small parcel into my hands, "you need but ask. I am at your disposal."

I took the parcel only because it would seem rude not to, trying hard to ignore the mystery in my hands. "Remember your promise, Princess. The letters are destroyed, but you must tell your parents everything."

She nodded. "I will, I promise, no more secrets."

Tears flowed from both sides, though not from me, until finally Elaine and I took our seats in first class. Elaine waved all the way until we were out of sight of the platform and then sat back with a sigh.

"Well?" she said, leaning forward.

I laughed. "All right, what is it I have not explained to your satisfaction?"

She threw up her hands. "Everything! Nothing! How did you figure out that Lorenzo and Lia were Marco?"

I settled back into my seat. "I didn't for the longest time, I swear. The only lead we had was that the letters signed Marco were written by a right-handed woman. Lorenzo was very convincing as the flirtatious Italian gardener. I only started to be suspicious of him when I began eliminating the suspects he kept throwing into my path. And then when Carlo warned me to be careful, it made me all the more observant of Lorenzo."

"Lorenzo wanted you to believe that Pina was the blackmailer, while blackmailing her as well," she answered with a scowl. "Imagine threatening that poor lady with the kidnapping of her charge. Monster."

I nodded. "Driving her to cloister the princess, restrict her movements, fill her days from breakfast to dinner, and limit her correspondence — making Pina seem like the source of the problem. Even the staff became resentful of Pina because of this."

"You took a chance revealing what you knew to Pina, though," Elaine said, shaking her head. "When I left our room that morning, you still didn't know who the blackmailer was or where the letters were — don't deny it."

"I wouldn't deny it. But by the time you left the palace, I knew who was lying to us and who was not."

Elaine threw up her hands incredulously. "That was a five-minute difference, Portia Adams! What could you possibly have realized in the five minutes it took me to walk out the bedroom door, arrange for a car and leave the premises?"

I thought back to the sight of Lorenzo bathing himself with the fountain water. "Suffice it to say, it became obvious that Lorenzo was not a portly man, though his vest made him look that way. The same uniform was worn by several others, and none of them seemed to go from slim to portly in donning the vest, so I surmised that something was odd. Add to that Carlo's warning, and I guessed what was making the vest bulkier than it should be."

"Then why did you send Pina to his rooms to investigate, the same way you had in her rooms?" replied Elaine, pushing her hair behind her ears as she spoke.

"Well, I couldn't very well go; the man was obviously suspicious of me, which was why he took it upon himself to follow me around," I answered. "Better that I distract him in the kitchen while she looked for the letters in his room."

"Of course, the only reason a handsome man would follow you around was because he suspected you were the consulting detective from Baker Street," she said with a wry twist of her mouth. "Regardless, I thought you suspected the vest; why check the room?"

"I didn't know how much Lorenzo understood of my presence in the palace," I answered, turning over the package in my hand. "Remember, he had been intercepting mail addressed to the princess, and you had earlier sent wedding photos which she claimed to never have seen. It was possible he had seen me as part of your wedding reception, where I was not dressed like a personal maid."

"I did not think of that," Elaine said, tapping her mouth with her index finger. "So you and Carlo arranged to light his vest on fire to get it away from him."

I nodded, undoing the string on the package. "Once I realized from his footprints that Carlo was the one standing under the balcony when we each made our evening climbs, I knew that he was on our side and allied myself with him. He revealed his hatred of Lorenzo for ruining his cousin Lia, and he was correct in his assessment of the man. He did not know what they were up to, specifically, but he knew it involved the princess, so he started following her around to protect her while he worked on Lia, trying to convince her to leave the palace and leave behind any criminal plans."

"What do you think will happen to Lia?" Elaine asked.

I stopped unwrapping for a moment. "She will have Lorenzo's bastard child in exile from the palace and her family. They will have none of the blackmail money he was planning to use to run away with and none of the satisfaction of hurting the princess or the king."

"You really believe she was the mastermind behind the plot, though, Portia?"

"I do," I answered, my eyes meeting hers levelly. "She was studying to join the church when she became pregnant with Lorenzo's child, and that, of course, forced to leave her studies. Then she got back to Racconigi and was given her notice by Pina, who equally could not allow a member of her staff to birth a child out of wedlock. Desperate and angry, Lia had access to the right players, the right knowledge about the political situation and the resentment born out of her place in society and that of the princess.

"Most assuredly, they were working together from the beginning, but it was she who wrote all the letters except the last two: the one to the princess demanding the money, and the one to Pina requiring that she leave the palace in the dead of night with no explanation. Those two were written by an entirely different mind — Lorenzo's."

"So it is what you said, then. Lia's motive was emotional and political," Elaine murmured. "She fully intended to use the letters against the king."

"And Lorenzo's were entirely financial," I finished. "Perhaps Lia thought to regain her standing with the church; perhaps she just wanted to strike out at the royal family. Who knows, really? She would not speak at all when we confronted her. Not even when Carlo was trying to get her to explain her actions. Lorenzo was far more talkative, because his motives were simpler — he wanted money."

"What changed then, do you think? Why did Lorenzo write those last two letters?" demanded Elaine.

"Lia wouldn't admit it, but I will bet that our appearance at the palace frightened her into wanting to back down, at least while we were in Italy. Until we got there, she was in it for the long con and was patient enough to wait for the perfect moment to destroy the Savoy family. Lorenzo initially agreed with her strategy and took the princess's letters, sewing them into his vest for safekeeping."

I pulled off the last of the wrapping to reveal a sparkling treasure.

Elaine gasped at the same time as I did, moving from her seat across from me to sit beside me on my padded bench.

In my hands lay a pearl-and-diamond brooch with the crest of the House of Savoy rendered in gold leaf.

"How gorgeous, Portia," Elaine whispered, lifting it up gently so that another smaller package was revealed beneath it along with a card.

"The broach is an heirloom of my family that I now pass on to yours, Portia Adams, that they will always know the service you have done for Italia," I read aloud from the note. "The earrings are so you remember me and come back soon."

I carefully unwrapped the smaller package to reveal a pair of pear-shaped diamond earrings.

"Not bad for your first trip to Italy, eh, Portia Adams?" Elaine said, poking me in the side with her elbow.

"Not bad at all," I replied with an answering smile.

CASEBOOK EIGHT
SETTLING THE SCORE

CHAPTER ONE
LONDON, FALL 1931

I admit that my apprehension about returning to college for my third year of law school had many layers to it. For example, since my return from Italy, I had still to lay eyes on either of my grandparents or my boyfriend.

To be sure, I had letters from my grandmother, Irene Adler, explaining her extended trip to the United States, so I knew her to be safe, if not entirely forthcoming about her reasons for being away from London. But my grandfather had disappeared with no word at all. All but one of the letters I had written to him while I was abroad had been waiting for me at my townhouse on Baker Street, having been returned to sender with the stamp "addressee unknown."

This made no sense in light of the letter he had written me before I left, so the day after my return from Italy, I set out bright and early to visit the residence in Marylebone my grandfather had given as his address.

Nerissa and I took two wrong turns after exiting the tube stop but finally made it down the right street to find a burned-down husk of a building. Nerissa sniffed around the debris as I looked on with shock, my heart in my throat at the fate of my grandfather. I had just recently wrapped up a case of arson, so I was alert for evidence of a crime, but the neighbors were quick to tell me the story.

An elderly woman who had lived on the first floor had fallen asleep with a lit cigarette in her hand, causing the fire and killing the unfortunate culprit.

Her neighbors attested to her having frightened them before with smaller fires, and since she had no relatives that anyone knew of and no real assets other than the house she had owned and burned down, everyone had accepted it as a tragedy and moved on. No one could remember if anyone was living in the flat above, and since the arsonist in the case also owned the house, there was no one to ask about a potential tenant. The sick feeling in my stomach remained even when I was assured that no other bodies had been pulled from the wreckage, and I knew I wouldn't sleep easy till I spoke to the police.

I hailed a cab straight away, my mind buzzing with possibilities, and asked to be dropped off at Scotland Yard.

Because Sherlock Holmes had purposely dropped out of society, and because a spare number of people knew of our relationship as grandfather and granddaughter, there were very few people with whom I could discuss this troubling issue.

Sergeant Michaels was one of those people. Through the machinations of an evil man during the casebook I had titled "Box 850," the sergeant was now aware of both my grandfathers, Dr. John Watson and Sherlock Holmes, former partners who shared a granddaughter.

"Now then, Adams, where you off to in such a hurry?" a voice called out as I took the stairs at the Yard two at a time, Nerissa quick at my heels.

It was none other than Sergeant Michaels, standing outside smoking a cigarette with another officer.

"Sir, I was coming to speak to you, actually," I said, allowing myself to be introduced to the other man, who quickly excused himself, putting his butt out with the heel of his shoe. I waited until he was out of earshot before directing my questions at Michaels.

"The house fire in Marylebone, number 327 Gloucester Place, what do you know of it?" I blurted out.

Michaels looked surprised but answered, "Nothing much, looks like an accident to me n' my boys. Poor old lady fell asleep with her cigarette. She'd done it before but got lucky when a milkman smelled her rug burning as he walked by on his route." He tapped his nose for emphasis. "This time the whole place caught fire. The evidence box is on its way here from the local station. You can have a look if you like."

"But was there anyone found ... anyone else found?" I said.

"Who else?" he asked, giving Nerissa a scratch under her chin. "What's this about, Adams? Have you found some evidence there that I need to look at?"

"My grandfather," I said, glancing around us before continuing, "Sherlock Holmes. He lived in the upstairs apartment of that building. Or at least the address he gave me was for the upstairs apartment. I had never actually visited him there."

"Well, that's a whole new kettle o' fish," Michaels said with a grunt. "No, Adams, we found no other bodies, only the old lady's. And it wasn't so burned down, that place, that we couldn't identify her or anyone else if we had found them. The firemen got there in good time, and only that house was affected. They took down the walls themselves to get the fire out, but no, we would have been able to see if there was anyone else in the house." He frowned. "But I got the report from Simmons himself on that. The neighbors said she lived alone, the old bird did."

I let out my breath with difficulty. It was entirely possible that Sherlock Holmes did not live at the apartment but picked up mail there. Michaels reached out to put a steadying hand on my shoulder. "Adams, I tell you, he wasn't in there. Your own Dr. Whitaker was the coroner on the scene — go talk to him if you don't believe me."

"I believe you, Sergeant, I do," I said, and I did. The more I thought about it, the more I believed that Holmes had never lived at that house. And hearing that Gavin had been assigned to the case was reassuring as well. "Thank you so much for explaining. And yes, when you get that evidence box I would like to take a look at it."

"Well, all right then, off you go, Adams," Michaels said, tossing down his cigarette and shooing me away from his offices.

I headed back home to drop off Nerissa. She was thankful for the return, curling up on the rug between my two easy chairs while I grabbed my book satchel and headed back out my door.

So deep in thought was I that I practically walked into my downstairs tenant on the main floor landing.

"Oh! So sorry, Miss Adams," Brian Dawes said with a tip of his uniform hat.

"Not at all. My fault, Constable," I replied, trying to step out of his way.

We both moved left at the same time, and then right, in lock-step.

He gave a tight smile and extended a hand in front of him, inviting me to exit the tight foyer first.

And that was the state of affairs with the only other person I could speak to about this, I thought, opening the front door, only to run directly into Annie Coleson. Her trench coat was new. A gift, I would guess, from her boyfriend, its sky blue very flattering against her pale skin and blonde hair.

"Portia!" she exclaimed. "Brian said you were home, and I came right over to get the whole story. How was Italy?"

"I ... well ... it was fine, Annie," I said, submitting to her hug in the congested hallway.

"Brian, let's bring Portia out for our breakfast. We want to catch up," she said around my shoulder. Being a half-foot shorter, she had to look around me to catch her boyfriend's eye, but without waiting for his response she turned around, looping her elbow through mine and started chattering as she led us to the Rose Café. I was sure Brian wanted no part of this party, but I barely got a word in edgewise with his girlfriend telling me all about the happenings in London while I was away.

"And Lady Grace has suddenly reappeared in public," Annie said, as we crossed the street to the café. "I have been trying to get an interview with her father for more than a month about his stance on women's suffrage. I may try to go through her to get to him now that she is socializing again. She had almost dropped out of society, you know. And quite transformed her look. Her social secretary must be thrilled."

It was only when we were seated by the window with our tea and scones ordered that Annie realized I had not said more than yes or no to her since leaving Baker Street.

She looked back and forth between Brian and me, neither of us making eye contact, he finding great interest in his hat on the table, and me looking around at all the other patrons.

"What's going on?" she asked finally, a nervous giggle popping out of her pink lips. "I feel like I'm the only one who doesn't know a big secret."

Brian swung his gaze back toward her, and at first I thought he was going to deny it, but he hardened his jaw and looked straight at me, a challenge in his brown eyes.

I swallowed, wishing myself away from this place, but said, "Annie, I wasn't entirely honest with you when I left London with Elaine Ridley."

"What?" she said, confused. "What do you mean, Portia? You didn't go to Italy?"

"Oh, she went to Italy," Brian said, his tone controlled but his eyes betraying his anger. "But she didn't go for a jaunt, Annie."

"Then why..." Annie started to say, and then understanding came fast and she looked from her boyfriend to me. "That's why you've been in such a bad mood, Brian?"

Brian opened his mouth to deny that vehemently, I am sure, but I interrupted. "It's my fault, Annie. I could have told you all the truth before I left, but I didn't want to worry you."

"But you told Brian?" she asked, her eyes on her boyfriend, who immediately shook his head.

"No, Brian just figured it out," I answered immediately. "On his own."

"Of course he did," Annie said, turning her attention to the waiter as our food was delivered on small plates.

Quickly, and with little embellishment, I filled my friends in on the casebook I had called "Principessa."

"But you didn't need to lie to us about that," Annie admonished, spreading clotted cream and jam on one half of a scone and placing it on the plate in front of Brian. "Of course we would have understood that you wanted to help Mrs. Ridley. She is, after all, your friend!"

Brian said nothing, choosing to stir lemon into his tea.

Taking a sip from my own cup, I had to admit to myself, at least, that part of my reason for keeping the truth was about proving myself on a solo assignment.

"I'm sorry, Annie, I was at least partially trying to avoid the press and public that seemed so interested in my life since that press conference," I said, looking down at my plate because I couldn't look at Brian anymore and see the disappointment in his eyes.

Annie sighed heavily. "Well, for heaven's sake, just promise from now on you'll tell us when you're going off on an adventure! What if something had happened to you over there and we found out after the fact — imagine how upset we'd have been. Imagine how upset Dr. Whitaker would be!"

I raised my eyes at the mention of my boyfriend and found myself actually wondering what Gavin would feel if I had been harmed while abroad. Would he react this way when I told him the truth about my trip? I hadn't really thought about it until now. We both valued our independence above everything else in our lives. I believed he would be curious about my adventure but not hurt at all by my keeping it secret. I would feel the same way if he were pulled toward something that interested him. I caught Brian looking at me and dropped my eyes again. He did not take the same view, obviously.

"Promise," Annie said, putting both her hands over mine on the table.

"I promise," I mumbled, unused to making such a promise and already wondering if it was one I could keep.

"Good, then," she said, throwing herself back into her meal with gusto, "that sets things to rights, doesn't it, Brian?"

But it didn't. I could see that from the set of his jaw and the way he smiled with his mouth but not with his eyes.

Pride kept me from asking his forgiveness again. Hadn't I already apologized?

"At least since I've been back from Italy no reporters have come knocking on my door," I said.

She shook her head. "I think the true test of whether the press has sated their appetite for you will become clear when you solve your next case. That's when we'll know for sure."

I agreed and then said, "I've been looking for Gavin, actually. Is he busy with the Yard these days? Because I haven't been able to find him since I've been back."

Brian looked at his girlfriend before answering. "He has been at the Yard quite a lot, though not on cases, as far as I can tell..."

When I raised my eyebrow, Annie piped up, "He's been spending a lot of time with Constable Simmons. Did you know they were both at Pellam Orphanage when they were young, Portia?"

I thought about the slightly smarmy constable and couldn't recall Gavin mentioning him before, but it was only recently that he had opened up to me about his life at the orphanage.

Brian opened his mouth to say something and then seemed to think better of it. I reminded myself to ask him what he was holding back when we were next alone. For the moment, I listened to Annie telling us all about the latest political machinations in London.

Chapter Two

Professor Archer scanned his audience before picking up his notes from the lectern. Something about his clothing or the way he was standing caught my eye as he said, "Before our next class, be sure to memorize page 394, because we'll be talking in detail about the welfare of the accused."

I dutifully put a note in at page 394 and mimicked my classmates, shoving books and notes into my satchel and listening to the rising hum of chatter start anew.

"Miss Adams, a moment?" Professor Archer called as we began filing out of the lecture hall.

A few of my peers snickered as I passed, but I ignored them, well used to being seen as different and therefore worthy of gossip.

I made my way down to his side. "Professor Archer, very good to see you again, but you have lost some weight, have you not? I hope you are not unwell?"

"Ah — no, I am fine, Miss Adams, I assure you," he replied, glancing down at himself a little abashedly, "and it is not as though I couldn't stand to drop a stone, anyway."

He led the way out of the hall as we spoke. "I was wondering if I might interest you in a little side project I am working on."

I followed his steps, recognizing our direction. "What project is that, sir?"

"It is for a paper I am writing on criminal psychology — specifically, on the psychological profiles of suicides," he explained in hushed tones, his eyes on mine.

"I'm surprised," I replied. "I had no idea the subject was of interest to you."

"Well," my professor admitted, "it *is* a controversial subject, and one that can be rife with grisly and upsetting details, but it has never really been taken on from a legal and police angle — only from a psychological angle, from what I have read. I am, as you know, coming up on my retirement, and it would be something to solidly attach my name to."

"I see," I answered, thinking about it as we came to his office door. "And how do you see me contributing to this paper?"

"Oh, as a full and equal coauthor, Miss Adams," he replied, shaking out a small ring of keys and applying each one in turn until the right one was found. "You've had your own experiences this year with those women who were suspected suicides — from that case with the reverend in White-chapel?"

The casebook I had titled "Truth Be Told" did indeed begin with a suspected suicide but had resulted in a kinder sentence, depending on whom you talked to. The prostitutes who had been tricked into thinking they had been damned by God had in fact been coerced into joining the cloth and faking their own suicides. When told the truth by the reverend's wife, who had done the coercing, they all chose to remain in the church, preferring the quiet, simple life of a nun to the violent life of working the streets and begging for scraps.

"I have reams of research and decades of case notes," my professor declared as we gained access to his paper-filled office, "and you have the energy, the mind and the writing skills to put it all together into academic form."

Looking around at the stacks of papers and boxes of stacked files, some might have been intimidated. But I, for the first time since my return to London, felt the spark of curiosity blaze anew.

"Count me in," I declared, extending my hand for a firm shake.

CHAPTER THREE

Two days later, on my evening walk with Nerissa, I stopped to speak to a few of my Baker Street Irregulars as they streamed by me in a noisy little herd.

I pulled out a bag of sweets, and that got some smiles out of even the filthiest of them, and then I got caught up on the street-level whisperings this group was so good at gathering for me. Other than some oddities in the intimidation tactics of a few known thugs, there wasn't much to report.

Nerissa finally agreed to leave, despite the amount of attention being directed her way, and we made a slow loop back toward home.

Stepping into our foyer, I could smell the faint scent of rosewater, signaling Annie's presence. Normally this was a night of the week when I was invited to join the Dawes in the downstairs apartment for their family dinner, but I didn't hesitate as I went upstairs to my own rooms.

Nerissa immediately set to drinking at her water dish as I peeled off my outerwear and proceeded to making a solitary supper of cold meats and bread.

Two hours later, a knock sounded at the door, surprising me. I looked over at Nerissa, who headed straight to the door to sniff at it. Popping a bit of cheese into my mouth, I tip-toed on sock feet to the door to look through the peephole so efficiently installed by Jenkins months ago, to see Annie at my door.

"I knew you were home," she said as soon as I opened the door, breezing in carrying a plate of food covered by a checkered napkin and somehow managing to avoid Nerissa's curious nose. "You can't fool me twice, Portia Adams."

I sighed, following her to the countertop, where she flipped up the corner of the napkin that covered the plate she had carried up and stole a roasted potato from under it.

"I was just ... I just wanted to be alone, Annie. I wasn't trying to 'fool' anyone," I said as I peeked under the napkin and saw nothing of immediate interest.

"I thought maybe you had Gavin up here," she said, grinning from ear to ear. "Perhaps catching up on lost time?"

I snorted, and she giggled. "But you *have* seen him, haven't you?"

"I left him a message at the college, but no, I have not spoken to him yet. Though there is a lingering proposition that we really must discuss..." I said, enjoying her surprised annoyance a little too much.

"Portia Adams!" she declared, nosiness interrupting her filching for a second. "Is this what you and the doctor were talking about on our walk before you left for Italy? You had better tell me something, chum — you owe me after that whole ramble with royalty!"

I smirked. "That is what I should have called the casebook — "Ramble with Royalty," instead of "Principessa.""

She glared at me, so I removed the napkin from the plate entirely, hoping to mollify her with more starch.

When she stubbornly withdrew her salty fingers, reminding me of the first time we had shared a meal in this room, I said, "Dr. Whitaker is going to be traveling soon, and as part of his trip," I hesitated slightly, "before I left for Italy he asked if I would join him abroad — to celebrate his birthday, and I agreed."

Annie gave up all pretense of anger, reached for the plate and started munching anew.

"Fabulous. Romantic. About time," she whispered. "Just the two of you off on a romantic vacation. I love it."

I laughed at her reaction.

"Excuse me, ladies," came Brian's voice from my still-ajar front door. Nerissa had already nudged it open again on hearing his footsteps on the stairs.

"Oh, Brian, I am sorry, I was to come directly back down, wasn't I?" Annie said, passing me the half empty plate. I remembered my childish act of announcing my answer to Gavin loudly enough that Brian would hear it, and I bit my lip.

Brian had his overcoat on and was obviously dressed to walk his girl-friend home, and despite his smile and the way he was patting Nerissa, the tension in his body was evident.

"Apologies," I said, stiffer than I intended to, reacting to his body language. "I did not know you were waiting."

He inclined his head in response and stepped aside for Annie to pass through my doorway.

As the door closed firmly behind them, I could clearly hear Annie say, "I don't know why you didn't just come up with me ... after all..."

Any answer he might have offered was lost to my ears as they headed out of the front door of the townhouse.

CHAPTER FOUR

A s planned, I rose early the next morning, intending to stop in at Gavin's office before heading to Bruiser Jenkins' place for some training.

I waited until I heard Brian leave for the day before knocking on the downstairs apartment door to return the plate from the night before. Mrs. Dawes was her usual friendly, talkative self, reminding me that in Mrs. Jones' absence, she was available should I need anything.

I thanked her but demurred, wondering for a moment if she was going to ask why I hadn't come for dinner last night. When she did not, I surmised that the combination of my antisocial behavior and her son's disinterest in my attendance meant that she saw nothing amiss.

I tried on the whole cab ride over to the college to put the matter out of my head. Why should it bother me so much that Brian had partitioned me from his life with such ease? What did we mean to each other, really, other than owner and tenant? Flirtation and attraction were all well and good, but wasn't a strong relationship built on trust and matching ambitions? The kind of relationship I had with Gavin — steady and without all this energy spent on whose feelings were hurt and who needed to know what. Gavin allowed me to be an individual while being a couple. Wasn't that the relationship I wanted?

I got out of the cab and quickly made my way to Gavin's office, trying to outrun my thoughts. I knocked at his door several times, with no response. I craned my head around the corner to see if he were perhaps in conversation with his students but instead saw Chief Inspector Archer fiddling with his keys outside his office.

He dropped them, cursing roundly as he stooped to retrieve them, bending gingerly.

Dr. Beanstine approached him from his right, even as I approached from the left, leaning down to get his hand under the older man's arm.

Archer was obviously surprised, because at first he jerked away from the offered help and stared up at Dr. Beanstine.

"Oh dear!" Beans (as he was nicknamed by his Scotland Yard peers) said. "Terribly sorry. I did not mean to startle you."

By now, I too had reached Archer from his other side and could see that my professor's face had turned from surprise to suspicion and that he hesitated before taking the younger man's hand.

Dr. Beanstine glanced up at me with a small frown before Archer turned to both of us with, "Blasted keys. Why I have so many I will never understand!"

"Here, allow me," I said, taking the round circle of keys and applying the same one I had seen him use yesterday.

The door swung open before I saw the return to my professor's usual demeanor. "My thanks, Miss Adams, and of course to you, Dr. Beanstine."

"Not at all, sir, not at all," replied Beans, scratching at his new vest as he spoke, a ticket to *Doctor Faustus* peeking out of the top of the vest's pocket. Beans gave me a smile and headed off to his own office. Usually he would have stopped and tried to draw me into conversation, so I noted his quick exit and smiled at the reason. Beans had a new woman in his life, if his haircut was any indication. It was the second time he'd had it cut in less than a month, and that was an increase in frequency for the man I knew.

"Did you need to see me before class, Miss Adams?" Archer said, gathering up a few folders from his otherwise pristine office.

"Actually, I dropped by to speak with … someone else," I admitted, casting my eyes around the room. "But I can't help but notice, sir, that all the files that were here yesterday are … well, not here now."

"Files?" Archer said, ushering us back out the door.

"Yes, the ones we were going to use for our paper?" I replied, watching him deftly lock his office door.

"Ah yes, Whitaker volunteered to deliver them to my office at the Yard. Had to make three trips for all the boxes, good man," he said finally, glancing down at his watch. "We should regroup there and discuss our next steps — perhaps tomorrow afternoon."

I nodded and then watched him head off toward the doors, no doubt headed to the lecture hall. I lingered for a moment, looking thoughtfully at my boyfriend's office door, and then followed Archer.

I took the tube to Bruiser Jenkins' flat in Brixton, my mind still on Archer.

"Adams," Jenkins said as soon as he opened the door, "no dog training today?"

"No, just me today, I'm afraid," I answered, hanging my satchel on the large hook and pulling out my worn old trousers and shirt for our lesson. I couldn't help but smile at the music coming out of his gramophone. It was mellow jazz, and I could feel some of the tension I had been carrying around seep out of me in response.

I had turned toward the bathroom, where I intended to change, when a knock sounded at the door.

"Aren't you going to answer that?" I prompted the large man, who was glaring at the door.

"No," he said, crossing his arms over his large chest. "This is your time. I don't need interruptions."

I could see through the basement window that the knocker had started to walk back up the basement stairs, his wide shoulders encased in a worn suit jacket that showed much care.

My curiosity was aroused, but I paid heed to my instructor, choosing to keep my mouth shut and get dressed for our lesson.

"All right now, I thought we'd pick up from last time," Jenkins said, his back turned as I reentered the large room, my dress under my arm. He was fiddling with his gramophone when another knock could be heard at the door.

This time I stepped forward to answer it before Jenkins could say any-thing and swung the door open to find the same man in the worn suit, now joined by a wiry man in his thirties, wearing thick glasses.

"Gentlemen, can I help you?" I said imperiously, ignoring their goggling at my apparel. Trying to move quickly in a dress was harder, so I did my practice in a pair of very old trousers and a loose short-sleeved shirt.

"We, uh ... we're..." the shorter of the two started to say, but was inter-rupted by a squeeze to the elbow from the initial knocker.

"Sorry to have bothered you, miss, we must have the wrong place," he said with a tap of his hat, taking his friend by arm and tripping quickly back up the stairs.

I watched them leave with a frown, taking in the second man's obvious reluctance. Both were working-class men, though the man in the suit had taken some pains, at least, to look like he was a professional. His suit was not tailored, but it showed signs of repair, and his shoes had been buffed more than their cheapness would normally warrant. He was putting on airs for somebody.

Closing the door behind me, I turned to see Jenkins come out of the loo. He had ducked out of sight when I opened the door.

"Mr. Jenkins, it is obvious you are avoiding those two gentlemen," I said. "Are they troubling you?"

"Nah," he said, back at his gramophone, where he turned it off.

"They are lying. They were looking for you, and when I answered the door instead, they lied," I answered, crossing my arms over my chest. "They are not done with you, Mr. Jenkins. They will be back."

"Nothing I can't handle," he said, turning back to me with a raised chin. "Now, let's do some work here. I think I should show you some moves I've been learning from a tough little Chinese fellow at the fights."

Despite stopping in at King's College again on the way home that night and again the next day, I had yet to run into Gavin. I rang as well, both his office and the flat he rented. Still nothing. Finally, I stooped to leaving a note for him in the administrator's office in the hope that he would retrieve it there. The secretary happened to mention that it was the tenth note that had been dropped by for Whitaker, and then quickly corrected herself, assuring me that the other notes were from an older burly man with an accent, not from another woman.

Never having suspected anything untoward of my boyfriend, I frowned at her hasty correction and found myself more intrigued by the burly man than I would have been of a woman. Nine notes seemed excessive, so I was even more surprised when she admitted the notes had all been left in the space of seventy-two hours.

I couldn't convince the secretary to let me see the notes, no matter how insistent I was, and since I had no solid reason to worry about his safety, nothing I said could move her on the subject. She did describe the man, when I pressed, as a redhead dressed in work clothes and bearing a slight limp, though she could not remember which leg he favored. His accent was European, though she couldn't place it, admitting that it was neither French nor Spanish, but she was able to speculate no further.

Part of me wanted to linger around the office to see if this man would make a tenth attempt, but remembering Gavin's remarks about not needing to know everything about me, I decided he might prefer to deal with this on his own. Still, I only left when the secretary locked the door for lunch, apologetically ushering me out and putting up a chalk sign that said she would be back in an hour.

So dismissed, I headed down to Scotland Yard, avoiding the small cluster of reporters that circled a constable on the front steps.

The notoriety of my parentage had been public for months now, and thankfully the public's appetite for stories on 'Dr. Watson's long-lost granddaughter who had taken up the family business' had finally been satisfied. However, I had yet to take on a big public case since my return from Italy, which Annie and I agreed would be the true test of my celebrity.

I nodded at several officers as I made my way between desks and down corridors, my hard-won relationships having fully recovered from the lying pen of Dick McGregor, a reporter for *The Daily Mirror* who, during the course of the case "Truth Be Told," had claimed to have access to one consulting detective P.C. Adams, faking the entire thing, including hiring an actor to play the detective.

"Miss Adams," Constable Bonhomme said with a grin as I approached his desk, "aren't you a fine sight this afternoon."

"Likewise, Constable," I replied. "I do hope your little one is recovered from her cold?"

He looked nonplussed but nodded and said, "You must be here to see Sergeant Michaels — he's been storming around all morning, so you might want to rethink that."

That piqued my interest, so I asked for the sergeant's whereabouts.

I was directed to the basement, where I could hear Sergeant Michaels' bellows well before I actually laid eyes on him.

"And the next time you bring me such a cock-and-bull story on the sequence of events, Mr. Abner," he said, his rotund face an alarming shade of red, "I'll have you doing overnights in Whitechapel for a month!"

The unfortunate Constable Abner slunk past me and the five or six others in the room. I could see Constable Dawes standing beside the fuming sergeant, holding an open notepad. He stiffened visibly when he saw me enter the corridor where they all stood but quickly glanced back down at his notes when Michaels turned his attention to the next man beside him. My heart sank at our continued estrangement, and then I reminded myself that I had someone in my life who never made me feel this way. Someone who affected my mind more than my heart.

"And you!" Michaels started to say and then caught sight of me and redirected his statement, only lowering his volume slightly. "It's about damn time, Adams. Where the hell have you been?"

All eyes swung toward me, half relieved not to be his next target, the other half sympathetic that I was.

I folded my hands in front of me with more patience than I felt. "Apologies, Sergeant, my telepathic abilities seem to be failing me. I did not *sense* that you required my presence. It will not happen again."

You could have heard a pin drop in the silence as the six men waited for Michaels to explode at my sarcastic comment.

But I knew how to bully a bully, and instead of resuming his tirade, some of the flush left his cheeks. "See that it doesn't, Adams," said he, his eyes giving away his amusement at my answer.

The men let out their collective breath, greeting me quietly and with smiles until Michaels ordered them to "Clear out before I remember what lazy sods you all are!"

They didn't need to be told twice, fairly bolting up the stairs like a herd of frightened sheep.

"Not you, Dawes," said Michaels, halting the tall man in his tracks. "Now, Adams, have you been down here before?" he demanded, gesturing for me to come closer, which I did, shaking my head.

That earned a *harrumph*. "Dawes, you need to keep Adams here up to date so I don't have to waste my time with basic training..."

Brian said nothing; he just nodded stonily.

Michaels frowned, glancing between us. "Oh-ho, so that's the lay of the land, is it? A little lover's spat?"

We both started to protest at the same time and were shouted down.

"I couldn't care less what is happening b'twixt the two of you, and I want that made crystal clear!" the sergeant boomed. "What I need is a team of investigators who can work together. Dawes, your pay packet is dependent on it, so unless you want to join the bread line out there, I'd straighten up!"

"And you..." he said, turning toward me with a glare, "not only do you owe much of your new celebrity to the men in this department who involve you and watch out for you..." I glumly nodded, taking his words to heart. "But for the sake of your family — this particular problem deserves your undivided attention."

Both our heads came up at these hushed words. Michaels nodded, tapping a thick finger on the page that Brian still held open.

"Down here is where we keep the evidence and case files of current and older cases," he said, pointing down the hallways as he spoke. "Most of these rooms are filled with boxes upon boxes of these here notepads, along with the relevant physical evidence from the cases they are about."

As he spoke, one of his men attempted to shinny past us with just such a box and was stopped by the sergeant.

"This here case is unsolved — you can see because there's no end date on the label," he explained, pointing to the top of the box and then lifting it open to reveal a few sheets of paper, a child's doll and some opened letters.

"Go on, go on, man," Michaels said brusquely, replacing the box cover. We watched the young man stop to talk to another constable sitting at the bottom of the stairs and go through a checklist of items on a clipboard. They each signed the paper before the man carrying the box continued up the stairs.

"A missing child? Kidnapped by one of his parents?" I asked, turning my attention back to Michaels, who looked surprised and then nodded.

"Ay, with her mum, we hope," he replied. "Now, this list Dawes has here. This is a list of evidence that has gone missing from our basement."

I blinked and then leaned over Brian's notepad. "I don't understand. What do you mean 'missing'? As in removed from the building? How do you know?"

Brian pointed at the clipboard in the other constable's hands. "Because we have a sign-in, sign-out sheet that must be filled out every day. In fact, there is a junior officer assigned to that clipboard at all times to make sure no one leaves with evidence without signing it out. This is the only staircase that leads down into this basement area."

"When Cullingham came down here two days ago to pull the papers for a stolen vehicle, he found the box empty!" Michaels cut in, waving his arms around. "Totally empty! And Cullingham swears he had a notebook plus the papers plus a photo of the car as supplied by the owner, in that box!"

"And he's the only one on the sign-out form as having checked it in or out," Brian added, taking the clipboard from his peer and walking it back to us. "Which makes sense, as he is the officer assigned to the case."

"So that got me to thinkin'," Michaels said, tapping a thick finger against his temple. "How many other boxes have we got in here that are missing their evidence? Well, let me tell you, so far we've found five boxes empty, and I will bet my dinner tonight that there are more!"

I frowned and was scanning through Brian's neat handwriting when he said, "And so far, we have been unable to come up with a pattern for the thefts."

Brian compared his notes against the clipboard in his left hand. "Different officers who checked them in and out, different dates as to the original crimes and different states of solution. Some of these boxes are purely archival, the crimes and cases solved decades ago."

"But one at least — that of the fire in the two-story house in Marylebone — was fairly recent," I said, pointing to it on the list as my eyes met Michaels'.

He nodded, pulling out a cigarette and lighting it. "Not much evidence in there, Adams. I had a look at it myself before it was filed away," he said. "But still, even with an open-and-closed case, missing evidence is a huge problem."

"And possibly evidence that it is not as open-and-closed as you might have hoped, Sergeant Michaels," I said, looking down at the list again. "But surely this happens from time to time?"

Michaels just puffed angrily at his cigarette, so Brian answered, meeting my eyes for the first time in a month. "Items go missing. Even boxes of evidence go missing. But the items in a box missing entirely while the box remains?"

He looked at Michaels, who nodded and dismissed the young constable at the bottom of the stairs to take a break.

"What can I do?" I asked finally, looking to the sergeant.

Michaels tapped his cigarette before answering. "Look at the list, will you, Adams? If there's a pattern, chances are you'll see it. In the meantime, I'll catch your partner here up on the house fire."

Brian obligingly handed the list of missing items and their corresponding cases to me and then stepped back to talk to his superior. I took it and started pacing, scanning for similarities, flipping back and forth through the notebook and doing the same with the clipboard.

Common items leapt out and were discarded when the similarities ended before all five boxes could be linked. Types of crimes? No, that wasn't it either. Gender of the victims? Locale in London? Size of the missing items? Constables assigned to the cases? Nothing seemed to fit.

I focused on the list of items from the Marylebone fire: three burned photos, an intricate eagle pin holding a standard, a silver dragon ring and the remnants of a blue ceramic vase that the officer who wrote this list had described as 'fancy-looking.'

"I wish someone would have told me," Brian was saying, calling my attention back up to him and Sergeant Michaels. "And nothing has been heard from Portia's grandfather since?"

Michaels shrugged, raising his open hand in my direction.

"No," I replied, "nothing." I handed the notebook and clipboard back to Brian. "There are no obvious patterns here, I'm afraid. Even if I limit the pattern to four matches."

"Are you sure?" Michaels said around his cigarette.

I shrugged. "There are, of course, elements I cannot know ... like the condition of the evidence, the value of the items, though that seems to range from expensive to worthless. Also a full list of who was on duty upstairs in the Yard during the windows when the missing contents were stolen — that kind of thing. If this were purely financial, some of the choices of items that were stolen make no sense at all. They are worthless. And if it's not financial, then ... perhaps it is more about the police being deprived of the evidence. But there is no one obvious person who benefits from all these items being stolen."

Michaels frowned. "And that tells you...?"

"Well ... it's possible that only one of the evidence boxes were of interest to the thief," I answered, wondering at the items that might have belonged to my grandfather. "The rest are meant to distract you from the only important case that would lead back to the thief."

To Sergeant Michaels' growing frustration, two more boxes were discovered during the search to be completely empty that week.

Despite once again looking through the list of missing items, I saw no new pattern emerging, though I was able to solve a case of stolen identity from the list of missing items in the box.

That mollified the large sergeant, though upon bringing in the perpetrator, he spent almost three hours interrogating the poor man about his involvement in stealing the evidence. The man confessed almost as soon as the officers had their hands on him to impersonating a dead neighbor in order to double his dole money but unfortunately knew nothing of the theft of the box of evidence for his case or any other.

I was witness to this, first-hand, working in Chief Inspector Archer's office at the Yard, knee-deep in case files about suicide and suspected suicide.

Archer's office was next to one of the interrogation rooms in a corner of the second floor. The center of the room was an open space with desks and wooden chairs for the various officers.

The first day I came in to work alongside the professor, it became obvious that little work had been done to organize the notes and boxes all over the office, which was why every day after class found me wading through box after box with my own clipboard, organizing the papers into usable case studies and discarding the ones that were off-topic or wrongfully filed (of which there were many).

This meant that for the first time in over a month, Brian and I spent hours in the same space working away on cases. It wasn't the same as before, but at least we were working together again. However, my presence meant that Sergeant Michaels could tap me on the shoulder whenever he wanted. The thing was that the cases he wanted my opinion on were invariably to be found on the desk of one Constable Dawes.

We both knew what he was doing, but after the talking-to we had received in the basement, neither of us chose to challenge him.

On Friday night, I headed down to the Yard, my satchel packed with snacks and a Thermos of tea, anticipating hours of work ahead. I was determined to finish the last box of case notes tonight so that tomorrow I could start writing. Archer and I had already agreed on an outline, but now I was anxious to put pen to paper and stop all the organizing and list-making.

It was after 9:00 p.m., so I knew the police staff was reduced to a skeleton shift, but I was forestalled by Sergeant Michaels as I climbed the stairs.

"Ah, Adams, good timing," he said, putting out his cigarette under his heel.

"Don't you ever go home, Sergeant Michaels?" I blurted out before I could stop myself.

He answered without a pause. "Go home to what, Adams? My wife left me almost five years ago, and she took all our friends with her. Turns out my name's not as golden outside this office as I might like, and the reason is exactly what you think it is."

I chose not to speak my thoughts, so he continued, "Because me being here at all hours makes me a good sergeant and a bad husband and a worse father. That's right."

Never having thought of the man as either of those last two things, I just gaped at him.

"Amazed you, didn't I? Guess there's no tell-tale evidence on my person anymore for you to suss out and decode. Yeah, I have a daughter. Millie's her name. Only a few years younger than you, though more homely, poor little mite. She doesn't want to see me. Prefers the uppity Irishman my wife took up with after the divorce." He shrugged his massive shoulders. "Maybe she'll come around when she gets a little older. Maybe not. Point is: I got nothing else to do but be here till she does."

"I ... I don't know what to say," I managed to stammer, wondering how to get out of this awkward conversation, "I'm only here to ... to finish up the cases I have open on Professor Archer's desk before tomorrow." I hoped to forestall a new assignment. "I promised myself I would start writing tomorrow, and there is only one way to do that."

"What a wonderful work ethic you possess, Adams," he replied, grasping my elbow. "I would very much like you to apply that drive toward the Westminster Bank."

I sighed, opening my mouth to turn him down less politely when he said, "I hear your very own Dr. Whitaker is already attending the body, along with Constable Simmons. They were having a drink at a pub across the street when the alarm was raised." He took out a notebook, hastily scrawled a message and handed it to me. "Now surely you're not too busy to stop in and give your boyfriend a hand?"

I flushed but recognized that I could solve at least one of my problems by agreeing, so I took the notepaper in defeat.

He responded with a clap to my shoulder. "Now let me hail you a cab, Adams."

Ten minutes later, I arrived at the designated coordinates to find Constable Simmons at the locked front doors of the bank. Looking around as I exited the cab, I noted only one pub in the vicinity, and it looked more like a gentlemen's club than a drinking establishment.

"Constable, good evening," I said, climbing the stairs to the front door.

With a frown, Simmons answered, "What you doing here, then?"

Used to his rude manner, I simply answered, "Sergeant Michaels sent me down."

"What for?"

"I assure you, it was not my idea," I replied, starting to get annoyed when he showed no signs of getting out of my way. Remembering that my boyfriend was on site, I said, "You were here with Dr. Whitaker? At the King's Arms?"

If anything, my words seemed to frustrate him more because he licked his lips before answering. "Who told you that?"

I rolled my eyes, deciding this conversation had extended beyond my patience. "I believe I will speak to Dr. Whitaker myself, if you don't mind."

· Simmons looked for a moment like he was going to deny me entry, but I simply stepped around him and opened the large doors to the mostly deserted marbled offices of the Westminster Bank.

I glanced around at the additional security features that had been recently added, including a security guard who was sitting around at the top of some stairs and jumped to his feet on seeing me. I introduced myself and found that the man spoke little English. I managed to explain my involvement and was directed farther into the bank. From the top of the stairs I could see the barred door that led down to the vaults and the crouched figure of Gavin Whitaker at the bottom of the stairs just outside an open vault door.

I made my way down the long flight of stairs. "Gavin, finally I have found you! Honestly, I had no idea that following you around from crime scene to crime scene was the only way to get your attention!" I said with a large dollop of humor in my tone, but I started in surprise when he turned my way.

His usually lean face seemed even leaner, his cheekbones more pronounced. There were deep, sunken circles under eyes that seemed almost feverish in the way they flicked over me. He was surprised to see me here, to be sure, but there was more to his look than I could put my finger on.

I continued my visual assessment as I dropped to one knee at his side. "Gavin, are you unwell?" I asked, worried for him and remembering the man who had been so zealously seeking him at the college. I thought of the strange way Simmons had reacted to my arrival and wondered if he were a part of this as well. Was Simmons part of the past Gavin was trying to escape, or was he tied to Simmons because of it? Had their shared experiences at Pellam Orphanage made them friends even a decade later?

He smiled, but it was his cold smile, the one usually reserved for people he didn't know or didn't care to know. "Tired only, trying to get prepared for this trip as well as continue to teach my classes and serve in my capacity as assistant coroner ... even a much better man than I would feel the burden."

I couldn't help but frown at his choice of words. "Then you must let me help you, of course," I said, reaching out to touch his arm.

He looked down at my hand, and I saw a brief look of regret pass over his face like a cloud over the moon on a dark night, so quickly did it pass.

The body at our feet finally drew my attention. "Come, you are obviously finished with your assessment of this unfortunate man, at least without the tools of your lab. Let me take you for a meal. In truth, you look as though you haven't eaten since last we spoke a month ago."

He glanced down at the body and then pulled a sheet up and over the man's face. Then he nodded and stowed his instruments in his half-opened bag.

He stood and straightened his long frame with a wince, and glancing back toward the open steel vault, door, he called out, "Constable, do you need me to sign anything?"

Brian Dawes stepped out of the vault in answer, surprising me, but then, thinking back to Sergeant Michaels' words, maybe I shouldn't have been surprised.

"Not yet, Doctor, I have one more item to clear up in here." He raised his eyes to see me next to my boyfriend, and his handsome features registered shock.

"Of course, Constable," Gavin said. "Perhaps, Portia, you should go on ahead. I would not want you to wait for me, and you obviously were on your way somewhere." He pointed to the weighted satchel over my shoulder.

I looked between them and then put my hand on Gavin's arm again. "Why don't you ask that security guard at the top of the stairs to load this gentleman into your hearse?" I suggested, stepping over the vault's threshold to stand next to Brian. "Perhaps I can help the constable with this one last item? And then by the time you are all loaded up, we will be done as well, and we can finalize the paperwork for tonight?"

I looked hopefully at Brian, who understood quickly and agreed. "Yes, of course, Doctor, it is late. I promise a few more minutes, and you two can be on your way."

"But surely, Portia, you need not trouble yourself..." Gavin protested, looking to the constable for aid. "I assure you there is nothing mysterious about this death."

"Actually, this is one of those questions that Miss Adams usually answers in seconds," replied Brian, looking distractedly back into the vault. "If you can spare her, of course, Doctor?"

Gavin looked like he wanted to argue but decided against it, his weariness perhaps convincing him to let us have our way, and he trudged up the stairs to call upon the help of the men at the top.

"Thank you, Constable, I appreciate it."

"Not at all," Brian replied, glancing at me and then at the receding form of my boyfriend. "Did Sergeant Michaels send you down as well?"

I nodded. "But why? He knew Simmons was here, so why send you and me as well?"

Brian thoughtfully ran his hand over his chin, speaking in an undertone so only I could hear. "Simmons has been acting strangely, to the point that Michaels has asked me to keep a bit of an eye on the man. Any idea why he was drinking with Whitaker? Do they do that often?"

"To be honest, I don't think so," I replied with a frown, "but I agree Simmons is being dodgier than usual."

So was Gavin, come to think of it, but I didn't say that.

"How has Simmons been acting strangely?" I asked instead.

Brian grimaced. "Michaels followed your lead of looking for patterns in the staff at the Yard and found that Simmons has been at the offices even when he was off-duty, sometimes late at night. In light of the missing evidence, the sergeant's suspicions were aroused, so he asked me to keep a weather eye on the bloke. This is another one of those odd incidents. Simmons is off duty but determined to investigate this case."

"What would Simmons gain by stealing evidence from the Yard?"

"I honestly don't know," Brian admitted, "but Michaels didn't like how Simmons sounded when he called in this dead body, so he sent me down here."

"Do you think someone hired him to steal evidence?" I said.

"Lord, I hope not," Brian answered, "but the thought has crossed my mind, and I'm sure the sergeant's. If you think so too..."

"No, no," I said with a wave, "I don't have any evidence of such a thing, and I wouldn't want to point fingers without it. Tell me what it is you have found that keeps you from closing the crime scene," I said, determined to get this work done and find out the underlying reasons for Gavin's worrying appearance. If he were in trouble, I was determined to help, regardless of our earlier agreement to stay out of each other's personal business. And if Simmons was involved, I was more than happy to gather evidence against the man; he was not someone I wanted around Gavin, regardless of their history.

Brian held out a small brass button. "This was Mr. Victor Trevor's, obviously," he said, pointing at the older gentleman on the floor who had been the focus of Dr. Whitaker's work.

"It was in the vault?" I asked, taking the proffered item. "Why does that bother you? It is from the suit he is wearing, so it fell off today."

Brian walked further into the vault, around a small corner to point to some of the empty shelves. "Only because it was tucked all the way back here. How did it get there?"

I frowned, holding up the button. "There is a tiny sliver of wood or wool, I think ... at the edge of this."

I pulled my small magnifying glass from my satchel to peer at it more carefully.

I glanced back at Brian and handed him the glass and button, doing my own circuit of the vault.

"If he caught the button on something in here, I don't recognize the wood," I said, peering under boxes and metal struts.

"It isn't here," concurred Brian, "but it bothers you, right?"

"A little," I admitted, "but maybe he lost it earlier in the day, and then came back down afterward to look for it?"

"And died in the exertion?" Brian suggested. "Does he strike you as the type of man to go hunting all over the floor for a lost button? That button cost more than my most expensive pair of boots, I'd warrant."

I grinned at that, forgetting our disagreements for a moment as I watched the stretcher bearing Mr. Trevor back up the stairs.

"Cardiac arrest?" I asked, looking back at Brian, who nodded.

"If not cardiac arrest brought upon by exertion, then what?" I challenged as the lights flickered briefly.

Brian shrugged. "Like you, I don't like coincidences, what with missing buttons, missing wood and a dead body, but Dr. Whitaker is positive that an autopsy will bear out his initial assessment, and you know how averse he is to speaking in absolutes so early in a case." He looked worriedly up at the flickering bulbs.

The flickering was a harbinger of the blackout that fell not a moment later.

I could hear the surprised calls from the men upstairs, and I instinctively reached out for a wall to orient myself, feeling my way along a metal strut.

"Portia, are you alright?" came Brian's voice from out of the darkness.

"Quite alright," I replied, feeling my way toward the vault door, which was less than five meters to my right, if memory served. "If you're headed to the vault door, remember you have to step over the raised edge."

"Portia?" called Gavin's worried voice from far up the stairs.

"We are safe, Doctor," I called back. "Please do not risk injury by attempting to come down the stairs in the dark."

"We are bringing the torch, Dawes," called Constable Simmons from even farther away, but even as his voice died away, the hum of electricity foretold the relighting of our situation.

"Ah, there," Brian started to say, a step behind me, and was cut off as the giant vault door swung closed in front of us with an ominous slam, followed by three consecutive sliding sounds as the bolts slid home.

CHAPTER SIX

W e stood for a second in shocked silence and then looked at each other. "Automatic lock?" I asked, stepping to the steel door and giving it a good push.

"On a timer, most probably," Brian agreed, adding his own shoulder to the effort.

I banged on the door as Brian called out, "Whitaker, we are still inside!"

We heard nothing in response, which was understandable given that we had several feet of steel and concrete between us and the outside of the vault.

"They know where we are," I assured Brian, stepping back to assess the door. "They will no doubt find the right person to get us out."

Brian ran his hands over the door again before answering. "That may give them some trouble, seeing as the bank manager is the one with the code to override the timelock."

I frowned and then understood. "And he was just carried up the stairs and into Gavin's vehicle ready to be transported to the morgue."

Brian nodded as the lights flickered on and off. We both tensed for the actual blackout that would possibly turn off the electricity long enough to push the door back open. The flickering resolved into the still light of the vault, and we let out our respective breaths. I shrugged and lowered myself to the floor so that my back was leaning against the cold steel door. Brian did another complete circuit of the vault room, moving in and out of my sight, his pace quickening as he made his way back to the door, running his hands over it for the fourth time.

"Brian, there is naught to do until the good doctor and the constable figure out a way to get us out of here," I said, opening my satchel to pull out my Thermos. "Fortunately, though, I have a few provisions to get us through a few hours at least."

Brian glanced down at me oddly and then started to repeat his circuit. I cocked my head, watching him repeat his steps until he again arrived at the door. Suddenly a loud banging could be heard across the room from us, and Brian whipped around, his face as white as fresh cream. I carefully placed my satchel back on the ground and got up, following him as he shakingly searched out the source of the sound.

"It must be the air-filtration system," I said, concerned at his behavior. "It is a good thing."

"A good thing, yes," agreed Brian, pulling on his collar.

"Brian, do you have issues with ... enclosed spaces?" I asked, putting my hand on his arm and feeling it trembling. I searched my memory for a time when I had seen him in such a small space.

"I ... don't like being locked in here, if that is what ... what you mean ..." he admitted, his eyes flicking around us.

"They will get us out," I assured him. "It is only a matter of an hour or two at most, even without the bank manager. There are locksmiths and welders, and any number of options. Perhaps they could even cut the power to the bank and emulate what got us stuck in here in the first place."

Brian looked up at the tiny grate where air could be felt coming in and took a few deep breaths before saying, "Well, they might, but they don't have you out there coming up with those solutions. You're stuck in here. With me."

I couldn't argue that logic, though I put more faith in Gavin. "Do you want to sit there under the grate?" I asked, looking up at his pale face. "I will sit against the vault door just in case the electricity goes off, and then I can give it a push immediately."

He gulped and nodded but stayed standing as I walked back to the door and sat down next to my satchel.

Brian paced back and forth in agitation like a caged tiger I had seen at the zoo many years ago in Montreal. That brought back a sharp memory of my mother's kind face, laughing at my first view of these wild animals. I smiled in spite of the situation, thankful that I had arrived at the point where memories of my mother brought me more joy than sadness.

"Do you feel as though it is getting warmer in here?" Brian said, pulling again at his collar.

"I do," I lied, tugging off my jacket. "Why don't you remove your hat and coat? No need for the formality locked in a bank vault, after all."

He nodded, removing the articles of clothing with shaking hands and placing them on the shelf next to him alongside his notebook. Sweat sheened his brow and the back of his uniform shirt, which stuck to his frame like a second skin. He opened his shirt at the collar, and that seemed to give him a moment's relief.

Claustrophobia, I thought, *or something like it,* trying to distract myself from the material clinging to his lean torso. He continued to pace, looking up worriedly at the tiny grate each time he passed under it, as if doubting its continued function.

"So ... the piece of wood ... it came from something that was in this vault, but no longer is," I said aloud.

Brian glanced at me, stopping in his tracks, confusion on his face.

"The sliver of wood on the button," I reiterated, pointing at his closed fist.

He seemed to have forgotten he still had it, because he stared down at his clenched fist. Slowly, he opened his hand to reveal the brass button in his reddened palm.

"Do you agree?" I pressed, determined to take his mind off our predicament.

He looked up from his hand with a nod. "That would seem plausible. More likely the wood got caught on the button while it was still on the suit than the wood attaching itself to a button already lying on the ground."

"Exactly," I said, rising to stand next to the shelf where he had found the button. "So let us postulate that Mr. Trevor leans in here to pick up a heavy box — a wooden box — and as he stands, his button is pulled off, taking a tiny piece of the wooden box with it."

I didn't wait for Brian's affirmation before continuing. "Now you might ask if Trevor is the type of man to actually do the work of carrying a heavy box out of his own vault. Perhaps we are making assumptions about the man based on his position and how he is dressed. Perhaps he is exactly the type of man who works hard with his hands. I did not take the liberty of examining them before he was taken away."

Brian piped up. "But there was no box around him outside the vault. Not near the body, nor anywhere on this floor, as far I could tell. I did a thorough search, and the place is basically empty."

"So then, he lifted the box, dislodging the button, and handed it to someone else," I described, again mimicking the actions, handing my imaginary box off to an imaginary person.

"And that person did not notice when Trevor clutched at his chest and toppled over? I find that highly unlikely," Brian put in, resuming his pacing, though this was thoughtful pacing rather than fretful.

I bit my lip. "But you're making the assumption that the incidents happened at the same time — that he lost his button while moving a box and that he suffered his attack. What if he moved the box, lost the button, and then later in the day came down here and had his attack all alone?"

Brian tilted his head, admitting the possibility. "So there might not have been a second person at all in that scenario. He could have done it all — moved the box, lost the button, taken the box upstairs and out of the bank and then come back down here and died."

I thought about it. "I would need to know more about the circumstances to figure out a sequence of events. Obviously, this branch has been around for some time, but this vault is nearly empty. I take it they were shut down for a period of time? To install new machinery for security?"

"Exactly right," he answered. "The bank has been closed for three weeks. Trevor was cognizant of the rash of bank hold-ups in recent months and decided to have the vault upgraded."

"So the bank was closed today?" I asked, of course knowing the answer by the state of the lobby upstairs, the dust apparent on the tellers' booths and the unwashed state of the floors.

"Yes, it was to reopen Monday. The only person here today was the bank manager."

"And the security guard," I put in.

"No, the man upstairs is Trevor's bodyguard, not a bank security guard," Brian corrected. "He waited outside while Trevor was in here. When he didn't reappear for an hour, the bodyguard came in and discovered his body. When he ran back out to the street, Simmons happened to be leaving the pub with Whitaker, so he called it in and started the investigation.

"I've never known the man to be the type to leap into action, especially when he was off duty, but there you have it. He was with Whitaker, who came down to assess the body, and then Simmons called the Yard to let Michaels know that they were on site. Overstepping his bounds a little by involving the coroner before the sergeant, but..."

"Yes, exactly what I was thinking," I said, fighting the urge to get up and pace, more intrigued by Simmons' actions than by the clues we were discussing. "How did the bodyguard know Simmons was an officer if he was off-duty?"

"Not sure..." Brian answered after a pause.

"And Simmons was with Gavin at the King's Arms? Seems a little fancy for Simmons. Are they members?"

Brian looked surprised by the question but answered, "I ... I'm not sure. And wouldn't you know better than I?"

I didn't. We didn't really talk about our friends, possibly because we each had so few. "So then, when you arrived, Simmons and Gavin were already at work?"

"Yes, Simmons was outside. He let me in, seemed a bit annoyed that Michaels had sent me down, as he was already here," Brian answered. "And the doctor was working on the bank manager down here. I found the button, and when I compared it to Trevor's suit, Whitaker tried to convince me to replace it on the body out of respect."

I frowned, because that was an oddly emotional reaction from Gavin, but I didn't interrupt.

"Something about the button and how it was lost bothered me, so I kept it as evidence. Then I tried to take a statement from the bodyguard, but his English is not very good. Will have to find out a translator, I think. I think he's German — Egger is his name."

"Egger..." I repeated thoughtfully. "Actually that sounds ... Austrian."

"Austrian, right," Brian replied, scribbling in his notebook, not realizing that my insight had started a queasy feeling in my stomach. Austrian, giving more of a connection to Gavin and his recent meetings with high-ranking Austrians. I wondered if the burly man with the European accent leaving messages at the college would also turn out to be Austrian.

"And Saturday and Sunday were no doubt to be busy with the cleaning of the bank and restocking the cash vaults and this one down here?" I asked, my mind still circling the Austrians like a Handley Page bomber.

Brian nodded again and then said, "So tonight was perhaps the last night to get something out of the vault without prying eyes seeing it."

I had reached the same conclusion. "Something in a heavy wooden box that could have been carried out by the bank manager."

"It still doesn't mean that the contents of the box are nefarious, though," Brian put in, crossing his arms. "After all, everything of value was taken out of the vault weeks ago. Why would someone leave something precious in here while the vault was being worked on?"

"How did Gavin's hearse happen to be nearby?"

"I don't know," Brian answered. "Perhaps he drove it down here to meet Simmons at the pub? And I will ask Simmons about the King's Arms. You're right, it's not his usual type of haunt. The more I think about it, the more I agree that there is something odd there."

I was glad that Brian was focused on Simmons instead of Gavin. I myself was not happy with the suspicious nature of Gavin's involvement, and I found myself dreading my next step after I got out of this vault — to check the hearse parked outside for a missing wooden box. I had no idea why he would have taken it, but he and Simmons certainly had the opportunity to steal the box and conceal it before Brian had arrived on the scene. Simmons stealing evidence was one thing. Why in the world would Gavin do something like that? I shook my head. Surely he wouldn't. Surely I would find nothing but the unfortunate Mr. Trevor in the hearse parked outside the bank.

Brian closed his notebook, staring down at it, and I wondered how much of my worry about Gavin I should share with him. If Simmons were acting suspicious so, too, was Gavin. I knew enough about my instincts to trust them, but I had to be sure my closeness to the subject wasn't affecting my judgment. I had come to the decision to spill my concerns when Brian spoke.

"You could have asked for my help, you know," he said, still looking at his closed notebook.

I realized we had switched topics. "You mean before I went to Italy."

"Of course, I know you never actually need my help per se," he continued, still not looking my way, "but I thought we ... work well together. And I would have kept your secret, even if I weren't in Italy with you. I could have helped from here."

"Brian, I thought I explained the details of the case to you and Annie at the café," I replied, walking over to him. "The ruse of my waiting on Mrs. Ridley was precarious enough without adding you to the mix. Even correspondence from Italy was a risk."

"But that wasn't why you lied about it," Brian said, finally looking up at me, halting me in my steps with his accusing eyes.

I looked away, unable to hold his gaze.

"Is it?" he pressed.

"No," I admitted, looking back up and fighting the defiance that wanted to bite back for being interrogated thus.

"Right, so you lied to me because ... why?" He shook his head, trying to understand. "We all know you're brilliant, Portia, that your mind is ... exceptional..."

I twisted my mouth. "You must think me terribly arrogant, Constable Dawes..."

"Brian," he corrected automatically, "and yes, you are. And what's more, you know you are. I don't even think you see it as a personal fault. And what is odd is that in you I don't see it as a fault either. I think it's vital to who you are. That surety — that confidence — it's what allows you to see the world the way you do."

I nearly snorted at his description of me. Confident? Didn't he see how insecure I was about being compared with Holmes and Watson? At how bothered I was by losing Brian's friendship for even a short time?

He stepped forward, closing the last foot between us. "The thing is that I fooled myself into thinking that didn't apply to us." He smiled ruefully. "How's that for arrogance? I allowed myself to think that you saw us as equals."

My mouth dropped open as I considered his words. "Dear God, you cannot believe that I am so far gone!"

"No, no, hear me out, because I want us to have no more secrets between us. Let us have everything out on the table," he said, raising both his hands. "Like you, I have read everything in the bookshelves of your apartment. I knew that Mr. Holmes' intellect raised him above the minds of the people around him — even above the mind of your other grandfather, his best friend. It's why he never allowed himself to get close to anyone. It's probably why he decided that your father could not be his son. It was because he couldn't be a father. He isolated himself. He was above 'friends'."

I grasped his arm with both my hands, feeling its coiled tension mirrored in my own body. "Never. Do you hear me, Brian Kevin Dawes? I am *not* Sherlock Holmes, and even if I were exactly like him in every other way, it would never extend to you — never to you."

He must have seen that I was telling him the God's honest truth, because he reached down to run his finger over my cheek.

"Tears, Portia?" he whispered down at me. "I don't believe it."

I hadn't realized I was crying either, but before I could explain it away, he leaned down to kiss me. But before he could, we jumped apart, hearing the sound of the large bolts being pulled back one by one out of their sockets in the vault door.

We instinctively raced to the heavy door as it slowly swung outward to reveal Gavin Whitaker and Constable Simmons.

"Finally! Portia, I am so sorry," Gavin said, stepping over the threshold of the vault, arms extended. "This is entirely my fault."

I took his hands willingly, hoping my voice wouldn't shake when I spoke, which it did. "Nothing to be sorry for, Gavin. I knew you would get us out as quickly as humanly possible."

"That he did, miss," responded Simmons, entering directly after. "Near moved heaven and earth to get a locksmith. Drove there himself in the hearse, he did, with the body in it and all!"

I couldn't help but run my eyes over Simmons and found no outward sign of his profession, making me wonder again at the series of events that had led the bodyguard to calling Simmons into the bank. The knowledge that the hearse had left the premises before I could check for the wooden box did nothing to improve my mood.

"That's quite enough, lad, let them all get out of there to take a breath of foggy air before they hear it all," came the loud voice of Sergeant Michaels from somewhere outside the vault. "Get out here, Adams, before this contraption locks you in with a few more companions."

CHAPTER SEVEN

A re you quite sure you are well enough to be out?" Gavin asked me for a third time over breakfast the next morning. The small restaurant he had escorted me to was sparsely attended. A few couples sat at tables to our left and right, but the staff far outnumbered the customers.

I fought down my impatience at his uncharacteristic concern and just smiled and nodded again. "I am. Please stop worrying and tell me about your plans."

He picked at his eggs. "Not much to tell, really. I am busily wrapping up my work. Mr. Trevor's autopsy was my last one for the Yard, so that is well. His body is at the crematorium. I intend to sublet my apartment here in London, as I will be provided with housing along my tour."

I had very carefully dressed for our breakfast in a pale gray suit that I knew he favored because it went so well with his own taste. I had picked it when he showed up in the pinstriped suit and waited for me to dress for breakfast. At my breast I wore the lovely silver pocket watch he had presented to me earlier in the year, and as far as I could tell, despite his overt concern, he had noticed none of this. That was fine, because I was also hoping he wouldn't notice how distracted I was.

I kept reminding myself that Brian and I hadn't actually kissed ... so why did my lips feel different? I shook my head for probably the tenth time this morning. This was ridiculous. I wasn't this person. I refused to be this person. Mooning over a kiss that hadn't even happened and might never happen! The height of stupidity. Instead of any romantic thoughts, I should be feeling guilty at the idea of kissing my best friend's boyfriend. Or kissing any man but the one sitting across from me. Better that it hadn't happened.

"You finished his autopsy already?" I asked, determined to move past these distractions to more worrying concerns. "That must be a new record. Nothing untoward, I must assume?"

"Hmm?" he replied, and then shook his head. "As I thought, the man died of cardiac arrest. I suspect by the time the guard found him, the poor fellow had already been dead for a few hours."

I frowned, wondering at the lividity of the corpse I had seen on the floor of the basement, but I was not an expert in forensics like Gavin.

"Lucky that you and Simmons were so close by ... I had no idea you were even friends," I said, leaving the question open-ended.

Gavin rearranged his napkin on his lap. "I wouldn't go so far as to call him a friend. We were at the same place. We had a drink. Naught but co-incidence, really."

He didn't want me to know his connection with Simmons, I realized as he distractedly continued to push food around his plate. I took note of the missed patch of stubble on his cheek — something that I would have be-lieved impossible, but there it was. His tie was ironed, but tied badly, and his eyes had a bloodshot look. I wondered suddenly if he had heard about the true reasons for my trip to Italy from Brian. Was that why he had been avoiding me? Why there was this sudden coldness between us?

"Gavin, there is something I should tell you about my trip to Italy."

"Oh? Did something happen? Pray tell me you did not fall in love with an Italian prince?"

"Not at all," I answered. "But it was not purely a vacation for me ... or for Mrs. Ridley."

Gavin nodded. "I never thought it was."

I cocked my head. "You knew I was going overseas for a case?"

"Portia, we each have our pursuits, and we each have our secrets. I knew by your excitement that this trip to Italy was more than you were able to say at the time, and I accepted it. You do not need to explain anything to me, save to share any interesting facts from the case or the countryside."

I smiled but felt a frown fighting to displace it. I couldn't want him to be worried, could I? When I resented it in everyone else around me when they worried about me — shouldn't I be pleased by his trust in my abilities?

"I'm guessing your friends Annie and Brian were not as happy to discover your real reasons?" he asked astutely, pulling my attention back to our conversation. When I simply shook my head sadly, he said, "No matter. Smaller minds mean smaller ambitions, my dear. You and I are destined for greater things, and greater things are not always done in the full light of day. Take, for example, the lengths the press is taking to learn more about you..."

That derailed my thoughts for a moment. "Surely they are not pursuing you?"

"Oh yes," he replied with a grimace. "We haven't tried to hide our relationship, after all."

"I am sorry for that, Gavin." I put my hand on his arm, feeling the flex of his strong biceps hidden beneath this suit. "I did not mean to inflict this celebrity on you."

"While you were away, I will admit, it was easier," he said, almost to himself. "Lonelier but less dramatic."

I felt a little stab of guilt but shook it off. "Is that why you were spending so much time at the Yard in my absence?"

He looked startled. "What makes you think I was spending time at the Yard?"

His answer reminded me of the way Simmons had dodged my questions outside the bank yesterday, and the queasy feeling in my stomach returned full force. "Brian mentioned it, I think. Just that you seemed to be spending a lot of time with Simmons..."

"I can't think why my personal comings and goings would be of such interest to the constable!" Gavin burst out, interrupting me and causing a couple at the table next to us to glance over in surprise. It made me glad that I hadn't asked him about the missing wooden box from the vault. Something I had been pushing down bubbled back to the surface, and I felt concern being displaced by a growing anger.

"He is a detective, after all, Gavin, he will notice things that are out of the ordinary," I replied. "As do I."

Gavin swallowed, his eyes hardening as he tried to bring his emotions to heel. "What is that supposed to mean?"

I leaned toward him, not intimidated by the set of his jaw. "It means something is going on with you, Gavin. I know there is. At first I thought you might be in trouble, that this burly man trying to contact you at the college meant you harm in some way."

His dark eyes dilated as I spoke, but I continued. "But now I suspect you are an active participant in whatever is ailing you. What are you involved in? What is going on between you and Simmons? What is this connection with the Austrians that has made you so paranoid and tense?"

"I assure you ... nothing is going on, as you put it," he bit out, keeping his voice low this time so that the rest of the room would not hear. "But if courting the consulting detective at Baker Street means that my every move is over-analyzed..."

"Over-analyzed?" I hissed back, my anger rising to match his. "Ever since your second meeting at the Austrian embassy, you've been acting strange! You're hiding things, you've been avoiding me, and you're outright lying about your relationship with Simmons for reasons I cannot begin to fathom. What were you doing outside that bank yesterday? Why did you have your hearse parked nearby? Why were you willing to remove evidence by replacing a missing button on the dead body? What is going on, Gavin?"

He bent at the waist to pick up his napkin that had slid to the floor at his outburst, and when he came back up his face had entirely changed. No longer strained and angry, it was calm, his eyes the only indication of the fury he was holding within.

"I am sorry that it has come to this, but the one thing I cannot stomach in a woman is suspicion," he said, his voice steady, his gaze locked on mine. "I must therefore call an end to this relationship and ask that you accept my sincere best wishes in your future endeavors."

I gaped at him, shocked. He meanwhile reached into his wallet, pulled out a few banknotes and laid them on the table as he rose to say, "Good day, Miss Adams," and walked out of the restaurant without a backward glance.

CHAPTER EIGHT

I wished my grandmother was around to talk to about this. She was always so good about cutting through the politics of something and focusing in on the underlying cause. Despite my claims to the contrary, my emotions, namely anger in this case, were making it hard to concentrate on anything at all. Gavin was tangled up somehow in Mr. Trevor's case at the bank. I refused to think that he was actually involved in the man's death, but he was helping to cover up evidence. For money or friendship to Simmons, I did not know, but I was going to find out. And then I was going to save Gavin. I owed him that much.

I had gone straight to the Yard to talk my suspicions out with Brian, but he was out on his patrol, and since I had no real evidence, only coincidence and gut feelings, I couldn't take it to Sergeant Michaels.

I was in Professor Archer's office waiting for Brian's return when a knock at the door finally drew me out of my own head.

"Miss Adams, you are diligent! I've been knocking at my own door for almost five minutes now," said Archer with an indulgent smile.

"I am so sorry, sir," I said, opening his door wider to let him in and noticing his further weight loss. "I was engrossed."

"Not at all," he assured me, picking through some papers on his desk, lifting one and then another in his search. "How goes the research? Found any patterns in behavior? Have you started writing?"

I gave him a moment before offering to help. "No, no, Miss Adams, just my cursed keys. Can't seem to find them anywhere today."

I frowned, easily able to see the outline of his key ring in his front shirt pocket, though it looked smaller than last I had seen it. "Yes, I am on to the writing part, finally. I actually have a couple of pages for you to look through, if you have time."

"Oh, but you had asked about a missing box in the bank case?" he said. "You and Dawes were right. According to one of the bank employees, there was an unclaimed wooden box left in the vault."

"What was in it?" I asked excitedly.

"The employee doesn't know," Archer answered with a slight shake of his head. "He only knows that there was no record of it in the list of items, and that it had been unclaimed for almost twenty years."

"Odd," I said, tapping a finger against my lip. "So Trevor may have arranged to have it picked up after hours?"

"Perhaps even more so, because Trevor's bodyguard has gone missing since his employer's death," Archer said. "We tried to contact him for a follow-up interview, and the flat he had given Dawes was cleared out."

We were interrupted by a knock. "Adams, you busy?" Sergeant Michaels asked, poking his head in. "Oh, good morning, sir. Could I borrow Adams for a moment?"

I handed a couple sheets of paper to Archer and then patted his shirt pocket as I passed him. He reached into his pocket and drew out his smaller circle of keys, smiling at me in confusion.

"What can I do for you, Sergeant?" I asked, exiting the office.

"What do you see here?" he asked, handing me a pocket watch and stepping back, puffing on his cigarette.

"Old. More than twenty years old, I'd say. This watch company doesn't exist anymore, at least under this name. Passed down through family until recently, by the pristine look of it, except for two very recent scratches," I said, turning it over. "If I had to guess, I'd say it made its way to a pawn shop through a downturn in fortune rather than being stolen and then pawned. No effort has been made to scratch out the personal inscription, so I would guess that the person who sold it to the pawn shop hopes to buy it back."

Michaels was nodding, only raising his brows when I finished my analysis.

"You don't say, you don't say," he murmured around his cigarette.

"Sounds like I should plant a bobby at the shop in case our friend here comes back with the money to buy it back."

Not knowing the rest of the details of the case, and quite frankly not caring, I shrugged and handed the watch back to the sergeant.

"The one you've got there is a sight nicer, Adams," he remarked, pointing to my gift from Gavin Whitaker.

"Yes it is," I agreed, briefly touching the watch and looking around for Simmons. Actually, thinking about Simmons and his after-hours interest in the Yard turned my mind toward a new angle.

"Sergeant, the process you outlined for the evidence room downstairs ... the officer you have assigned to check things in and out — he looks *in* the box and goes through the list as the box is taken out and brought back in — correct?"

"Yes, he and the officer checking the box in or out do that together," Michaels answered, pocketing the watch with a frown. "So two of them are accountable for missing items that way."

"So the items go back into the evidence room, having been accounted for, and the box goes back on the shelf."

"Yes, yes, but the boxes are empty, so how did all that evidence get out of here without the officer seeing it leave, eh?" Michaels snorted. "Did it up and walk out of its own accord?"

"No, sir," I answered, walking briskly toward the flight of stairs to the basement, forcing the stout sergeant to keep up. "The evidence never left."

"It what?" he puffed at me, catching me halfway down the second set of stairs.

"By emptying the box, the thief made you think that the evidence had been stolen," I explained, slowing my pace. "As Constable Dawes said, one item missing could be a mistake — something misplaced. Everything in the box missing is suspicious. That is preplanned theft. And it would take some planning and some bravado to do it here, of all places."

Sergeant Michaels waved away the freckled constable who stepped forward with the clipboard as I walked around, looking down the hallway at the various rooms.

"Brian told me that this was the only route in and out of this basement, but are all the doors down here locked as well?" I asked, walking down a hallway and randomly testing doors.

"Yes, the keys are held by the man assigned to the clipboard," Michaels answered, following me. "I have a copy on my ring, as does the chief inspector."

And the chief inspector was becoming quite forgetful about his keys.

I got to the end of the hallway and found the door I was looking for. The knob turned easily. "Except for this one, which is not locked."

"Well, no," admitted the sergeant. "That's just a caretaker's closet."

I looked back toward the stairs and noted that I couldn't be seen from this angle, nor could I see the constable I knew to be sitting there. "Nothing in there but brooms n' such. But we searched in there as well, and spoke to all the cleaning staff too."

"Do the cleaning staff have to sign in and out too?" I asked, flicking on the light to have a better look around.

"Of course," Michaels answered as I perused the small space. "If you're thinking that the evidence was transported out in a rubbish bin or something, that's not how it works at all. They take their equipment up· and down the stairs, to be sure, but rubbish is collected upstairs and thrown out upstairs. The bins are checked by the constable on guard every day, and they are empty, as they should be by the time they are stored in this room. The only other thing big enough to hide evidence would be the mop bucket." He pointed at a medium-sized metal bucket in the corner near a small grated drain. "And what would be the point of that? It would just wreck the evidence."

"You forget, Sergeant, that whoever did this might be pleased with the items being destroyed," I replied, getting down on my knees and trying to pry up the grate with my fingertips. "Either way, you, the police, are deprived of the evidence."

Instead of answering, Michaels demonstrated his agreement by joining me on the floor to help me wrestle with the grate. A few moments of struggle rewarded us, the grate pulling loose in our now-grimy hands with a metallic screech.

We both peered down into the small sewer pipe below, only a hand wide at its widest visible point.

There you could see remnants of notebooks and papers dissolving in the water and whatever chemicals were used to clean the floors of this building.

Michaels started bellowing for his staff to bring us towels and water as I carefully began removing the missing evidence from the sewer pipe, mindless to the muck and refuse it was mixed with.

"Someone is looking for something," I said aloud, my mind whirring, "something here at the Yard, at my grandfather's flat and at the bank. Simmons was present at both locations ... are they connected, or is it all coincidence?"

"What?" Michaels said as he came back into the room.

I sat back on my heels, holding my filthy hands out in front of me so they didn't touch my clothes and hoping I was wrong, because to be right meant Gavin was probably involved. He, too, had been at both the Westminster Bank and at the Yard. "Sergeant, is there an Austrian connection to any of the evidence boxes that were tampered with?"

The sergeant's eyes showed confusion. "Austrians? No, not that I can recall. Why?"

"Good," I said, hoping against hope that my instincts were wrong and leaning back over the grate to keep my hands busy. "The bodyguard standing over the bank manager was Austrian, we think..." I broke off suddenly, my hand pulling at a small circular item.

"Adams, we can take care of that," Michaels started to say impatiently. "You go get cleaned up..."

He trailed off as I pulled on a long string attached to a silver ring.

"Son of a...." Michaels swore. "He's pulling evidence right out from under our noses!"

"Fascinating," I murmured, careful not to pull too hard on the string. "There is a small pipe leading out of this sewer down into your general sewer below, where the other end of this string obviously goes. But how did he get it down the pipe?"

"Who the hell cares how, Adams?" Michaels barked. "Bonhomme, you get five men into the sewers underneath this here room and find where that string goes!"

"Coincidences be damned! If I am not mistaken, this silver dragon ring comes from the evidence box of a certain house fire," I said, attracting Michaels' attention, "which means that the thief wasn't satisfied with having it washed out of your hands and into the sewers below — he wanted this ring." I met his eyes from my crouched position. "Perhaps the same way he wanted that wooden box at the bank. This crime is personal, Sergeant. Not financial. And it personally involves Sherlock Holmes."

CHAPTER NINE

I t was obvious that the thief had tugged on this string leading up and into Scotland Yard's basement offices. The ring must have gotten stuck between some refuse in the pipes, which was why it was still in our possession rather than the thief's. Also obvious from the thin striations in the muck of the pipe (once we got close enough to it with a torch) was that several strings and items had been pulled through in this manner.

From the list of the items that had been in the evidence box, we had managed to recover only two: the ring, because it was still attached to the string, and a small piece of ceramic vase that had either been discarded in the sewer or had fallen out of the pipe before the thief could grab it.

Amidst the frenzy of officers searching the sewers, I took Michaels aside to tell him everything I suspected about Simmons. Then, pushing down my feelings of guilt, I also relayed my suspicions about Gavin Whitaker. I told him about their connection through the orphanage, about the burly man pursuing Gavin, and about the meetings at the Austrian embassy that had so changed my former boyfriend's personality.

Michaels said that Brian had already talked to Michaels about Gavin's odd reaction to the button found at the scene of Trevor's death, so the sergeant added it to his list of suspicious behavior, along with their sudden shared interest in hanging about Scotland Yard. Trying to keep anger out of my voice, I quietly explained that when I had confronted Gavin about his recent behavior, he had ended our relationship and dropped out of my life.

Michaels' only reaction to this last bit of information was to raise his eyebrows, and I appreciated that he didn't ask for details I didn't want to share about that horribly awkward breakfast.

Neither of us could come up with a reason as to why they would steal from Scotland Yard or from the Westminster Bank, but Michaels agreed to at least confront Simmons on his coincidental appearance at the bank and then take on Whitaker next.

I left the police waist-deep in the tunnels under Scotland Yard searching for those items and any others that might have been dropped into the liquid below the pipes.

I got back to Baker Street at a reasonable hour, stinking to high heaven from my sojourn into the sewers of London. Amusingly, I had met with two members of my Irregulars down there as they scampered about looking for refuse they could sell. It gave me a chance to catch up with them on other matters, and I gave them a new assignment that guaranteed a few meals for some of the children.

A letter from my grandmother in the front hall gave me pause, but looking down at my filthy hands, I decided that a wash-up was far more of a priority than satisfying my curiosity.

Upstairs, Nerissa backed away from me, whining, which I could understand given my state and her highly sensitive nose. I undressed right there inside my front door and jumped straight into the bath, washing my hair twice. I carefully replaced the silver pocket watch in its velvety box near the window, next to my mother's cross, my mind lingering on Gavin Whitaker.

Nerissa bounded around me as I exited the bathroom in my oversized robe with a towel wrapped around my head, so I gave her a bit of attention before quietly creeping downstairs to retrieve my letters. I had made it halfway back up my stairs when Annie Coleson poked her head out of 221A.

"Portia! I am so glad I caught you," said she, closing the downstairs door behind her and following me up.

"Annie, how are you?" I asked, letting her in before closing the door behind us.

"I'm fine, of course, but how are you?" Her eyes were concerned as she carefully stepped over my pile of smelly clothes.

Embarrassed, I gathered them all up. "Nothing to be worried about, Annie For reasons that I will not bore you with, I was traipsing around the bowels of London about an hour ago."

I dumped the clothes into my large bathtub, reminding myself to take them to the cleaner's tomorrow, especially the boots. I came back out to find Annie sitting on one of my armchairs, scratching Nerissa's chin.

Her dress seemed a trifle too fancy for a dinner downstairs, as did her makeup. Her hair showed signs of having been pinned up carefully but hastily undone.

I pulled off my towel and ran my fingers through my damp hair. "But you weren't talking about today, were you? You were talking about getting locked in a bank vault, perhaps?"

She surprised Nerissa and me by bursting into tears, covering her face with her hands. Nerissa whined up at her, trying to lick at her face, which was more than I could think of to do.

I finally settled for retrieving a clean hankie from my wardrobe, and pressing it into her hands, I patiently waited for the waterworks to recede.

"Oh, Portia! Brian has been so ... so different," she finally managed to get out when I handed her a glass of water.

"Since the bank vault?" I asked, of course referring to being locked in a vault for hours, swallowing past the guilt of what else had happened in that vault. I had succeeded in pushing the almost-kiss out of my mind for a few hours, but it seemed the time had finally come to pay the piper.

"Yes ... I mean no, for longer," she said, shaking her blonde head, her weepy eyes on mine.

"Keep talking. I'm just going to put some clothes on," I said, unable to hold her gaze with this secret still between us as I walked into my bedroom, leaving the door open.

"Oh, I am sure if I had your mind, I could lay it all out for you in minute detail," she said. "But I don't think like that! There have been changes, though, in the way he looks at me, in the way he talks, or just doesn't talk ... even in the way he holds me..."

I grimaced, glad she couldn't see my reaction as I pulled on a long tweed skirt, comparing her words with my own love life.

"You know," I called out from my bedroom, "Brian had quite a reaction to the confines of the vault. I've been meaning to talk to him about it since."

I gave up hiding in my room, joining her in front of my unlit fireplace. "Did he tell you about it?"

She shook her head again, her tears dried on her cheeks, her nose still quite red.

"I believe he may suffer from a phobia," I said, turning to my bookshelves and running my finger over the spines until I hit on the one I wanted. "I'm of course not a doctor, but the symptoms he was displaying while we were locked in there reminded me of claustrophobia."

"Oh dear God!" Annie whispered, her hand pressed against her throat.

"I don't believe it to be serious," I assured her, using the index to find the appropriate page and then bringing the book to her with it opened. "You see? Read this. It has a full spectrum of symptoms of which I believe Brian displayed only the most minor."

She did as I bade, reading the page while I twisted my wet hair into a knot and proceeded to feed Nerissa. Passing my window, I noticed a man smoking in the alleyway behind my townhouse. The sun was setting, so the glow of his cigarette stood out, but when he saw me looking down he quickly turned to duck between the houses, his limp evident even from this distance.

"And you believe this ... phobia may be causing the distance I am feeling between Brian and me?" she asked finally in confusion.

I tilted my head. "Not if you're saying you've been feeling it for some time. The claustrophobia was a recent reaction to a specific circumstance," I admitted, leaning back on my kitchen counter and crossing my arms.

Annie closed the book with a snap. "Then, putting this phobia aside, you've seen proof of a change in his behavior as well, Portia?"

I had seen proof in that vault for a few seconds, but since nothing had actually happened, I said, "Unfortunately, as you may have noticed, the constable and I have been on barely speaking terms since my return from Italy."

Annie sighed, coming to my side to help me with the tea. "You're right, of course. He was quite angry with you when you got back and told us the truth. And this change started before you came back. It came on while you were gone, so of course you have no information to work from," she concluded as I walked by the back window again, making a pretense of closing the curtains. Yes, I could still see a tendril of smoke rising out from between the townhouses. I was being watched by a smoking man with a limp.

"Never mind. Cheer me up, Portia, tell me of your plans to travel abroad with the dashing doctor."

I bit my lip, turning her way. "Sadly, I can only do one of those things Annie — either I can cheer you up *or* I can tell you about the plans to travel abroad. I cannot do both."

My letter from my grandmother was a welcome distraction, detailing her adventures in New York and promising to be back in London before Christmas. I missed her vivacious personality, undimmed even at her advanced age. I even missed her dragging me around to the social events I purported to hate and the restaurants I had never heard of in regions of London I never wanted to visit.

She chastised me in the letter for not spending more time with Jenkins practicing my self-defense techniques. I read the letter thrice, looking for any sign that she was in fact with my grandfather but found nothing in her words or references that indicated it. I knew that her relationship with Sherlock Holmes spanned decades on both sides of the Atlantic and that the word 'tumultuous' didn't even begin to describe it. Memories of the few good times they shared drove them to look past all their vast differences in morals and principles — at least for a little while. But their unions lasted far less time than the years of frosty silence that lay between them like ice sheets on a dangerously frozen lake.

That was actually an apt metaphor, I considered as I dressed the next day, packing up my smelly clothes from the trip to the sewers to drop off at the cleaner's.

My mind was strangely unfocused as I made my way down to King's College, careening between my last meeting with Gavin, my missing grandfather, and of course the distracting memory I had made in a locked bank vault with my best friend.

The lecture I attended was an interesting one, with the discussion centering on criminal rehabilitation — a subject on which I had read copiously and therefore had developed some well-thought-out arguments. I was still arguing with Wilson, one of my peers, as I took the stairs that would lead out of the lecture hall, when I walked straight into Dr. Beanstine.

Papers flew everywhere, as did limbs and spectacles.

"Oh dear, so sorry, ma'am," the young man spluttered, obviously not recognizing me without his much-needed glasses.

I couldn't help but grin despite my throbbing knee as I hunted under papers for his spectacles. "Not at all, Henry, entirely my fault. I was in a hurry to relieve Nerissa's dog-sitter."

"Portia?" he replied, squinting at me from his prone position. "Is that you?"

"Of course it is, my friend," I said, handing his spectacles to him and gingerly getting into a crouched position to pick up his papers, as did Wilson. Beanstine repeated his apology to us another two times as we finished picking up papers, and Wilson then said his goodbyes, pressing a note into my hand.

"Well then, you were certainly in a hurry as well, Henry," I said, restoring the last paper to the pile at our feet and tucking the note into my pocket. My brief glance at it revealed it to be a phone number and the words "Call me to discuss further over tea" written below.

"Yes, a class, of course," he replied, pushing his glasses back up his nose. "I am covering a few of Dr. Whitaker's labs this week."

I felt a pang of, not sadness exactly, but continued frustration with the reminder of that situation, but I looked around the lecture hall with a frown. "But either your students are all late, which seems unlikely, or we are in the wrong classroom..."

Beanstine blinked a couple of times, looking around the room, and then started flipping through his datebook.

"My mistake," he admitted with a sigh. "The class is tomorrow at this time."

"No harm done, Henry," I replied, clapping my glum friend on the back. "How about you join me for lunch, and I can ask you some questions about our good Professor Archer?"

At a restaurant called the Green Ivy, Beanstine admitted had also noticed the memory lapses in Archer but confessed that he had seen none of the physical changes I had noted. He promised to look more carefully next time he saw the man but humbly played down any concerns about either, pointing out Archer's age and chosen lifestyle.

"Chief Inspector Archer has always been a man of moderation," Beans said to me over a simple meal of soup and sandwiches as we sat at the back of the restaurant. To sit near the windows was just not possible anymore, since the growing number of hungry Londoners would haunt the paned glass.

The unemployment rate in this city and so many others made our positions in life more and more enviable. I thought about the disparity between the haves and the have-nots and wondered how my mother's friends were coping in Toronto. I couldn't wonder about my own friends back in Canada, since I could claim none there. But glancing up at Beans as he readjusted his glasses for the fifth time, I knew that had changed here in Britain.

"I suppose that could be true, but do keep an eye on him as well, would you?" I asked, patting at the corners of my mouth. "If he is slipping into anything serious, like dementia ... or..."

"Oh no! Portia, do not even speculate, I beg you," Beans entreated, his eyes sad behind their thick lenses. "I have read some of the most recent articles on Alzheimer's disease and dementia, and I tell you, in my medical opinion, we are nowhere near the seriousness of the symptoms in those cases."

I nodded, assured in his expertise on the subject, and told him so, returning a smile to his kind face.

"And when, my friend, will I get to meet the new lady in your life?" I prompted, taking firm hold of the tabletop before I spoke.

Beanstine bumped the table in surprise, but thanks to my preparation, nothing moved.

"Why ... how could you possibly? I don't understand..." he managed to sputter, his face reddening.

"Lady Grace, is by all accounts, a brilliant and scholarly woman — you and she have much in common," I remarked. "Surely your families do not protest?"

"Well, there is a slight matter..." Beans stopped his rather excited answer to ask, "Wait, I must ask, however did you know? We have been so careful..."

"And you have done fairly well, as I have seen naught of your relationship in the papers," I agreed.

"Portia!" Beans said worriedly.

"Oh, don't *fash* yourself, Henry," I said, using a Scottish colloquialism once used by a colleague on a train case titled "Unfound." "The clues are only there for those who are looking for them, and as you know, most people barely look up from their own feet to notice, well, anything, really."

I glanced around the room and then said, "That woman over there. She's getting up the nerve to break things off with that man. You can tell by the way she is playing with her ring finger, despite the fact that her ring is tucked away in her pocket ... she keeps checking that, by the way, to make sure it is still there." I waited for Beans to glance over at the table before continuing. "The man is oblivious that the woman is married. He's finished both his wine and his meal, while she, in guilt and misery, has touched neither."

Beanstine's eyes widened as he looked more carefully at their plates, readjusting his glasses to see better.

"Or that waiter over there," I remarked, looking to the front door of the restaurant, where a middle-aged gentleman stood erasing a chalkboard decorated with chalk drawings of ivy. "He is going to ask his boss for money."

Beans frowned as he looked the man up and down. "How can you tell?"

"He has dressed the part," I replied without looking at the man. "His jacket had a small hole in the elbow that had been mended but has been carefully unstitched so as to look in shabbier condition than it is. His shoes and trousers are well-cared for, though, so it is unlikely he could have left for work with an unnoticed hole in his elbow. And then there is the fact that he has demonstrated the issue with his clothing twice in view of his employer — in the hopes that said gentleman take him aside to correct his man, the waiter can lament his poor economic state. See ... watch — he's doing it again!"

And sure enough, as the owner of the café walked by, seating a couple of businessmen, the waiter erased the board again, his elbow obviously sticking out of the troublesome hole.

Beans shook his head. "Dead bodies I can read like an open book, but your skill with reading the living is truly amazing, Portia Adams."

I smiled at his odd compliment, thinking about my breakup with Gavin and deciding that yes, to date the consulting detective of Baker Street did mean you would be subject to over-analysis. If he couldn't handle that, then it was best that we parted. The question was, why he was so defensive?

"Did you by chance have a look at the body of the bank manager, Henry? Mr. Victor Trevor?" I asked all of a sudden.

"Bank manager?" he replied, blinking at the change in topic. "I don't think so. For a police case?"

I nodded, and he shook his head. "Hadn't heard a thing about it. Must have been handled by a different coroner."

I knew it had but hoped Beans could corroborate Gavin's findings and relieve me of suspecting him of worse than evidence-tampering.

"Returning to you, I can always tell when you have been home to see your family," I said, pointing to the pin on his jacket with his family crest, "though usually you remove it when you get back to London. This time it has been secured there for more than a month, judging by the crease it has left on the fabric. I must therefore surmise that your relationship with your family is improving, or that they approve of something. As you have not changed careers to something more 'lordly,' shall we call it, I look for some other reason your family is pleased with you. Or some other reason that your family's status is suddenly of use to you."

He looked at his jacket hanging over his chair as I took a sip of tea and pushed away my finished plate of food. "You are wearing cologne, which I have never known you to do, and I have seen you once a week since I've been back from Italy, and you have had a haircut each week, all key indicators of a new romance — in any gender, by the way."

Beanstine blushed at these observations, but looking around to make sure he wasn't overheard, he whispered, "But how did you know of Lady Grace, specifically?"

I grinned. "A guess, that one, but a good one as it turns out! Lady Grace is not someone you read about often in the society columns, preferring her privacy and the pursuits of the mind. Which, by the way, indicates that she and I will get along very well."

"But if you didn't read about her..." Beans interjected, leaning forward.

"I said you don't read about her *often*," I corrected, looking up at the ceiling. "Quite suddenly, at least for the lady in question, she was reported attending *Doctor Faustus* a few weeks ago, which I knew you attended as well, and in the papers was remarked upon as looking 'remarkably healthy and youthful,' if I recall *The Sunday Times*' words rightly."

I looked down again at my friend. "She is dressing younger than her age, and you are dressing a little older. She would be ideal in your family's eyes, and therefore you are finally in their good books. Put two and two together, and I honestly could not be happier for you."

Beans finally allowed himself to grin, probably reassured that no one else would have put these clues together, though he made me promise to keep all I knew quiet (especially from Annie Coleson) before he launched into a half-hour monologue about his new relationship.

I listened to this speech with half an ear, my eyes for some reason drawn to another pair of diners I had not described to the now verbose Dr. Beanstine.

In my head I was going through the list of missing items from the evidence box collected at the fire that burned down my grandfather's flat. One of those items was a distinctive pin featuring an eagle holding a standard in its claws.

A pin much like the one I was staring at on the gentleman seated a few tables away. The man was uncommonly handsome, wealthy to be sure, in his forties. He was making very little effort to disguise his interest in me, his eyes flicking in my direction every few minutes in between heated conversation with the red-headed man sitting across from him, tapping his cigarette on the ashtray between them.

I did my best to collect information about the two while trying to seem interested in what Beans was saying. The man with the pin facing me was easier to analyze. All I could see of his companion was the back of his hair, which was unkempt and closely cut, and his manner of dress seemed much less moneyed than his companion. But his profile reminded me of the man I had seen smoking outside my townhouse. I'd have to see him from the front to be sure. He crushed out the cigarette and waited while the redhead took out a silver cigarette holder before taking one. He let the redhead light the cigarette, his eyes on me.

"...and with Dr. Whitaker's departure..."

I switched my attention back to Dr. Beanstine with what felt like an audible snap. "Wait, whose departure?"

Beans looked surprised and then worried as he got up the nerve to nod slowly.

"Of course, he has left," I murmured to the table, smoothing out the napkin in my lap.

"Oh no, do not tell me you somehow did not know," Beans said, his eyes concerned as he reached across the table, knocking over a cup that was, thankfully, empty.

"I ... of course I knew, Henry," I assured him, attempting to smile around the knot in my stomach as I leaned over the table, righting the cup.

"Of course you did," Beans said, letting out his breath with a nervous laugh. "I mean, just look at what you could tell me about a bunch of strangers in this room! How would you not know about the departure of your very own boyfriend?"

I managed to hold back the wince that threatened and instead looked around the room to see that the man who I had been observing so carefully had left with his companion while I was distracted. I sighed as Beans motioned for the bill. So much for my vaunted observational skills.

CHAPTER TEN

I was not the first woman to be treated thusly by a man, and I surely would not be the last, but my brain refused to accept that this was a simple rejection. We were no longer together. He didn't owe me a call before he left on his trip. He didn't owe me anything at all. But the manner of his leaving just added to the pile of suspicious behavior he had been exhibiting.

I walked into my apartment, leashed Nerissa, and walked right back out on our usual walk through Regent's Park, taking our time and stopping to pick up some of my dry cleaning along the way.

I dropped Nerissa off downstairs to have some social time with the Dawes' dogs, and then I headed back up the stairs alone.

Turning the handle to my door, I swung it open to a different apartment than I had left. I stood at the doorway for a moment, running my eyes over my home, checking off things in my head as I did so.

"Portia?" called a voice from somewhere behind me, and I acknowledged the draft of cool air that signaled that the front door had opened and closed.

"Yes?" I answered, not turning but also not entering my apartment.

"What is wrong?" asked Brian, now directly behind me.

"Someone has been in my apartment while I was at the park with Nerissa," I explained, finishing my mental cataloguing and entering my rooms, heading straight to my bookshelf to tap my finger on a notebook that had been tucked in further than I had left it. I pulled it out and flipped through it for a minute, my brain whirring. It was one of Watson's journals, detailing seven cases the duo had solved in the year 1902.

"What? No," he said, following me in and looking around. "How can you tell?"

"My things are not as I left them," I answered simply, still holding the journal but walking back to my front door to check my lock and finding nothing amiss.

He turned and hurried down the stairs, where I could hear him checking in on his parents as I walked over to my small jewelry box by the window, pleased to see my mother's silver cross still nestled in its velvet folds.

Brian had returned by now, out of breath, to say, "My mum and dad heard nothing at all."

He walked around the rooms, checking for himself that we were alone while I sifted through the clothes in my closet, unable to find the silver pocket watch given to me by Dr. Whitaker.

"You think they got in through the window?" he asked, calling my attention away from that problem to the window, where he now stood looking down onto the alleyway.

I nodded without turning, still looking through pockets for my watch.

When I didn't speak for a few moments, he strode over to stand beside me. "What were they looking for?"

"The only thing that seems to be missing is the silver watch Gavin gave me. And I'm sure I had left it in my jewelry box by the window. My necklace is still there, but the watch is not."

"Odd to be sure," Brian agreed and then dropped his gaze from mine as I riffled through another pocket. "It was important to you?"

"It was," I said thoughtfully. "But not for the reasons you might think. Gavin has left London, Brian, and I see no reason to gloss this over — he has put me aside."

He seemed surprised by my admission, but his surprise quickly turned to happiness as a grin spread across his face. I felt my chest tighten at his reaction.

"He took it back."

Brian blinked at me. "He? He who?"

"Gavin. He is the only one who would take the watch and nothing else," I said, my stomach clenching at the realization.

"What?" Brian replied. "Why would he do that?"

I turned over the journal, flipping through the pages. "Because he wants me to know something. He's warning me that I'm in danger."

Two evenings later found me sitting on the roof of my townhouse, a modest picnic before me and a telescope propped up and at the ready. Instead of surveying the stars, as was its usual practice, it was pointed down toward the street.

I stretched my legs, wiggling my feet out of their pins and needles, and then leaned back in to focus on the man standing on the south side of Baker Street a block south of my own building. It was the same man who had been facing away from me at the restaurant, wearing the same scuffed, size-eight shoes and rather threadbare blue coat. He limped slightly, the injury to his right leg making me think of the man described by Gavin's secretary. He was not the only red-headed foreigner with a limp, surely, but his connection could not be ignored.

He had been standing, leaning against an alleyway wall, for more than an hour, his gaze fixed on the row of townhouses. He had walked by four times before finding his resting spot, which was how I had first noticed him. My team of intrepid homeless children had sought him out on my direction, assessed that he had a foreign accent and then followed him to the servant's quarters of the Austrian embassy on Belgrave — the same building that had changed Gavin from the ambitious professor I knew to the paranoid ex-boyfriend he had become.

I chewed thoughtfully on a biscuit as I used my pencil to jot down his bent nose in my notebook. I heard a noise behind me and tensed until I recognized the footsteps on the metal balcony that led up here.

"Portia, do you mind if I join you?" asked Brian.

I considered it honestly for a few seconds before answering, and he waited patiently.

"Please do. I think this would be a most opportune moment," I replied finally, turning to watch him negotiate his tall frame onto the roof from the stairs. "But if you could please crouch down just in case, so no one can see you?"

"Opportune?" he asked, arriving at my side and crouching down beside me.

I turned the telescope his way in answer, pointing down the street. "That gentleman in between Vellums and the meat shop."

He settled down into a more comfortable position and then carefully focused in on where my finger was pointing.

"Ah yes, the gentleman rooting around in his nose? Quite charming," he said with a smile.

"What? No, no," I said, pulling the eyepiece toward me, nearly bumping heads with him.

I couldn't see the nose-picker anywhere, only my limping stalker. I turned my face to Brian's, which was still bare inches away, to see him grinning. I rolled my eyes at his childish behavior.

"What of the man?" he prompted, taking the eyepiece back but not moving at all, comfortable with the closeness of our bodies in a way we hadn't been before our time in the vault.

"He has been following me for at least three days," I admitted, getting a small measure of revenge from the constable's reaction. He jerked back, nearly knocking over my telescope.

"Days?" he demanded and turned quickly back to look through the eyepiece. "Why did you not tell someone?"

I shrugged. "He hasn't approached me at all. He is obviously waiting for something. He is the same man who was inquiring about Gavin at King's College. I believe he is the Austrian Gavin was trying to warn me about by displacing my grandfather's journal."

"Wait, what?" Brian said.

"'The Case of the Illustrious Client'," I said, referring to the title Watson had given that case. "Did you look into what happened to Baron Gruner?"

"He was quite the cad," Brian answered. "Keeping a ledger like that filled with the names of his past conquests? A horrid little hobby for a horrid man."

"A murderous man," I put in. "The ledger was not the worst of his offences."

"We're not sure what happened to him after he was attacked by Kitty Winter, but surely he would be in his eighties by now? And she threw vitriol in his face — he would be very scarred."

"I wondered if he might be financing this endeavor from afar," I said.

"So it wasn't just the pin they were after, or they wouldn't be here watching Holmes's old office. We still don't know what they're after, only that it has some connection to the Baron Gruner case."

I nodded. "Do you recognize the fish truck parked on the street?"

"Yes, I think I know it." Brian answered. "It's from a shop in Old Ford, isn't it?"

"I believe it's his, but I didn't actually see him drive up in it. We'll have to wait till he leaves to see."

"Do you really think Whitaker was the one who broke into your flat and pointed you to that specific journal?" Brian said quietly.

"There was no other reason to take the watch but to make sure I knew it was him," I said. "He wanted to warn me, but he also wanted me to take it seriously. Which I do."

"But was he working with these Austrians?"

I looked back through the eyepiece, wondering the same thing. "Yes, I believe he was. Though I would also like to believe that when he discovered my involvement, he got out as quickly as he could. That's why they left so many messages for him. He was dodging them even as he dodged me. I think he is worried for my safety."

"You think better of him than I," Brian muttered. "I could see this of Simmons, who would do anything for a quick shilling, but Whitaker?" .

"I know," I said sadly. "I had my questions about how he was making so much money so fast, and now I think..."

I sighed, allowing myself to feel the regret that I had been holding at bay before finishing my thought. "I think he was trying too hard to pull himself up to the upper echelons he had always aspired to be part of. He was so insecure. So brilliant, but so insecure. I saw it but hoped against hope that his efforts were on the right side of the law. I suspect you will have to go back over his casework, especially those that involve Simmons, to make sure there haven't been other incidents where they took money to steal evidence, or, God forbid, cover up a crime."

We sat for a moment, letting that depressing thought hang in the air.

"I'm going down there to arrest this red-headed vermin, but first I have to know: how long have you suspected Whitaker?" Brian said.

I glanced his way with a defeated expression. "Weeks. But I had no evidence. It was just a gut feeling. And you know I don't trust gut feelings. Well, *my* gut feelings, at least."

"Weeks," he repeated, shaking his head. "Next time do yourself a favor and share your gut feelings with your partner right away."

I squinted at him in surprise. "Partner, Constable?"

"Brian," he answered, interrupting me, his eyes brooking no argument.

I swallowed, attempting to retain my poise. "When did we agree to be partners? You haven't spoken to me for over a month..."

"And you lied to me when you left the country," he reminded me.

Instead of arguing, I nodded emphatically. "Indubitably. Which only provides more evidence of a lack of partnership."

He looked again through the eyepiece before speaking. "Then it is time to call this what it is, Portia Adams. Even the greatest detective in the world had a partner. If you are going to continue to follow in his footsteps, you cannot tell me that you can do what he could not: work in isolation. He had Watson. He needed a partner, and so do you. A man you can rely on, a man who knows how your mind works, and a man with access to the official world of coroners and evidence and courts."

Lifting his chin, he said, "That man is me."

I wanted to disagree, but to what end? He was my partner. The person I trusted above all others. The only person in my life to whom I had told all my secrets, and who held them close, as protective of them as I was.

I nodded again. "I would be honored."

He smiled broadly, finally betraying the insecurity he had felt making that small speech. He extended his hand in the small space between us, and I shook it readily, wondering how far this partnership could go, remembering a few stolen moments behind a concrete- and steel-reinforced wall.

"Now, wait here while I arrest our ugly friend down there," he said, carefully exiting the roof.

CHAPTER ELEVEN

The next week was one of emotional highs and lows, a circumstance to which I was wholly unused, preferring to have as little emotion in my life as possible. I supposed I was still mourning the loss of Gavin. Not the boyfriend, but the man. The friend I had thought I knew.

The good constable did his best to try to apprehend the man who had been following me, but he had obviously seen us on the roof and run away. Brian even went to King's College to try to officially retrieve the notes left for Whitaker, but he was too late. Gavin had picked them up before he left town.

Worst of all, Simmons had disappeared before anyone could question him, and without him Michaels didn't feel we had enough evidence to demand Gavin's return to London. He changed up a few of his constables' beats to walk by Baker Street more often. After five complete days without any sign of the red-headed man's return, he decided that the added security had scared away my would-be stalker. I didn't agree with his assumption, but since I disliked being watched by anyone — even a well-meaning policeman — I had not protested.

When Brian asked (over dinner at his parents' downstairs apartment, a tradition I was happy to reinstate when he asked me to), I admitted to him that I didn't think my stalker was out of my life.

"He does seem to have given up a little too easily," agreed Brian, pouring a glass of water for his father.

"This is very good, Mrs. Dawes," I remarked.

She beamed. "Glad you like it, little miss. Any word from your Mrs. Jones, by chance? I've been meaning to give her back her hat. She left it in the front hall."

"She told me in her last letter that she was due back before Christmas," I answered. I was looking forward to my grandmother's return.

We ate in amicable silence for a few more minutes till Mrs. Dawes asked hesitantly, of both of us "...and Annie? I haven't seen her in almost a week now — I hope she's not unwell?"

The entire table seemed to tense slightly. Even the usually half-asleep Mr. Dawes Sr. cleared his throat uncomfortably.

Guilt continued to nip at me when it came to Annie, so I had not sought her company since that night in my flat, but it was odd that she had not been by. She was much more social than I and carried the burden of nurturing our friendship, often in the face of my isolationist tendencies.

"She is well, Mother," Brian answered, his eyes on his plate. "Just busy with work, I am sure."

"Ah," replied his mother, not pursuing the subject but sounding unconvinced.

"Did you have any luck ascertaining the identity of the second gentleman, Brian?" I asked, deciding a change of topic was required, "The man wearing the eagle pin?"

Brian shook his head. "No, though I was able to verify your own findings that the pin is not of a known design to any of the manufacturers in the London area. Are you sure that the pin from the evidence box is the same one you saw that man wearing in the restaurant with Beans?"

"I can't say it's definitively the same pin," I admitted, "but it does seem more than coincidental that the pin discovered at the site of a house fire I have connections to looks like a pin worn by a man who seems interested in me and Baker Street."

"But you have not seen the man?" Brian pressed, his eyes assessing.

"Not at all," I assured him as his mother picked up my empty plate. "Neither he nor his red-headed accomplice since we were on the roof."

"And nothing from Whitaker?"

"Not a word."

"Good," he said, picking up his plate and his father's. "Let us hope it stays that way."

I waited till he was out of earshot before muttering under my breath, "It won't."

Several days later, I was knocking on the Haywards Heath door of my uncle, Dr. Hamish Watson.

I was following the butler to the east wing drawing room when I was buffeted by my young second cousins. I greeted the younger ones with hugs and shook hands with the older children as they peppered me with questions about the cases I was working on.

"Now, leave Portia alone," said Mrs. Emily Watson from the mantelpiece, where she stood with her sister-in-law, Sarah, who was holding the newest member of the family.

"She's gotten so big, Sarah," I said as the children peeled away from me to chase each other around some more. The baby was named Mary and had lovely blue eyes, a smattering of freckles and a shock of silvery blonde hair.

"Such pretty hair," I remarked, touching it softly. "Whose side of the family does it come from?"

"From Mary's side," said Sarah, wrapping an arm around me and giving me a peck on the cheek. "You don't know him because he is something of a black sheep in the family, but Regulus and Hamish's youngest brother had that color of hair when he was a small boy."

"You look well, Portia. Italy has been good to you," Emily said with a wide smile, nodding at her husband, who extended a glass of champagne to me.

I was wearing a black velvet, straight-fitting dress that featured a striped lace-and-velvet capelet. I was not normally attracted to evening dresses, but when shopping with an Italian princess, one learns to listen to her advice. I had paired the dress with the pearl-shaped diamond earrings she had presented to me before I had boarded the train.

"Thank you, it was," I replied, taking the wine and the kiss from my Uncle Regulus.

"So glad you could join us tonight, Niece," he said, and then seeing his butler enter the room, "and just in time, it seems. We're being called to supper. Shall we go through?"

I was distracted by a small frame on the mantelpiece, so I didn't answer right away, walking up to it to touch the medals displayed within.

"John Watson was mentioned in despatches for his actions in India and in Afghanistan as part of the Northumberland Fusiliers," said Hamish, walking over to join me.

I touched the medals reverently, wishing I had known my grandfather and could have heard his stories of the wars in which he had fought, both in the east and here at home.

"I'm surprised they haven't caught your attention before," Hamish said, extending his elbow so that he could escort me to the dining room. "They are always here on display for the family to be proud of."

I automatically took his elbow. I had noticed the medals before, of course. It was just that at that moment one of them reminded me of an eagle pin missing from evidence and worn by the man at the Green Ivy. As soon as I left there, I determined to search the Bodleian Library for books on war medals, for the eagle holding a standard. I had a sinking feeling I knew from which country it originated.

CHAPTER TWELVE

I hurried home from the library with my two borrowed books, anxious to share my findings about the eagle pin with Brian. I ran into him as he was leaving the house.

"Portia!" he exclaimed, pulling his trench coat over his uniform in a mad rush. "They've discovered a body just off Waterloo Bridge, and they suspect..."

He grasped my upper arm, and my heart clenched, a vision of Gavin's limp body suddenly clear in my mind. "They think it's Simmons!"

"Oh my God!" said the voice of Annie Coleson. She had come up behind me on the small walkway that led up to 221. Behind her I could see the fish truck Brian and I had observed when we were on the roof with the telescope.

"Annie?" Brian said in surprise, and then, "Do not print this. This is not for public knowledge yet."

She stiffened immediately, the hurt on her face obvious even in the failing light, so I dropped an arm around her shoulders, my eyes on the truck. There was no one in the driver's seat, meaning my limping stalker could be on the street right now. "She wouldn't," I said to Brian as I looked up and down the street, not seeing anyone who would fit the redhead's description.

"No, of course not. Forgive me, Annie," he said, looking contrite. I decided not to slow him down further by pointing out the truck. "Portia, I'm for the morgue. The scene has been cleared already to allow for traffic to continue around the bridge. Do you want to come with me now or wait and see if it is Simmons?"

The return of my stalker made my decision. "You go ahead, Constable. Please do let me know when you know something definitive. Especially..." I paused and then said, "if it is Simmons, and cause of death looks like ... poison."

He looked shocked but nodded, racing off, slamming the metal gate behind him as he exited the property.

Annie managed to keep up her brave face, but her slim shoulders slumped forward immediately after he was out of our sight.

"I actually came to see if you wanted to see a late film, Portia," she said. "But I suppose in light of this drama..." She was looking sickly again, much like the first time I had met her and declared her to be suffering from malnutrition.

"Nonsense," I declared, taking her hand and pulling it through my arm, marveling at how far I had come in terms of my views on Gavin Whitaker. From boyfriend to suspected murderer in a month's time. Did I really think him capable of such a descent?

"Come inside, Annie. I need to ring someone up quickly, but then we have the evening to ourselves," I said, scanning the street again and seeing nothing.

"That sounds lovely," she said, smiling up at me through unshed tears.

As soon as we were in the door, I shooed Annie up the stairs and used the telephone in the hallway to ring up Jenkins. He immediately agreed to come to Baker Street and have a surreptitious look around for either of the men I described.

Annie, meanwhile, doing her best to shake off her dour mood, had put a kettle on in my kitchen. I was tense with possibilities, certain I was being watched, but did my best to be attentive to my friend.

I had observed enough of my mother's interactions with other women to at least know my expected role in such situations, even if it didn't come naturally to me. I nodded a lot and tried to look sympathetic as she listed the various ways her relationship with her boyfriend had recently deteriorated.

Annie had become very dear to me over the last year or so, but her issues with a man we both cared about seemed, well, trivial when compared with everything going on around us. In addition, my own feelings for Brian made my judgment rather biased — best that I stay neutral and logical than unfairly influence a relationship that so directly affected my life.

Standing by the window, I tensed, seeing a shadowy figure slip between the houses, but the figure was large and looked up to salute me. Bruiser Jenkins. I felt some of the tension leak out of me as I watched him casually walk the alley using a cane he did not need. If my stalkers were here to-night, they would soon be discovered.

About a quarter of an hour later, when our teapot was empty and Annie was starting to look sleepy, a knock at the door startled her out of her re-laxed state.

I knew it was Jenkins but looked through the spyglass he had installed anyway so he wouldn't give me a lecture.

"Evening, ladies," he said, taking off his hat to nod at Annie. "I was just walking by and thought I might pop in and say hello."

"Won't you come in, Mr. Jenkins? You remember Miss Coleson?" I asked, opening the door wider to let him step in.

"Of course, Miss Coleson. You look well," he said, taking a small step into my apartment.

"Thank you, Mr. Jenkins, but it's Annie, remember?" She extended her hand and gave him a lovely smile. "You must excuse me. Portia, I'm going to dash some water on my face before I go."

She headed off to my bathroom, and as soon as she was out of earshot, I said, "Anything, Mr. Jenkins?"

"The lorry was gone by the time I walked by," he replied, replacing his hat on his head. "And I walked two blocks in each direction, saw no limp-ing redheads at all."

I bit my lip, glad but annoyed at the report.

"Do you want me to stay close?" he asked. "I could fetch a spot in the alleyway across the street for a bit, see if they swing back around."

"I don't think that's necessary, Mr. Jenkins, but could I bother you to escort Annie to a hackney?"

He nodded. "Good idea. I'll put the girl in a cab, and it will seem like I've left. Then I'll come back around and double-check on you."

I couldn't argue with that logical suggestion.

Annie demurred, of course, but Jenkins and I insisted, and I followed them down to the street, an idea popping into my head. Maybe it was time to reverse our positions — the red-headed man and me. Maybe I could solve two of my problems at once.

"It will all work out, Annie," I said, pulling my friend into a hug. "Just talk to him. He is a reasonable man."

She looked surprised at the return to our earlier talk of her misgivings about Brian, especially since my answers up until this point had been mon-osyllabic. "But Portia..."

"Don't take no for an answer," I stated, giving Jenkins a nod. "I may, in fact, take my own advice and surprise Dr. Whitaker in Germany. Perhaps it is best to have everything out in the open."

She gaped at me but took Jenkins' large bicep and walked with him down Baker Street and out of sight.

I turned and slipped between the houses into the alleyway. I remember looking up at my curtained window, but that was where everything got a little hazy.

Chapter Thirteen

I woke groggy and bound on a hideously patterned settee. I slowly swung my bound feet to the floor, adjusting to the spinning room. The lack of a gag meant either that I was isolated enough not to be heard or I had awakened earlier than expected. The lack of a blindfold was more worrying, because it meant my kidnappers didn't care if I identified them — most likely because they intended for me to never leave this place alive.

Regardless, information was power, I thought, assessing my surroundings. A basement level, to be sure, with rooms of covered furniture in various states of disrepair. There was only a small lamp lighting the area, but I could see equipment strewn all over the place, broken barrels that smelled terrible and a set of stairs leading up to the main floor, I assumed.

I closed my eyes and listened for outside traffic — which I could hear. That meant somewhere in this room there was at least one window open or broken. I listened to the honking of cars and common sounds of people walking by — though not a great quantity and not at a frenzied pace. There was another sound. I squinted, concentrating. Not cars but ... the honking sounds of ... boats maybe? My eyes flew open as a lock turned at the top of the stairs, and two sets of footsteps came down toward me.

Coming down were the two gentlemen I had originally seen at the Green Ivy with Dr. Beanstine.

"So yer up, are ye?" said the older redhead with the bent nose, his limp more pronounced on the stairs.

"I am indeed, sir," I replied, surprising him with my calm. "And if you could please remove my bonds, I believe you will still find me within your power and unlikely to try and overpower you and escape. The Old Ford docks are, after all, a loud area, and even if I were to yell at the top of my lungs, I doubt anyone out on the street could hear me."

The surly man looked at his handsome companion for direction, and I was not surprised to see that man's mouth turn up in a sneer before he said, "Quite right, Miss Adams. We are all reasonable people, and you must know that your safety and comfort are paramount to us."

"At least until your true mark arrives," I agreed, my eyes upon him even as his partner stooped to undo the ropes at my wrists.

The sneer widened into a true smile. "By God, you truly are his grand-daughter."

I nodded once, rubbing at my wrists as my ankles were similarly freed. "My question is this: what makes you think he will come alone?"

The man at my feet finished his work and stepped back to stand beside his partner. "An' tha's what I've bin sayin' all along, yer Lordship — *aargh!*"

His cry was in response to the cuff he received, and I raised my hand to try and forestall any more violence. "The former baron is right in his denial, though it need not be so physically demonstrated," I said, my eyes remaining on the gentleman of the pair. "He is not a baron, though, so you shouldn't refer to him as his lordship. The nobility was dissolved in Austria more than ten years ago, when his father was still Baron Gruner."

This time neither man could hold back his surprise, and the rougher-looking one stepped forward menacingly, only to be stopped by a well-manicured hand on his shoulder.

"Careful now, Mr. Fuchs, remember that Miss Adams has a purpose here as our guest," he said soothingly, his charisma fairly oozing out of his pores. "Be a good man and do a round of the perimeter, would you?"

Fuchs blinked stupidly at his master but then nodded and with a small bow headed directly back up the stairs.

"You sound like you have spent most of your life in Britain," I observed. "College?"

He gave an imperious nod.

"His manners are not those of a butler, even a former butler fallen on hard times. Your father's former chauffeur, perhaps?" I asked.

"Heavens, no," replied my captor, pulling a wooden chair toward the couch. "One of the outdoor staff — chief horseman in his heyday, I believe. At least when that position existed."

Of course, the baron's estate would have lost much of their staff in the last few decades, Mr...?" I replied, clasping my hands before me as I ran my eyes over the now-seated man.

He flashed a cold smile again before answering. "You may call me Fabian. But you well know that they were never my staff, though with your help, I hope to change that."

Finally, the last piece of the puzzle slid into place.

"You see, your grandfather has something I need — something that will change my fortunes forever," he explained, ignorant of the realization I had come to. "I will trade your life for that one little thing, and all will be right once more between the houses of Gruner and Holmes."

"How will he even know that I am taken? Or where to find me?" I asked, honestly curious. "I have been unable to contact him since the two of you burned down his postal address — killing an innocent old lady, may I add."

Instead of defending himself, Fabian shrugged slightly. "The old woman was very kind. She invited me in of her own accord and over a few cups of tea confirmed my suspicions about her upstairs tenant — that it was just a posed space where an older gentleman would pick up his mail every few days, and where he stored some of his things in her basement."

"Yes, you do seem to share your father's skill with the womenfolk," I answered, nodding.

He took it as a compliment, his chest puffing out with pride. "She was a talkative one, Mrs. Birch, which is understandable given that she had no living relations left to talk to ... talked herself right to sleep, holding her cigarette in her hand like she probably did a hundred times before."

He shook his head in mock empathy, and I felt disgusted and a little fascinated at the same time.

"Even though you could have waited there for my grandfather the way your Mr. Fuchs waited outside my apartment?"

Fabian shrugged again. "Fire would cover up my search through the house, give me a modicum of revenge and bring your grandfather running."

"Except he didn't come," I filled in. "But I did."

"That you did, my sweet," he said, reaching out to grasp my chin. "You don't look much like the old man, thank heavens, but he wasn't careful enough about picking up his letters, so I knew you existed before I set fire to the place. Such sweet writing. Who knew that Holmes had a living granddaughter? And that she was so handsome?"

He spread his hands. "When you showed up and he did not, well, I knew I had at least one more string to pull."

"Speaking of strings, why in the world did you go to so much trouble to retrieve your father's medal?" I interjected, pointing at the eagle pin on his jacket.

"I had no idea that the medal was in that flat, or I would of course have taken it before starting the fire," Fabian explained, looking down at it with fondness. "I needed to destroy the evidence from the fire, but when the medal was described to me, I recognized it and couldn't leave it in the hands of Scotland Yard!"

"Described to you," I repeated. "By Constable Simmons, I take it?"

He inclined his head. "Though he refused to actually remove it from the evidence room, coward that he was."

"An ingenious solution, by the way, pulling the medal through the pipes because you couldn't take it back out past the police," I replied. "Though I doubt you actually got your hands dirty yourself. Who came up with that idea?"

The man simply smiled.

"Unfortunate, because I would love to know how you snaked the string all the way from the drain under the closet down into the sewers," I said, shaking my head with honest admiration. "And no offense to your former chief horseman, but I don't think he is capable of such a scheme. Nor do I think Constable Simmons worked alone."

This time he shrugged. "I cared not how the item was retrieved, just that it was."

"And your connections at the Austrian embassy gave you access to just the brilliant mind to help you do that," I said, still wanting to hear Gavin's name on this man's lips. I was angry on his behalf. They had taken advantage of his insecurities, offering money, status and who knew what else for his soul. Yes, Gavin had sold it, but it was this man who had bargained for it.

Instead, he just curled his lip. "I repeat: I cared not how, just that I had my father's belongings back."

"And the box in the Westminster Bank? It belonged to your father, too?" I asked, trying a new tack.

"It did, but it was useless," Fabian answered with an angry look. "It was unclaimed for so long that the bank manager contacted the Austrian government. I have many contacts in that government, and I knew I had to see what was in the box before anyone else. It was nothing. Some useless files on people long dead. Nothing I could use. Not even anything I could sell."

"But the manager ... he was working with you...?"

"Yes, he was paid handsomely for his efforts," Fabian replied, waving a hand. "The man was of a nervous disposition. A few heated questions from Simmons and Fuchs, and he collapsed. It was entirely his own fault."

"And then you had to cover that up as well," I murmured, understanding how Gavin had been drawn into this deeper and deeper and wishing he had just come to me before he stepped over the precipice. His old partner, Simmons, with whom he had probably worked before on smaller petty crimes, had called him up, forcing him to come down to the bank and deal with the corpse before a real coroner could be called and perhaps question the death.

"Why did Simmons have to die?" I asked, though I suspected I knew the answer.

"He was a liability. Not a man who could be trusted to keep his word," he answered, and then gave me a wink. "Unlike others still in my service."

"Who killed Simmons?" I asked, my heart thudding dully.

Fabian shrugged. "Fuchs is willing to do much to restore me to my position. Slitting a few throats is of no great consequence to a man like him."

Gavin hadn't killed his former partner. That was something. Maybe he could come back from this. "The pin — it's a medal of honor that your father received. I believe from the Austrian army? For service in the Great War?"

"Exactly," he answered, pleased I understood the significance. "And after tonight, when Holmes brings me the ledger, I will at last have everything my father should have bequeathed to me. And in answer to your question about how he will find us, I am under no illusions when it comes to the great detective," he continued, leaning back on his chair. "Sherlock Holmes will find us because that is what he does best — especially with an incentive."

The baron pulled a small gun out of his suit pocket. "I left a message for him at your Baker Street apartment. A message that makes it clear that your life depends on his attention."

I met his gaze levelly over the gun's barrel. "Then I hope he doesn't disappoint you," I said.

"Oh, I am sure he will not," he replied jovially as we heard the door unlock upstairs again. "Just as you did not, my dear, so kindly telling your pretty friend that your absence should not be immediately noted since you are planning an immediate trip to Germany to join your boyfriend."

"My ex-boyfriend," I answered, trying to keep the anger out of my voice. "A state of affairs I blame entirely on you, by the by. And a bad situation I intend to rescue him from."

He chuckled. "As if he needs rescuing at all. Mr. Fuchs, is all well?" he called over his shoulder, using his left hand to search through his pockets. We could barely see the man in the dim light as he made his way limping down the stairs.

"Nothing stirring out there, and checked in with the boys, no sign yet," came the answer as new footsteps sounded down the stairs and headed toward us.

"Then the other boxes of evidence that were disrupted. They were purely to distract the police?" I asked, holding the man's attention.

"Perhaps," he said with a flirtatious curl of his upper lip. "Or perhaps there was someone else interested in getting something from the Yard's evidence rooms, and this was a convenient moment."

"The timing and communication of such a parallel venture would be," I breathed out, realizing that we still had no hard evidence connecting Gavin to this crime, "most entrepreneurial. Not to be overly dramatic, but are you suggesting a criminal mastermind is besieging London?"

Fabian's grin widened, but he waggled the two fingers in front of my face. "Now, now, my pretty. Some things you will have to discover for yourself."

"Allow me, sir," said his partner, reaching our side and holding out a packet of worn cigarettes.

Fabian barely looked up as he pulled out a cigarette, which his man duly lit with a match.

"Excellent, Mr. Fuchs. That leaves you here with Miss Adams, and I shall take my place across the street with Mr. Roe and Mr. Lee to await our prey."

Fabian had started to step away but then turned with a quizzical look, replacing his gun in his pocket as he spoke. "One thing surprises me, Miss Adams."

"What is that, sir?" I asked looking at Fuchs and then back at Fabian.

"By all accounts, you are a highly intelligent and thoughtful girl," he said, taking a long drag on his cigarette, "yet tonight you made it all too easy for us to follow and capture you. Even with a constable living downstairs and half of Scotland Yard guarding you for the better part of a week."

I nodded. "Because our goals were not so different — at least in the bigger picture."

He tilted his head slightly and listed a little in that direction, his eyes widening in surprise.

"You see, Portia wanted to find me almost as much as you did," the man disguised as Fuchs finally explained, straightening and turning toward the rapidly deteriorating Fabian.

"You!" gasped Fabian, managing to get that accusation out before his eyes rolled back in his head and he slumped to the floor, senseless.

"Grandfather!" I exclaimed, joyfully throwing my arms around the man.

"My dear girl," he replied, squeezing me tightly in his wiry arms. "I am very glad to find you safe, but all of this was really not necessary."

I leaned back to look him in the face. "You left me no choice! You dropped out of sight so completely, and I couldn't take the chance that you would come to the conclusion that I was safer with you out of my life."

He smiled his sardonic smile. "If I did, it would have been both necessary and temporary." Sherlock Holmes turned cold eyes to the prostrate man on the floor. "In demonstrating that he was willing to kill for his father's property, Fabian Gruner gave me no choice but to go into hiding."

"But that is over now, correct?" I demanded, crossing my arms. "No more running away from me?"

"I was never running away from you," he corrected automatically, and then, "But you are right. You have proven beyond a doubt that from now on, we stand together and fight. Mostly because I know what you will do if I don't."

I grinned, leaning in to give him a kiss. "What a disguise! If not for anticipating your arrival, I might not have recognized you myself!"

"Oh, I warrant my footsteps were recognizably different despite my attempt at imitating Fuchs' walk. The man was kicked by a horse when he was in his thirties, I deduced, a hard thing to reproduce," my grandfather admitted, scratching carefully at his fake nose and handing me the pack of cigarettes.

"Hold on to these while I deal with this blackguard. When do we expect the constabulary to arrive?"

I had opened my mouth to answer when the sound of the door being kicked in could be heard, and then Constable Dawes came pelting down the stairs, pointing his baton steadily at my grandfather as he breathlessly said, "Stand away from her, sir, lest I be forced to do violence on you!"

My grandfather barely looked up, finishing up binding Fabian's hands, so I stepped between them. "Brian, the man you seek is at your feet, brought to bear by ..."

I hesitated here, but my grandfather pulled the knots tight and then stepped around me gracefully, extending his hand in greeting. "Constable Dawes, how good to finally meet you. I am Sherlock Holmes."

Brian gaped at us, his baton slowly lowering as he took in my grandfather's words and we heard raised voices from the upper floors calling down to Brian.

My grandfather bemusedly pointed up the stairs. "You should assure your men that you are safe, Constable, and that they will find three suspects out in the alleyway who are related to this matter. All trussed up and ready for transport, watched over by Mr. Asher Jenkins, who aided me in that part of the plan. One of those men, a Mr. Fuchs, was the one who killed your fallen Constable Simmons."

That got Brian moving, and he called up the stairs. "I'm fine, Bonhomme. I have found Miss Adams. Go to the alleyway — there are three dangerous suspects tied up and ready for jail."

He turned back to us, looking at the man on the floor and back up at us. "But how ... how did you ... manage to...?"

I gingerly picked up the half-smoked cigarette and answered, "I'm guessing some kind of drug in the tobacco of these cigarettes?"

"Of course," replied my grandfather, scratching at his fake nose again, eliciting a wide-eyed stare from Brian as the appendage moved. "Nothing too potent. They should be fully ready for questioning within the hour."

"And you," Brian said, his eyes filled with concern as he replaced his gun in its holster. "They did not harm you?"

I shook my head. "I am well, Brian. Thank you for finding me so quickly."

"I found a note on my apartment door when I got home, describing the reappearance of the fish lorry, and I got here as quickly as I could," he said, stepping forward to examine my reddened wrists, which I had been absentmindedly rubbing.

"Yes, that was Jenkins' note, by the way. Fabian had left one for me inside Portia's apartment, and Jenkins used the weathervane to contact me. We are fortunate that my granddaughter is as stubborn as she is brilliant and kept her wits about her while we took care of her captors," my grandfather remarked, smiling at the two of us and then backing into the shadows as larger, heavier footsteps could be heard on the stairs.

"Adams!" called the voice of Sergeant Michaels. "You've got to be the luckiest lass this side of the River Jordan!"

"Indeed I am, Sergeant, especially to have such prompt and helpful comrades," I remarked, stepping forward to meet him at the base of the stairs.

On Brian's direction, three men lifted Fabian off the floor and dragged him up the stairs, and I followed with the large sergeant, answering his rapid-fire questions as best I could.

"*Harrumph*, Dawes, are you joining us or considering renting the basement down there?" Michaels yelled over his shoulder as we reached the main level.

I knew why Brian lingered, so I slipped my arm through the surprised sergeant's and prompted him. "Now, let me tell you the story of Baron Gruner and his ledger, so you and I can figure out how much of this story need come to light, and how much we can keep in the dark."

CHAPTER FOURTEEN

L ord almighty, Portia, the amount of trouble you can get into in so short a time!" my grandmother exclaimed over tea a few days later. I had just caught her up on all the events she had missed during her travels, wrapping up with my rescue from the docks of Old Ford.

"Imagine knowing that you were about to be abducted and then actually creating a situation where you were vulnerable in order to help the kidnappers kidnap you." She shook her head, her gray curls bouncing in the morning light. "You are an original, my girl, that much is true. But how did you know they weren't going to kill you?"

I tipped the teapot over her cup before answering.

"You mistake me, Grandmother. I didn't know they would kidnap me. I didn't even realize that Fabian's objective was the leather-bound ledger his father wrote in to document his conquests. Not until I was in the basement. I thought the man simply sought my grandfather out of some delayed revenge scheme.

"Once I recognized the medal of honor and noticed the casebook that had been replaced in the bookshelf, I put two and two together and figured out I was being stalked by someone related to the Austrian Baron Gruner."

"A clue you owe to the at-large Dr. Whitaker," my grandmother pointed out as she raised her cup. "A topic we will be returning to in much detail, I promise you."

I ignored the last remark and answered the first. "Indeed."

"And then the night you went out with Miss Coleson, who, if I may observe, has been checking in less than I would have expected..."

"She came by the very night I was rescued..." I protested but was cut off.

"That night, you recognized the fish truck and dropped the bait that you were vulnerable," she continued.

"Yes, either to allow him to do a further search of this apartment while I was investigating the alleyway," I explained, "or to try and apprehend me — which he obviously did."

My grandmother snorted, so I felt the need to defend myself further. "I called Jenkins! I did what I could to minimize the danger."

My grandmother took another sip of tea before asking, "And the ledger, Fabian needed that to prove his parentage, correct?"

"*Exactement,*" I affirmed with a smile. "He was most forthcoming during questioning at Scotland Yard. Claiming that he had no intention of harming me but simply sought his father's rightful property. A ledger that would prove he was the illegitimate son of Baron Gruner. And with the baron's only legitimate child dead at forty-five without an heir, the person next in line to inherit a considerable fortune."

"More than enough reason to pursue your grandfather and kill you both if he'd had his way," she said.

"Well, he didn't 'get his way,' did he?" I replied tartly.

"What of Mr. Whitaker's connection?"

I felt my shoulders tense before I opened my mouth to answer. "Despite his admissions about his own crimes, the man was unwilling to speak of anyone but Fuchs and Simmons. We don't know why, but for now, Fabian is tight-lipped about Gavin's involvement."

Brian had been especially aggressive in his interrogation of Fabian, refusing to believe that Gavin's appearances at crime scenes and at the Yard were coincidental. I knew how he felt and shared his frustration, if not his fervor, to bring the former coroner to justice. I still didn't want to see Gavin behind bars, but I wished we could talk, somehow, to bring resolution to this whole case. Maybe even find a way to bring him back from his dark journey into greed and politics. Sergeant Michaels promised that on his return to Britain, Gavin would be brought in for questioning, but while he was abroad, they had no way to bring him in without real evidence or testimony from Fuchs or Fabian.

"And where, pray tell, is this ledger that caused such a commotion?" she asked, drawing my attention back her way.

I clapped my hands. "That is the beauty of it, Grandmother. It was right under his nose. My grandfathers turned it in to Scotland Yard decades ago as part of evidence in 'The Case of the Illustrious Client.' He could have claimed it directly from the Yard had he just petitioned for it with his lawyer, claiming that he needed it to prove parentage!"

"He assumed Holmes had it and wouldn't give it up." Irene Adler nodded. "Would have been nice if Holmes had told you when he realized who was pursuing him — so that you not be involved in his unfinished business. He can be entirely selfish, you know, my dear."

I rolled my eyes. "My grandfather held onto the Medal of Honor as a curiosity, one of the chosen few keepsakes he held," I said, ignoring the jibe. "The ledger was evidence and therefore at the Yard."

"What of his claims, though, Portia?" prompted my grandmother, leaning forward again, her eyes alight.

A knock at the door interrupted us, and I was enjoying her frustrated curiosity, so I answered the door instead.

"Portia, they are calling us to King's College, right away," said Brian quickly, his jacket half-on as he glanced through the open door at my grandmother and apologetically tipped his hat.

I quickly turned, trusting Brian's sense of what was important, and pulled on my coat. "I am sorry, Mrs. Jones. I must go."

"Portia Constance Adams!" my grandmother declared, standing up and using her cane on the floor like a gavel.

I stopped in place, as did Brian, his eyes confused, looking between us.

I shook my head, fighting the urge to smile. "It was all for naught! Gruner never had an affair with Fabian's mother, or at least never deigned to write it down in his ledger. So Fabian is not a Gruner and does not stand to inherit."

"What a shame," my grandmother said, sniffing, and sat back down casually, her curiosity satisfied.

Thus dismissed, I followed Brian out of 221 Baker Street and to the hackney that waited below.

Brian had nothing further to add in the car except to say that he had received a frantic call from Sergeant Michaels to come to King's College and to bring me along if possible.

We jumped out of the hackney less than ten minutes later and rushed past the cordoned area where students and teachers were being held back from one of the buildings.

"Bonhomme, what is it?" demanded Brian.

But Bonhomme just shook his head, the whistle in his mouth shaking also as he tried to keep people away from the center of the group of police.

I left Brian, squeezing through the crowd of men to the source of all the attention. Pushing past the last set of broad shoulders, I suddenly recognized the hand on the ground, a hand that had been the first extended my way from Scotland Yard.

There, in a puddle of blood and gore, lit up by the flashlights of his comrades, lay my professor, my friend, Chief Inspector Dillon Breen Archer.

CASEBOOK NINE
NO MATTER
HOW IMPROBABLE

CHAPTER ONE
LONDON, OCTOBER 1931, THAT SAME NIGHT

P ortia ... Portia?" A voice called me back from the concentrated analysis I was doing.

"Yes?" I answered, not looking up from the body I was carefully cataloguing, memorizing everything from the position of his arms to the smell of his breath.

The voice came closer as its owner crouched down beside me. "Portia, look at me."

I finally tore my eyes away from the ground to look into the eyes of my partner.

"I know, Brian, I know," I said, holding his gaze. "I need but one more minute. You know the evidence will change irrevocably as soon as the coroner arrives. Please. One more minute."

He clenched his jaw, looked up at someone behind me and then nodded once, standing up and out of my way.

I descended back into that place in my mind where everything but my senses faded out into a gray background of muted landscapes. The glasses

I knew the deceased wore were missing, as was at least one tooth, though that could have been a result of the fall. The position of the body and limbs was consistent with a frontal fall rather than a backward one. No alcohol smell was present when I leaned in close to his mouth, which wasn't surprising given the subject. I could also discern chalk dust under his fingernails, which were closely cropped.

My mind had taken all the 'photos' it needed, but I was pulled out of my mental cocoon by the flash of a crime photographer's camera.

Slowly, I stood, wavering slightly, and two different sets of hands reached out to steady me.

"Adams, you should sit down," said the usually gruff voice of Sergeant Michaels, his large hand remaining gripped around my upper arm.

"Whatever for, Sergeant?" I questioned, turning to him and registering how wan and old he looked.

The sergeant glanced at Brian, the owner of the other hands that had reached out to me, and then back at me.

Another constable stepped up to talk to the sergeant in urgent tones, giving me the opportunity to pull Brian aside.

"Did you observe that ... the deceased's glasses are missing? Did anyone find them down here?" I whispered at the man who had very recently declared himself my partner. When he shook his head dumbly, I pointed to the roof of the closest building. "I must get to the roof immediately. Are there already officers up there?"

Brian nodded.

"Then upstairs I go," I announced and stepped around the dozen or so men still gathered around the body. Still more bystanders and curious · Londoners formed a larger ring around the quadrant of King's College, and I could see that Constable Bonhomme and his peers were having trouble keeping them contained.

From the roof the spotlights and crowds were even more evident, and I walked out to see two bobbies speaking quietly together, and three more walking the roof with torches and notebooks, followed closely by another crime photographer.

"Have you found a pair of spectacles already?" I asked one of the constables standing closest to the edge of the roof.

"Er ... no, Miss Adams," the constable answered, not even glancing at his notebook, and then to the others. "Any o' you blokes find a pair o' spectacles up 'ere?"

"They would have been carefully set aside," I offered, looking around for a welcoming spot. "Perhaps on a raised edge somewhere, as there is no ledge to this roof."

The men all answered in the negative and then went back to their work. I looked out and over the edge of the roof to the body below.

I watched a man stride through the crowds, his pace frenetic as he made his way toward the body. From the way he moved and the way his peers sprang out of his path, I identified him even from fifteen stories up as Dr. Edwards, one of the Yard's coroners. He glanced from the body, wiping sweat from his brow, even in this cool weather. He didn't seem to see me at all but looked back at the ground and then, with a hesitation that was out of character for the man I knew, kneeled down to examine the body. He returned to his characteristic method of examination, poking and prodding at his victim, causing me to grimace as I watched.

Seeing my reaction, the constable I had spoken to reached out a hand to me. "Are you quite all right, Miss Adams? Do you need to sit down?"

I rubbed at my temples. "Why does everyone keep asking me that? No, I'm fine, Constable. Why is Dr. Edwards consulting? Surely Dr. Beanstine is on site?"

The constable shrugged. "I saw Beans, I mean Dr. Beanstine, earlier. He was here before the professor..." he hesitated here, and then, "before he died."

I whirled in surprise. "I must speak with him," and I headed off the roof immediately. I had assumed he had been dead when they found him, but if there had been witnesses to the moments preceding his death — if they had actually witnessed his death...

I stumbled on the stairs in my haste. I had made it down to the second floor landing when I ran into Brian on his way up.

"Portia, I was just coming up to find you," he started to say, frowning as I passed him and then turning to follow me back down the stairs.

"I need to find Beans. He may have eyewitness information," I started but was pulled to a stop, both physically and verbally.

"Portia ... Beans is in no condition to be interrogated," Brian said, his hand on my left shoulder. "Sergeant Michaels had him driven home to gather his thoughts, poor chap."

I shook my head, my mouth dropping open. "What could Michaels be thinking? Beans might have seen someone on the roof with ... with..."

"With the chief inspector?" Brian offered in a softer tone of voice than before, causing me to take a step off the first floor landing. He stepped down, blocking my way, and now put a second hand on my shoulder.

"I know what you're doing, Portia Adams," he said, "and I even understand why, but this is not a crime. Nothing points to murder. Nothing at all. I did talk to Beans before he left, and Archer was alone when he jumped.

"*Jumped,*" he said again, underlining the word as his eyes bored into mine.

I reeled back slightly, tripping back up the stairs. "You don't know that!" I declared unsteadily, my hand on the bannister. "You can't know that definitively yet."

Brian sighed, running his hands through his thick hair. "You're looking for spectacles on the roof because you know that suicides often take off their glasses before jumping. They think about it. They premeditate the jump. So your gut is telling you the same thing mine is."

I shook my head adamantly. "I was sure we wouldn't find them, and we haven't..."

"Yet," he interrupted, reaching out to me again.

I batted his hand away. "I must speak to Beans. Did he see all this from the ground or from up on the roof?"

Brian shrugged, giving me the answer before he actually said, "From the ground, but he could see that Archer was alone."

"He could see no such thing," I said as I stepped around him, my eyes daring him to stop me again, and threw open the staircase door to the cool air. The crowds had thinned slightly, but the number of policemen had trebled.

"Where was he standing?" I asked as soon as Brian followed me outside, my eyes on the rooftop I had just left.

"Who? Beans?" Brian asked, confused.

"Yes, Beans, of course," I replied, backing up, my eyes still on the roof.

"About there," said Sergeant Michaels.

"Exactly," I said triumphantly, pointing up at the roof. "From this vantage point you can see constables standing at the edge of the rooftop."

Brian and Michaels were now standing on either side of me, also looking where I pointed.

"I just left the roof, where five constables are searching the area with their torches. I only see three from this angle. In fact, I would guess," I looked behind us toward the medical building facing the square, "that someone in those offices could give us the most accurate account of the people on the roof at the time of the incident in question. Has anyone been questioned in those offices yet?"

I looked back at the two men, but to my frustration, their attention was elsewhere. Following their united gaze, I too watched the body being carried out of the area, covered in a white sheet. Dr. Edwards was almost as pale as the sheet covering his charge, and I found myself wondering at his response, even when all the officers around him began doffing their hats and helmets as the body passed them.

All eyes followed the progress of the stretcher on the way to the wagon where the driver waited.

All eyes except mine. Mine returned to the roof, searching for answers fifteen stories above my head.

Chapter Two

A knock at my door startled me out of my shallow sleep, jerking me awake and wrenching my neck from its uncomfortable position. Groaning, I rubbed at the back of my neck, cursing the wing-back chair in which I had fallen asleep, and looking with heavy-lidded eyes at the door, where Nerissa stood alert and attentive.

I knew my young bloodhound well enough to recognize that the person on the other side of my door was a stranger. Nerissa's tail was standing straight up, and her intelligent eyes seemed to bore right through the wood.

Still, I thought, rising and stretching painfully as a second knock sounded, she was not growling — a positive sign. I stepped around her as I smoothed down my dress, looking through the peephole to see a well-dressed woman on the other side.

"A client perhaps, Nerissa," I suggested softly, slowly opening the door so as not to upset the dog.

"Good morning," said I, noting my guest's wide-eyed stare at me, and then at the bloodhound at my side. The woman had been nervous even before I opened the door and hesitated as I tiredly ran my eyes over her dress, shoes, and the bag at her side, the contents of which rattled as she turned toward me.

"Good ... good morning," she answered finally. "I am sorry to disturb you ... but are you ... Miss Adams?"

I rubbed at my eyes before nodding, looking back at Nerissa as she carefully sniffed the air, her eyes locked on the woman.

"Portia Constance Adams?" the woman pressed, nervously watching every move my dog made while my eyes were drawn to the two tiny holes in the lapel of her jacket.

"Yes, Doctor, Portia Constance Adams. How may I be of service to you?" I asked, opening the door a bit wider.

Her eyes snapped from the dog to me in an instant, her pale features blooming suddenly with two spots of color. "How ... however did you...? My name is Dr. Heather Olsen — have we met before, Miss Adams?"

"Not to my knowledge, Doctor, but as it seems this conversation is becoming protracted," I stepped out of my doorway and headed toward my small kitchenette to put some water on to boil, "perhaps we could continue it over tea?"

She lingered at the door, peeking her head in but an inch, an eye fixed on the bloodhound, who had not moved since she had first knocked on the door.

I sighed. "Nerissa! Really! Make a decision — is the doctor a threat or no? Just decide!"

Nerissa finally glanced my way and then casually sat down in place, as if daring her prey to enter.

"Come in, Doctor. If Nerissa were going to attack, she would not do so from a seated position," I encouraged, setting out the tray and cups before passing them both and heading to the bedroom. "Take a seat, please," I said over my shoulder, "while I make myself presentable."

A glance at the clock in my bedroom made me wince. Almost ten thirty in the morning — not good at all! I quickly washed up, brushing out my hair and pulling on a pair of slacks and a green blouse. I quickly brushed my teeth, and, disregarding the dark circles under my eyes in the mirror, headed back out into the main area of my apartment.

"Forgive me, I thought it was much earlier," I called over the whistle of my kettle, noting that the woman had walked over to one of my bookshelves and was looking reverently at the books. She glanced at a photograph of Holmes and Watson, and then her eyes lingered on a cane in the corner before she peeked at me to see if I had noticed.

I finished my preparations, giving her a moment to get her bearings, and then brought the tray over to my little table that sat between the wing chairs, adding a plate of biscuits to assuage my growling stomach.

"Dr. Olsen, how do you like your tea?" I asked.

"Oh, black, thank you," she replied automatically, removing her gloves and sitting down beside me, fiddling with the pin holding her hat in place. I pegged her at late twenties or early thirties, married, though unhappily by the condition of her wedding ring, which, unlike her other jewelry, looked dull and uncared for. I noted the makeup carefully applied around her left eye and made a mental note.

I pursed my lips, observing her over the rim of my cup as the hat's removal revealed very pale blonde hair — almost silver, it was so pale — reminding me of someone immediately, the color was that distinct.

She had taken a sip of her tea while I made these observations, but now she met my curious gaze.

"You are not as I imagined, Miss Adams," she said, her eyes as curious as mine.

I smiled. "If you're getting your picture of me from the newspapers, then I am not surprised."

"Well, yes, of course, I followed the news of your ... exploits," she said, tilting her head slightly. "But I expected you to be ... I don't know ... more impatient, or impassioned, I suppose."

I frowned, thoughtfully chewing a biscuit, still worrying at where I had seen that fabulous color of hair. "Interesting. Well, if it helps, I can be both at different times, as I suppose can anyone."

"And this place, I've never actually been here of course, but it also seems different than I imagined," she said, looking around. "Smaller somehow, and more feminine, though that of course would come from you."

"From my former guardian, actually," I admitted, thinking fondly of my grandmother.

"Whom you obviously love very much," she replied, "to have kept her personal decorations when they are not specifically to your taste."

I smiled quizzically. "What an interesting observation, Doctor ..."

"And how it is you knew I was a doctor?" she interrupted, putting down her cup and leaning forward.

"Was it a secret?" I asked, a small smile playing across my lips. "Right, then: I can see there is a clipboard in your bag, based on the shape, and I heard pills rattling around in there as you stood at my door, more than would be reasonable for one person unless they were quite ill — which you obviously are not. Also, your coat has several evenly spaced, tiny holes, as if you often affix and remove something from it. Too wide for a fashionable brooch, especially one made of tin — which has left tiny black marks in the coat — therefore, a nametag. Not many people wear nametags consistently on their outerwear, especially when they don't wear a uniform, leading to my leap to medicine. But your shoes are not comfortable enough to belong to a nurse." I shrugged. "That left doctor. Now, why don't you tell me why you are here?"

"Oh, of course," she answered, sitting back, her eyes wide. "I have been asked to consult on the Archer death."

I flinched, spilling a few drops of tea on my well-worn rug. I glanced up at my guest to discover that she had been waiting for just such a reaction.

"You are here on the case from last night, then?" I asked, recovering my poise and replacing my cup on the tray, wondering at her strategy. "I was under the impression that Dr. Edwards..."

I trailed off, glancing at her hands again now that they were out of her gloves and then up at her delicate nose and taking in the scent of her perfume.

"But you are not that kind of doctor at all, are you, Dr. Olsen?" I breathed, leaning forward to look her over again. "No, not a doctor who works with chemicals or even blood, I would guess. Pills, but no strange-smelling salves, no stethoscope in your bag, so not even obstetrics or general medicine ... highly observant, used to interrogation techniques... What kind of doctor would be consulting on this kind of case if not a coroner but..." I tilted my head, reassessing her in this new light, "...a psychologist ... intriguing."

She recovered quickly from this intensive identification. "You seem surprised at my involvement, Miss Adams, and I would guess that you are seldom surprised."

I sat back, considering, when another knock sounded at the door. Nerissa, who had relaxed into a more comfortable sitting position, now turned on her heel, heading for her water and revealing the knocker.

I rose and opened the door to my grandmother, formerly known as Irene Adler, now under the assumed name of Mrs. Jones. I made the introductions, and Dr. Olsen very quickly excused herself, promising to see me again at the Yard, which I found odd, since she purported to be here on official business. She added to my suspicions when she took one more long look around the apartment as I handed over her hat and coat, and then she was gone.

I closed the door behind her, returning to my grandmother's side, finding she had in the meantime retrieved a new cup and was pouring herself some tea.

"Psychologist? Really?" She snorted as I sat down beside her. "Is that a profession now?"

CHAPTER THREE

My grandmother insisted on discussing the one topic I didn't want to linger on: that of the death of the chief inspector.

"I really don't want to talk about this, Grandmamma," I said for the third time, this time ducking into my bedroom to dodge the conversation. I carefully removed my mother's silver cross from about my neck and had walked back to press it into my jewelry box by the window when I remembered my missing pocket watch. That, of course, brought forth the image of the watch's giver and taker, Gavin Whitaker.

"Don't try to change the subject, young lady," Irene Adler said, wagging her bejeweled finger at me. "I know how Watson would take every death to heart, especially those closest to him. I just want to be sure you are dealing with the loss of your friend in a useful manner."

"I find it so interesting that when I am between cases, you look for clues that I might be like Sherlock Holmes in his most dangerous reactions to boredom, and now, in this case, you look for similarities to Watson's emotional reaction. Was it not you who told my grandfather that I am more than the product of my genes?"

She sniffed, disliking as always when I brought up her past arguments and used them against her. "I am not classifying John's reactions as wrong. Just that they existed. And don't try to tell me you are unaffected. You are still dealing with the new information about your ex-boyfriend, so there is a lot going on in your steely heart, my girl."

"I like that you call criminal activity 'new information,' Grandmother."

"Well," she said, rearranging her skirt, "I'm hardly one to throw stones from my glass house. Whitaker bent his brilliant mind to something more lucrative than a regular job. A choice I, myself, have been known to make from time to time."

"You can't possibly be defending him?" I asked, shaking my head with incredulity. "Or implying that I should pursue the man to reclaim the relationship he put aside?"

"Oh no, that would be impossible, given the young constable's latest move," she replied archly.

My heartbeat sped up. How could she possibly know about the near-kiss in the bank vault? Surely her spies were not so talented as to be able to see through concrete walls?

"The partnership he has offered," she explained, when I remained stiff and silent, a small smile playing across her lips when I let out my breath, "and Whitaker has made his choice. He chose ambition over you, which I can never forgive."

"Because you never made that choice?" I asked.

"You are an extraordinary woman who will make someone an extraordinary life partner," she replied immediately. "If I were choosing between you and any amount of money or fame, there would be no decision to make. The same cannot be said for the choices that have been laid in front of me."

"It does make it hard to trust again, though," I replied thoughtfully. "I suspected something was amiss for weeks, really, since he gave me that beautiful silver watch he has reclaimed. But even now, we have no direct evidence linking Fabian to Gavin other than that they met at the Austrian embassy. Fabian says he worked only with Simmons and had him killed by Fuchs when he was finished with him. He declares there was no one else on his payroll."

"So then Whitaker is still useful to Fabian," my grandmother finished.

"Yes, so it would seem," I replied, sad at the thought that Gavin was out there on the wrong side of the law. On the wrong side of me.

After receiving a few monosyllabic answers to her questions, she finally sighed and asked about Dr. Olsen, about whom I was much more interested in talking. The doctor's interest in me, my apartment and the case struck me as odd in many ways, and my grandmother agreed. She walked over to the cane in the corner, touching it thoughtfully.

"This was the original cane Watson brought back from the war," she said, looking down at it and then up at me. "It's not a prop, but the real thing."

I nodded, knowing its significance from prior discussions. "She seemed quite interested in it," said I, picking up the tray full of dishes and walking them to the sink.

"And you're quite sure she's a doctor? Not another excited reporter trying to gain access to you?" my grandmother prompted, wrapping her stole about her.

I tilted my head. "What was your impression?"

"I don't know about her profession, having come across very few in her field," she said, sniffing nonchalantly and then becoming more serious. "But that bruise under her eye is easy to recognize."

I nodded, and very shortly afterward we said our goodbyes. I assured her that I would do my best not to fixate on the death of my professor or on Gavin Whitaker. Of course, the best way not to fixate on that case was to focus on something else, so I headed down to the offices of my friend Annie at *The Sunday Times.*

Having only been inside the building a few times, I dressed up in the character of P.C. Adams, consulting detective, in brand new pumps and a matching chenille suit jacket and skirt. I treated getting into the character of P.C. Adams as an actor on a stage would — applying makeup carefully and doing my best to project a totally different aura from my real personality. I walked quicker and barely looked at people when I spoke to them, taking on a more elitist bearing.

Annie's desk was near the windows facing the Thames and reminded me of my friend in the way papers were scattered all round. A bouquet of drooping wildflowers somehow remained vivid in the ceramic mug they had been tucked into, and hand-drawn cards were pinned here and there to the cork board, no doubt penciled by Annie's charges, her twin younger brothers.

I stopped at her cubicle, smiling regally at the reporter who sat across from her desk. As expected, Annie flitted into the room a few moments later, her eyes widening in surprise as she saw me standing at her desk.

"Miss Adams, how good of you to come," she said as soon as she got within earshot. "Shall we talk here or make our move?"

The phrase 'make our move' was the one we used if either of us wanted some privacy, so I nodded approvingly. "I would like to seek out a coffee if we could, Miss Coleson, so yes, please, let's make our move."

She pulled her purse out of her drawer and threw a smile at her colleague, who was listening intently (though doing his best *not* to seem like he was).

I led the way back out of the building. "Thank you, Annie, this is not a topic for the rest of the office."

She sighed, her usually buoyant personality obviously in retreat today. "Even if it had been, Portia, I am in no mood to be on display ... even in my own office."

I glanced at her, taking in the bags under her eyes and tightness around her pretty mouth and strategically allowing her to fill the silence with an explanation — which she did in a few moments.

"I have put Brian aside," she said in a determined voice as we waited for traffic to disperse before crossing the street. Her eyes were fixed on our destination, and the determined way she said it brooked no useful response, so I simply walked with her to the café and pulled open the door.

We took a seat in the mostly deserted room before I acknowledged her statement with a noncommittal "Hmmm."

She pounced on my response. "You are, of course, unsurprised."

"Yes, Annie. We've been on parallel paths with our respective boyfriends, and you know how suddenly and absolutely my relationship with Gavin ended." I shrugged slightly. "Perhaps next time we will both be more observant of the signs and spare ourselves the frustration."

Her mouth dropped open, and she shook her head adamantly. "Portia, we cannot let ourselves become bitter old women just because of what has happened to us."

I shrugged again. "I'm not bitter. Gavin said he was leaving and left.

Do I regret how it ended? Yes, but I'm not sure how it could have been handled better."

"Surely you would have..." She hesitated here. "Brian did tell me in confidence of your suspicions about Gavin and his involvement with Constable Simmons."

"Exactly. What would I 'surely' have done? Even if he had come to me before he agreed to work with Fabian Gruner, there would have been the previous crimes he had committed with the late Constable Simmons to account for."

"Then they are finding cases where Simmons and Dr. Whitaker tampered with evidence?" she asked.

"They are finding cases where Simmons most definitely covered up evidence," I replied, my eyes hard, "but so far, the bodies examined by Whitaker have either turned out to be correctly documented or have been cremated so that we cannot determine if his coroner's report is false."

"Simmons was surely the duller of the two," she said with a nod.

"They are now going through cases where someone was exonerated by Whitaker's testimony in court to see if they can find payouts to either of the men," I finished. "So I return to the fact that Gavin did me a service by passing me over and warning me about Fabian. Better that I not have to be the one who brings him to justice. Surely someone else can."

She rolled her eyes this time and then ordered from the waiter who now hovered at our table. I ordered a black coffee. "Regardless, I didn't seek you out at your office to belabor our newly single statuses. I need your help with a case."

She pulled out her notebook. I described the morning's events, describing Dr. Heather Olsen in detail. Annie took notes and interrupted with questions.

Our coffees were half drunk by the time I had exhausted the particulars of my meeting with the doctor. Annie frowned at me. "Have you ever known a psychologist to be assigned to a case like this?"

"Not personally, and not in any of my grandfather's casebooks," I replied.

Annie's eyes lit up and I nodded. "And yes, of course I think it's just the kind of thing *The Sunday Times* should report on." She grinned. "I couldn't agree more. I'll chase this down, Portia, but I'll need to run it past my editor first."

I nodded, counting out change for the bill.

"Who did you say died, Portia?" she asked, looking down at her notes as I stood to pull on my jacket. "The case Dr. Olsen said she was assigned to? What was the name of the deceased?"

"Dillon Breen Archer," I replied, my eyes steadfastly on the task of doing up my buttons.

She had started to write down the first two names but glanced up at me on recognizing the surname.

"Wait — Professor Archer? Chief Inspector Archer? Portia!" she said, standing slowly, her notebook clutched to her chest.

"Indeed," I replied evenly, my gloves on. I raised my eyes to hers. "Will you let me know when you find out something about Dr. Olsen?"

She nodded slowly.

"Very good, thank you, Annie," I said and turned on my heel, exiting into the cool London afternoon.

CHAPTER FOUR

I had three open cases on my docket that kept me out of the Yard for the following week, in addition to my classes at King's College and all the homework that came out of them. October promised to be my busiest month yet.

Two of the cases were minor and really only pursued for the monetary gains they afforded me. The case of the "Fake Stained Glass Window," for example, turned out to be a genuine stained glass window that had been mistakenly attributed to a famous artist. The true (and until this case), uncelebrated artist turned out to be quite talented, and the church it belonged to was only too happy to keep it in place as part of the man's portfolio. The other case was solved within fifteen minutes of it being assigned to me, without my even leaving my wingback chair, and the client was more than satisfied with the resulting windfall of cash from his wealthy, if sneaky, father-in-law.

The third case was a personal favor to my trainer, Bruiser Jenkins, and it wasn't an easy favor to bestow.

Jenkins had never admitted it (and I had never asked), but I knew he still dabbled in activities on the wrong side of the law. The man was almost seventy, though, so I rationalized it the same way I rationalized my grandmother's dalliances. How much trouble could a senior citizen get into?

He was being pursued by a pair of young street thugs who wanted some information only Jenkins had access to. They had shown up at his house at one of our training sessions, and after poking and prodding at him, he had finally admitted to me that he was being bullied by the two.

Since his physical prowess, even at fifty years my senior, far outstripped mine, I offered to step in with my own skill set.

He turned me down flat the first time, and the second time I offered, and the third time, as I struggled to kick an apple off the top of a short ladder; my dress was severely hampering me. Laughing, he challenged me to a skill test. If I could knock it off in three tries, he would allow for my help. I grabbed at the hem of my dress and took another swing, missing by at least five inches, prompting him to scoff and stride up to the fruit, taking a triumphant bite. He took two more before putting it back on the ladder and backing up to show me how it was done.

That was when my grandmother surprised us, having snuck into the backyard without our knowledge and hearing everything we had said. I begged her to change his mind before he was seriously injured by the thugs. She had looked up at him appraisingly before knocking the ladder and apple over with one well-aimed kick at the ladder's leg.

The half-eaten apple rolled to a stop at Jenkins' feet.

One of the thugs, the larger man named Coby, was the easiest to track down, even without the help of Scotland Yard. Brian was spending much of his time at court, and we therefore didn't see much of each other at the house. So I went to my second best source of information: my Baker Street Irregulars. Ruby and her partner found out where one of the thugs lived, identified him and finally unearthed some information I could use.

Coby, it seemed, had a beloved grandmother he visited every Wednesday, delivering her flowers or sweets or some small gift every time. My further research revealed that she was his only living relative, and the two were very close, she having raised him and mortgaged her house to pay for his schooling.

I introduced myself to her one morning at her local park, using my middle name so as to disguise my profession, through Nerissa's ecstatic overtures, and made sure to make a good impression. Through the course of our interaction, I discovered that she had no idea what her grandson did to earn his coin.

The very next Wednesday, I returned to the park with Nerissa, who was more than happy to bound around the park sniffing other dogs and chasing squirrels while I waited for Coby to appear.

"There," said my own grandmother, pointing across the way to where a man in a suit entered the park.

I responded by throwing the ball I had been tossing to Nerissa toward the older lady we had been watching a few benches away. So it was that by the time Coby reached his grandmother's side, she was deep in discussion with the two of us. Mrs. Jones, as she was known these days, was almost unrecognizable in an old dress and worn coat with several scarves wrapped around her slender neck, but her charisma shone through the disguise, charming the older lady we had marked, and surprising Coby when he was introduced to Constance and Mrs. Jones.

I, of course, inquired as to how his work at the courthouse progressed, and he flushed slightly before continuing the lie he had spoon-fed his grandmother for a decade and which she had proudly repeated to me the week before.

"Isn't your friend Constable Dawes down at the courthouse these days, Constance?" my grandmother asked me, causing some of the color to drop out of Coby's cheeks when I nodded.

On schedule, Mrs. Jones brought the conversation around to the increasing crime in the city, the argument falling on receptive ears with the old lady, especially when the lamentable predicament of our friend Mr. Jenkins was brought up.

Coby looked stunned at first, his glance flicking back and forth between his grandmother and mine as they bonded over the downturn in morals of the younger generation.

"Can you imagine?" my grandmother said, shaking her head under the moth-eaten hat we had found for her at a second-hand store on the Heath, "a man in his seventies being harassed by two young ruffians? Is it to be borne?"

That was when Coby's grandmother turned to him with the sweetest look of adoration. "My Eddie would never let that 'appen — mayhap 'ee can look into it for you, Mrs. Jones, find out oo's causing such trouble to your friend."

Coby did his best to smile down at his grandmother, but all he could manage was a grimace.

"My Eddie is such a good boy," she continued, oblivious to her grandson's discomfort. "Visitin' his ol' grams every week." She patted Nerissa as she spoke.

My grandmother gave him an assessing look before, of course, agreeing with her new friend.

"And your own little gel 'ere," Coby's grandmother said, nodding my way. "Why, when she was over at m'house the other day for tea, did you know that she figured out 'oo had been stealing my laundry from the line?"

I shrugged nonchalantly, but she tugged on her grandson's sleeve for his attention. "Just sussed it out, she did — led me straight over to Mrs. Bello's shed two doors down, and we looked in those dirty windows, and what did we see but my very best linens folded up all neat as a pin!"

She chuckled, still pulling on Coby's sleeve. "Oh you should 'ave seen how red in the face she was — gobsmacked!"

We shared a laugh. (Coby tried to smile again, but failed abysmally.) Then my grandmother rose gingerly from the bench where they had been sitting beside each other. "Come now, Constance, we've taken up enough of these kind folks' time."

"Yes, ma'am," I responded, applying the leash to Nerissa and giving a tap of my hat to the slightly sick-looking grandson.

We walked away arm in arm, my grandmother moving slowly to remain in character, only speaking when we had gained the sidewalk and were out of sight of Coby and his grandma.

"That should do it, my dear girl," my grandmother said, chuckling and straightening as we rounded the corner, avoiding a young newspaper seller hocking his wears at the top of his little lungs.

"Oh, I think Coby is going to have a sudden change of heart toward Jenkins, and that he will do his best to convince his chum Ralston that they should leave him alone," I replied, hailing a hackney for the three of us.

My grandmother shook her head, the pride evident in her voice. "I've said it before, and I'll say it again, little one: you are wasted on this side of the law."

Chapter Five

Brian had slipped three notes under my door during the week, two inquiring as to my health and the third advising me of the date and time of the funeral. I had ignored all three, choosing instead to concentrate on my open cases, using the college library as my base, rather than my apartment, where I was sure to be interrupted.

With all three cases nicely wrapped up, some cash in hand from their solutions and nothing new on my plate, I decided on Monday to head to the Yard. My decision was in no small part influenced by my surety in the arguments I had constructed about my professor's death, which I was still determined to treat as a homicide. I was, after all, studying to become a lawyer and had to get used to the arguments coming from the other side — in this case, the short-sighted view that he had been suicidal.

The October air was crisp, and I was glad to be wearing my new skirt, an item I had held back from the P.C. Adams costume, deciding she would continue to be fashionably brightly dressed. I wore a pale gray sweater and a long overcoat and fit into the streets of London perfectly and anonymously, just the way I preferred.

Along Pall Mall, I stopped at the shop window of one of the beauty salons, where a film poster featuring Fay Wray was displayed. Peering through the window, I could see three young ladies sporting her exact hairstyle, and once again I considered cutting my long, dark hair. Annie and my grandmother agreed that my hip-length hair needed to be updated, and though I had never admitted it, my reasons for keeping it were personal. My mother had spent hours once a week rubbing olive oil into my scalp and brushing my hair out straight and smooth. Realizing that despite this sweet memory, were my mother alive today she would come down firmly on the side of fashion, I touched the tail, which was in its usual single plait, and entered the shoppe.

An hour later, I walked up the familiar front steps of Scotland Yard, nodding at the officers I knew and turning more heads than usual with my shorter hairstyle. Weaving through the desks, arriving at Chief Inspector Archer's office door out of habit rather than on purpose, I hesitated when I realized what had changed since last I'd been here, and I glanced over at Constable Dawes' desk, but he was nowhere to be seen.

"Dawes is working with the prosecutor on the Reed case, Miss Adams," said Constable Bonhomme, answering my unasked question as he passed me. "An' might I say that you look quite fetching today, Miss Adams."

I thanked him and then glanced at the closed door again, hating this hesitation in myself. It was a weakness I couldn't stand, and I shook it off with determination, turning the door handle, surprising the person seated at the desk as I did so.

"Oh!" said Dr. Olsen, for that was who sat at Archer's desk, a few folders open in front of her.

"What are you doing?" I demanded, my tone sharpened by my surprise at finding her there.

She blinked at me, her hair falling in soft curls around her face, her eye makeup less layered around her healing bruise. "Why, reviewing the final case of Chief Inspector Archer, Miss Adams. What, may I ask, are you doing here?"

I gritted my teeth and stepped back out of the room, heading straight for Sergeant Michaels' office. I heard the scrape of the chair as the doctor followed me, but I was undeterred, rapping sharply at Michaels' open door.

He jerked in response. "Adams, where have you been?"

"Busy," I replied shortly, entering his office. "And I have further work to do, hopefully without the interference of Dr. Olsen," I said, jerking my thumb over my shoulder to where I could sense her hovering in his office doorway. I didn't like her in my space. Not in my apartment nosing around, and not in Professor Archer's chair.

His gaze flicked between us as he ran his tongue over his lips, "Now, Adams, Dr. Olsen is here to help build a case against that Dr. Reed bloke. While she is here, it made sense to get her to look at the Chief Inspector's case. You, it turns out, were too busy getting your hair done, it looks like."

I wanted to wave my arms like he did when he was frustrated, but instead I leaned over his desk, my knuckles on his scattered papers. "Professor Archer and I were working on a paper together — remember?" I said through clenched teeth. "All the files and paperwork in that office are our intellectual property. *My* intellectual property, now that my coauthor is gone."

"The paper you were writing on suicide?" asked Dr. Olsen, still standing in the doorway. "You don't think that might be relevant, given the circumstances of the chief inspector's death?"

I chose not to answer, instead fixing my gaze on Michaels, waiting for him to respond to my claim.

He stood slowly, his gaze on the desk, before looking up at me. "I'm no lawyer, Adams, but my thinking is that intellectual property gets trumped by evidence in a crime — especially when that evidence is on police property."

He raised his hand at my protest. "Anything you got back at the college or at home, we gotta get permission for, but the contents of the chief's office are ours to fully investigate ... after Dr. Olsen's done, I'm sure she'd be happy to hand you anything that you need for your paper."

"It's tainting the case!" I said, banging an open hand on his desk, causing some of the officers in the outer room to peer in curiously. I pointed to Dr. Olsen. "*She* is tainting this case."

"Tainting this case or causing you to confront evidence you don't want to see?" Olsen said from her safe spot at the door.

"Adams..." Michaels started to say, sending a glare toward the doctor, but I cut him off, storming out of his office and practically running from Scotland Yard.

CHAPTER SIX

I went straight from the Yard to King's College, cursing all doctors, when I remembered my mother's terrible physician back in Toronto. The man had been entirely useless when it came to diagnosing my poor mother, actually making it my job to convince him of her cancer. Who knows; if he had realized it earlier, perhaps she might still be with me instead of gone. Blinking away tears, I cursed Olsen again. How dare she insert herself into Professor Archer's office like she belonged there? Another person who was important to me stolen away before their time, and me standing there, once again stymied by useless doctors.

Stalking through the deserted hallways, my anger slowly burned away to leave a frustrated wake of confusion and bitterness. My first meeting with Dr. Olsen had been uneventful, if curious, but her involvement in this case was ridiculous. She was not a police officer and could only add useless emotional speculation to a case that deserved logic and methodical investigation. My impression of Olsen soured by the experience in Archer's office, I remembered suddenly that it was winter break and that Beans would probably be off work this week. The realization did nothing to improve my mood.

I knocked on his office door regardless, even turning the handle when it went unanswered, and finding it unlocked, to my surprise.

The lamp had been left on, and on the desk I could clearly see that a thick-bottomed glass had recently held down the short stack of papers.

I bent over and found the empty liquor bottle and glass in the rubbish bin — exactly where I had expected them to be. So, he had run out of alcohol. Well, that gave me a pretty good clue as to where he went next.

On instinct, I put the glass in one of the desk drawers and carried the empty bottle out with me. I dumped the bottle in the rubbish bin behind the building and then turned right, heading east past two drinking establishments I knew were frequented by students and faculty of the college. I had walked about three blocks before I found what I was looking for, a seedy-looking pub that was open for business, even though it was before noon.

Trying not to curl my lip at the pub's filthy interior, I ignored the drunken catcalls from the bar and made a beeline for the darkest, most secluded corner of the pub.

"Dr. Beanstine, may I join you?" I asked the man slumped in the corner.

Beans raised bloodshot eyes toward me, frowning. "What?" he managed to whisper, not recognizing me at all.

I stopped a barmaid who was collecting empty glasses and paid his tab as he rubbed at his eyes, trying valiantly to figure out who I was. With the barmaid's help (bought with a very friendly tip), I managed to steer Beans out of the bar and back out into the leaf-strewn street. I passed the surprised barmaid one of my cards before she went back in. "Let me know if you ever want help finding your sister. I'd be happy to offer my services."

She gaped at me, one hand holding my card, the other pressed against her throat. I just nodded at her, tapping on my card in her hand. Then, with my arm around my friend, I guided him over to a nearby park bench, picking one with a large tin rubbish basket beside it.

Glaring at the snickering pair of students who passed us, I put my arm around Bean's shoulder. "Henry, how are you? Starting to get your bearings yet?"

He raised bleary eyes to me again, recognition finally alighting behind his thick glasses. "Miss ... Miss Adams?" he managed to stammer before his eyes went large, and he hastily turned to retch in the bin beside us.

I sighed, sure that this was going to be an all-night case, and stepped away from him to the curb, where I hailed a cab.

That evening found me sitting halfway down the stairs of my townhouse, reading old newspapers, waiting for my partner to finish supper in the apartment below.

The coverage of Professor Archer's death was minimal at this point, two weeks having passed, but I was reading the older newspapers because I had avoided them in the days directly following. Dr. Reed's upcoming trial dominated the papers, and I read up on the case that Brian and Dr. Olsen were both assigned to. The man was accused of experimenting on patients with drugs that were either not approved for their specific ailments or had been modified in some way from their original purpose. The case was suffering from the various defense ploys when such a prominent Londoner was involved, and it seemed that the judge was considering dismissing the case as the weeks drew on.

I had just closed up the papers, shaking my head at the ineptitude of the prosecutor assigned to the case, when Brian popped his head out of 221A. "Portia, good evening. Care to take a walk with me?"

"Perhaps a little later, Brian," I answered, rising as he left his apartment to stand in the hallway, looking up at me. His hair was still wet from a shower, and he looked ... well ... at ease was probably the best way to describe it.

"You cut your hair," he said, tilting his head to run his eyes over me as I tried very hard not to tense. "I'm glad you didn't cut it too short. Shoulder-length suits you."

I grinned, and he answered my smile with his own, putting his hand on our shared bannister.

"Maybe..."

"Beans..."

We spoke at the same time and then laughed at it, and I pointed my folded newspaper up toward my slightly ajar door. "I was going to say, we will want to wake up Beans, I think, and get him some coffee at the very least."

Brian looked around me, pointing at the door. "You've got Beans in there?" he asked, looking confused but following me up the stairs.

"Yes, didn't your father tell you?" I asked, opening the door wider and stepping through. "He helped me get Beans up the stairs a few hours ago."

Brian followed me in to see Beans sitting in my wingback chair, his head cradled in his hands. The blanket I had thrown over him while he slept was now in a bundle on the floor.

"What in the world, man?" Brian said, crouching at our friend's feet.

"Constable, please?" whispered Beans in an injured tone. "No yelling, I beg."

Between the two of us we managed to drag Dr. Beanstine out of Baker Street and to the Rose Café, where I usually spent my Saturday breakfasts.

Cradling a hot cup of coffee, his dark stubble standing out starkly against his pale skin, Beans started to look halfway normal, apologizing profusely for the burden he was becoming to us.

"Don't be daft, Henry," Brian admonished him. "Mates take care of each other."

"Exactly so," I agreed. "Stop apologizing to us and tell me what has driven you to this state."

The two men looked at each other in such surprise that I had to add, "Besides the obvious, of course."

"Isn't the obvious enough?" replied Beans, a tear escaping his eye and rolling down his cheek. "It's my fault Professor Archer is dead..."

I squinted at him, leaning forward, but felt Brian's hand on my shoulder as I asked, "Your fault? What are you talking about, Henry? Were you up on the roof with Professor Archer that night?"

"I may as well have been," sniffed our young friend, his broad shoulders shaking.

Brian shook his head at me before speaking. "Henry, this was not your fault. You have to stop blaming yourself — no one else does..."

"I am sure Miss Adams does," he said miserably, grabbing my hand as he spoke. "You warned me that the professor was exhibiting signs ... you asked me to pay attention to his weight ... his demeanor ... for signs of dementia..."

I nodded, shocked to feel tears threatening behind my lids and shaking off his hand to ensure the tears did not fall, trying not to notice Brian's frown at my actions. "I did, Henry, it is true, but I don't believe that the professor jumped from that building. Therefore, his state of mind was not a factor, so how could it be your fault?"

Brian's frown showed his disagreement with my statement. "We all failed the chief inspector. Whatever drove him up to that roof, we all failed him."

Braving Brian's ire, I asked, "Then you were not on the roof with the professor, Henry?"

Beans shook his head, rubbing at his eyes with the heels of his hands.

"How did you discover he was on the roof, then?" I pressed.

"One of the students ran into the hallway outside my office, calling for help," explained Beans. "I couldn't believe it, but of course I ran out into the quad with everyone else."

"And you saw the professor on the roof?" Brian asked.

"Yes," he answered, his voice dropping to a whisper. "I called up to him, a few of us did, but he didn't even look down. He seemed to be mumbling to himself."

I leaned forward again. "Or maybe speaking to someone else? Behind him, Henry? Where you couldn't see?"

Beans shook his head. "Four or five of the students ran back in, running up the stairs to the roof to try to stop him. They didn't get there in time, but they passed no one on the stairs and saw no one on the roof. And the professor, he never looked over his shoulder, Portia, never looked down at us, just looked straight out at the building opposite, and stepped off..."

He mimicked this action with his hand, his eyes far away as he relived witnessing it, and then his face began to crumble, and he started sobbing in earnest.

Brian patted him on the back, looking at me. "Enough?"

"Enough," I replied, my thoughts on the scene so clearly laid before me by our distraught friend.

Chapter Seven

Y ou didn't attend the funeral," Brian said, interrupting my thoughts. We had just dropped Henry Beanstine off at his apartment and were making our way back home.

"No," I replied. "I should have."

Brian looked surprised, so I clarified. "I wanted to ask some questions of his family, and that would have been an opportune moment."

Brian shook his head. "No, it wouldn't have..."

"Opportune for me, then," I further clarified. "Inappropriate for others."

"I suppose it is some small consolation that you see that, if not heed it," he replied, kicking at a pile of brightly colored leaves as we walked.

I shrugged. "I don't weigh myself down with cultural mores, and I'm not sorry for it."

"It's not simple etiquette I'm talking about, Portia," Brian said, his eyes still on the ground. "It's your reaction to the man's death I am worried about."

I chose not to answer, though he glanced my way before continuing. "Or more accurately, how you refuse to have a reaction."

"What good would a reaction do, Brian?" I answered, sounding colder than I meant to but being forced to because I was scared of a tremor in my throat. "How will that help anyone? For me to break down in tears like poor Beans ... how would that further our investigation?"

"How about just to allow yourself to grieve for him, Portia?" Brian pressed, slowing his pace. "Doesn't he deserve that from his friends? You were his friend, after all. You were one of his favorite pupils and a friend."

I clenched my fists and almost started in surprise when Brian wrapped his gloved hand around mine. Looking down at my fist within his hand, I found it easier to loosen it, feeling a tightness around my chest loosen at the same time.

"I do grieve him, Brian, I just ... I just need more time to figure out why he died," I explained finally, allowing our fingers to weave together. "It's my way. I need time."

He nodded, even adding a small smile, and we walked on in silence for a few minutes, hands joined that way. I wondered if anyone noticed but found I didn't care, glancing a few times at my handsome escort, finding my thoughts drawn once again to a locked vault door.

"Well, then, in pursuit of solving this crime, we found the chief inspector's spectacles. Did Beans tell you?" Brian said, continuing when I shook my head. "Almost twenty yards away from the body."

"So they didn't fall with him, then," I said, thinking aloud as we passed the Harrods department store, where two urchins were being roughly escorted out the front door by a burly security guard. Recognizing one of them as a member of my Baker Street Irregulars, I gave the boy a wink, and he ran to catch up with me. I handed him a coin, asking him to meet me at Regent's Park that evening, and sent him on his way. Dr. Heather Olsen was about to receive the full breadth of my investigative arm.

"I don't believe so, though Edwards was arguing that the glasses could have fallen off him as he fell and gotten blown away," Brian answered as soon as the child was out of earshot, used to my odd team of agents. "Edwards is an odd duck. I didn't even know he was close to the chief inspector, but he's taken his death terribly hard."

"Ridiculous," I replied, having assessed the same thing in Edwards the night of Archer's death. "Those spectacles fit him so well that they left creases on his nose. You could still see the creases even as he lay ... on the ground."

I took a breath. "No, he didn't lay them aside, and he didn't wear them on the way down."

"So...?" Brian asked.

"I'm not sure, Brian," I said, shaking my head again. "I'm assuming they were damaged enough for you to speculate they were not dropped while he was walking around below?"

"Large cracks, not shattered, lenses still half in the wire frame," Brian agreed. "Not dropped from face or pocket level, and no sign that they had been trodden upon."

I stayed quiet, thinking of the possibilities and not really liking any of the ones I came up with.

"Sergeant Michaels went to speak to the widow Archer the very day after he died," Brian said. "She admitted he had been acting withdrawn in the past few months but she was entirely surprised by his death — devastatingly so, poor woman."

"No doubt that is why Dr. Olsen has been asked to step in," I said, unable to keep the annoyance out of my voice. "To analyze his frame of mind. To prove with highly shifty science that he committed suicide. Wasting our time and distracting us from finding the true culprit."

"What true culprit, Portia?" Brian said, his voice gentle but firm. "You heard Beans. The man was alone on the roof and jumped. There was no one egging him on or pushing him over the edge."

"Not there, and not physically, no," I agreed, "but he showed no suicidal tendencies, Brian. I know this better than anyone, because I've been hip-deep in suicide cases for the past three months."

"Right, but don't you think it strangely coincidental that the paper you are working on, the paper Archer asked for your help with, was about suicide?" Brian answered, glancing sideways at me and then past me, across the street.

"No, because I don't believe he committed suicide," I replied easily. "Has it occurred to you that maybe he had me researching the subject so I would know his death was not a suicide and would find the truth?"

Brian frowned, his eyes returning to mine. "Hang on, so you're saying he had you reading about suicides, knowing he was going to jump off a roof so you could prove he didn't commit suicide?"

"Based on everything I have read, he didn't," I answered with a shake of my head that made me notice someone out of the corner of my eye.

"But I'm sure Dr. Olsen finds the paper I was coauthoring quite suspicious."

Brian shrugged. "I'm not sure what Dr. Olsen thinks, to be honest, but she certainly asks a lot of questions."

"Really?" I asked, feigning interest as I glanced around us to see very few people on our side of the street. Brian's hand was suddenly tense in my hand, making me a little more edgy.

"Yes," Brian said. "She had quite a few questions, for example, about our relationship..."

I answered without even hearing. "Did she, indeed?"

On the 'indeed,' I whirled around, raising my hand palm out in a halt signal toward the man who had been following us. He stopped abruptly, the cigarette dropping from his shocked mouth as he looked to each of us in turn.

"Good evening, Mr. Coby," I said, evenly.

"What the...?" my partner declared, his eyes focused on something across the street before they came to rest on the man I had stopped.

"Mr. Coby has been following us for at least two blocks, Constable, and I thought I would ask him his intentions before we went any further," I said, ignoring the annoyed passersby we were now.

Brian hesitated, but then stepped to the man. "You heard the lady," he said, pulling his copper badge out of his pocket and showing it to the increasingly worried Coby. "Why are you following us?"

"Me? No, sir..." Coby answered, beads of sweat popping out on his bald pate. "I wasn't following no one."

I cocked my head. "No? Then this has nothing to do with Mr. Jenkins? Whom you called on earlier today?" So saying, I grabbed a folded-up envelope out of his open jacket, handing it to Brian after a glance.

"Asher Jenkins," read Brian aloud from the address on the envelope and then used it to smack Coby on the forehead. "I suggest you stop lying to Miss Adams, my friend. It's a fool's errand, I'm afraid."

"Stealing mail is a crime is it not, Constable?" I asked, fully knowing the answer but wanting Coby to hear it from an officer.

"That it is," replied Brian, crossing his arms over his chest. "One I'd be happy to arrest you for, Coby, unless you get a bit more honest with us."

That was when a shot rang out, shattering the window next to us. Brian threw himself over me, and people all round started screaming and running. From the pavement, we looked around in the minimal light.

"Are you hurt?" he whispered in my ear.

"No, you?" I whispered back.

"No," he replied, easing off me slightly.

"I don't see anyone. Do you?" I whispered, my eyes wavering on each shadow.

"Short, dark hair, long nose, long gray coat," Brian answered, surprising me. "Military gun, I think..."

A few more tense seconds and then Brian was up, pulling me into the partial cover of the alleyway.

"I thought he was following us a few blocks back, but when I lost sight of him, I assumed I was just being paranoid," he said.

"No one in the alley," I said confidently, and then, ruefully, "and Coby is long gone."

"Not entirely," Brian answered, pointing at the trail of blood that led away from the sidewalk.

"Flesh wound at the most," I answered. "The bullet went through him in order to hit the window, and there's not enough blood loss to slow him down."

"I still have a chance of overtaking him," Brian answered then looked back at me, hesitation written on his handsome features.

I raised my hands. "Go, Brian! I am not interested in a foot-chase!"

"I'll see you at home!" he called, racing in the direction of the blood trail.

By now a bobby had made it to the scene, and I hurriedly explained that Constable Dawes was in pursuit of a wounded suspect and described the shooter as best I could from Brian's description. I had been so intent on Coby that I hadn't seen him at all. The bobby stepped away to ring it in, and I knelt down on the sidewalk, looking from there across the street and back again.

I carefully stepped over the broken glass of the shop window and into the shop itself, looking for the bullet. There! My torch lit on the crumpled piece of metal lodged in the back wall at about waist level, and then I looked back through where the front window had been.

"Miss?" said the bobby I had spoken to. "You'll have to clear out of this here crime scene, please."

"Indeed, but please note the bullet in the wall. I have not touched it," I said, pointing my torch toward it. "It is lodged in the wall and should remain so until the scene is documented."

I ignored his stare of surprise, stepped back over the threshold of the storefront, and, pulling out my notebook, I began canvassing witnesses.

"If I had known this trouble with Jenkins would escalate to such mortal danger, Portia," my grandmother said a few mornings later, reaching for me. "I am so sorry, my dear."

"I am fine, Grandmother, as is Brian," I assured her from within her arms, breathing in the heady, comforting scent of her perfume.

"And that snake, Coby?" she demanded, stepping back so her hands were still on my upper arms.

I shook my head, escorting her into the apartment. "Brian lost the trail in the tube. We think the man ran along the tracks between the trains."

My grandmother took a seat in her favored wingback. "Do you think it was Coby's partner, Ralston?"

"Not from what Brian described," I answered. "He thinks he got a good look at the shooter, and it doesn't sound like Ralston."

"Interesting," she replied, tapping her manicured finger to her lips. "Then can we even be sure you were the target?"

"I have been thinking the same thing, but what are your thoughts?" I prompted her, walking to my little kitchen.

She shrugged. "I wondered if perhaps your grandfather, looking to protect you, tried to scare off a would-be attacker. It would have been too messy for his own handiwork, but if he hired someone who was less of a perfectionist than he ..."

I shook my head. "My grandfather is in the south of India, according to his latest letter, and though that wouldn't preclude his finding out about this and stepping in, it just doesn't make sense to me.

"The timing of the shot seems odd for someone trying to defend me," I continued, plucking an apple out of a basket and offering it to her. She shook her head, so I took a bite, chewing thoughtfully. "Why wait until I had the upper hand to take the shot? At that point everyone could see I was talking to the man who had been pursuing us."

"So if Coby wasn't the target, that leaves you."

"Or Brian," I replied grimly.

Her eyes opened wide, and then she started to nod slowly in understanding.

."I agree that Coby was following me, probably to either beg me not to approach his grandmother again or to threaten me, we may never know," I said, finishing the apple and walking to my wastebasket.

"Disagreeable man," my grandmother muttered. "And not very bright, if you ask me, to approach you after we demonstrated our upper hand."

I shrugged. "Nerissa and I will return to the park next week to underline our persistence in the case, and you are welcome to join us again if you wish."

"Count on it," promised my grandmother, moving on to compliment me on my hair, as I knew she would.

CHAPTER EIGHT

The next day, I actually waited for Brian to get ready for work, and then we headed for the Yard together. I again brought up the idea that he had been the target of last night's excitement.

He shook his head, his breath coming out in puffs of white on this uncommonly cool autumn day. "I gave it some thought, I really did, and the more I think of the timing, the more I think the shooter was Coby's man. Perhaps not Ralston, but someone else of their acquaintance. It is simply too far-fetched to imagine that we were being followed by two different men for two different reasons. Much more likely that the second man, seeing that you had recognized Coby and realizing we were moments away from hauling him down to the Yard, fired at us to give his man a chance to get away."

"And missed so badly that he hit his partner?" I said incredulously.

"If he wasn't aiming to kill us, just to scare us, then certainly." Brian shrugged. "He could have aimed between us all, and Coby just stepped back away from us and into the shot."

I shook my head, not believing it but having no proof otherwise.

"That means that your friend Jenkins is into something much more dangerous than he let on," Brian said, blowing on his hands as we waited for traffic to abate at the corner.

"Actually," I admitted with a smile, "I asked for as little detail as possible when it came to *why* he was being pursued by Coby and Ralston."

Brian's answering smile was less confident. "If you don't want me digging into this, you just need to say it. Firing at a police officer is enough for us to pursue the man, but if we bring him in, and he is involved with your Jenkins case..."

"The man may impugn Jenkins," I finished as I carefully negotiated the icy stairs leading up to the Yard. The rain and then sudden drop in temperature had made them precarious, and when Brian extended his hand I took it, enjoying the natural way that felt.

"Miss Adams," said a voice to which I was beginning to have a rather negative visceral reaction.

I sighed heavily, glancing up at Brian to catch his bemused smile.

"Dr. Olsen, good morning," he said, extending his right hand to her, even as his left hand guided me safely up the last step.

"Good morning, Constable. I believe our friend the lawyer is looking for you again," she answered, shaking his hand with nary a smile on her lips and then redirecting her attention to me. "I am glad you're here, Miss Adams. I planned to call on Mrs. Archer again today and thought you might be interested in joining me."

I hesitated and noted that she anticipated my reaction, pushing me to say, "Yes, Dr. Olsen, I would. I will speak to Jenkins today, Constable," I said to Brian, "and see what I can do to minimize his ... involvement."

Brian tapped his hat at the two of us and headed into Scotland Yard.

"Shall we, Dr. Olsen?" I said, determined to keep the upper hand as we negotiated our way back down the stairs. I considered why she wanted my presence at this interview. Was it to keep an eye on me? Had Michaels asked her to pay attention to my reactions? What was her interest in me?

She meanwhile hailed an obliging cabby, and almost as soon as the door had closed behind her, she asked, "I take it Jenkins is part of another case? Possibly the one you and Constable Dawes were in pursuit of last night when you were shot at? Do you often take on cases outside of the Yard and involve its staff?"

I nodded noncommittally and redirected. "Tell me, what is it you want to know from the widow Archer? I take it you were with Sergeant Michaels when he previously interviewed her?"

She cocked her head. "Yes, I was. And as for today, I am not sure.

Mostly it's an instinct, Miss Adams. What is it *you* hope to learn from her?"

"I asked you first," I replied, allowing the frost to dominate my tone.

"And I asked second," she replied, dismissively folding her arms.

I smiled at the defensive posture. "Tell me, Dr. Olsen, are you still with your husband, or have you separated from him?"

She started, her mouth dropping open slightly, so I leaned toward her. "I do hope you left. A man who hits you once will invariably do so again, or so all my reading has taught me."

Some color came back in to her cheeks and she sputtered, "Y-your reading? Indeed? So experienced in the ways of the world are you that you gain all your knowledge between the covers of your grandfather's journals. I am sure he would be most proud."

I blinked, feeling the ground shift at the way she spat out the word *proud.* "Yes, his writings, amongst other things..."

"So kind of him to leave you with a legacy you could build a life on," she said, swallowing hard and then rooting through her purse. "A name, a business he handed down to you, along with the townhouse and connections."

"And a family," I answered, pressing the button she had revealed. "The Watson brothers have been very kind and accommodating since discovering I was in Britain."

She flinched at my mention of the family I had discovered on this side of the Atlantic and then shook her head, almost to herself, pinching her lips closed. What was her angle?

I assumed she was looking in her purse for a kerchief to compose herself, but instead she pulled out a few coins in preparation for our arrival and silently handed them up to our driver.

"Shall we?" she challenged, opening the door and exiting without waiting for my response.

I scowled, considering her remarks before following her out of the cab. She had by that time knocked on the front door of a modest bungalow.

"Dr. Olsen, your husband..." I started to say.

"Was only another in a long line of disappointing men in my life," she answered, cutting me off as the door slowly opened, and I suddenly realized where I had seen her freckles and hair color before. Family, connections, the men in her life ... Dr. Olsen's interest in me crystalized in my head, but before I could say anything, the door opened.

Professor Archer's wife gave Dr. Olsen a hug before ushering us in. She was almost exactly as I had imagined her: plain, not-too-bright, but kind and entirely distraught at the loss of her husband.

She actually started off the conversation by tearfully asking me not to believe that her husband had taken his own life. Since I already shared that view, I looked over at Dr. Olsen, a challenge in my eyes. She, however, ignored me, put her arm around the older lady and spoke to her in soothing tones until she calmed down.

"He was under a lot of stress, to be sure. We all are," Mrs. Archer said, her eyes wet with tears. Her black dress had seen better days, and her hose was far too loose, pooling at her ankles in a distracting way. "Retirement is supposed to be a time of less stress, of less work, but for us..." She trailed off, looking up at a photo of her and her husband on the mantelpiece.

"Mrs. Archer, your husband was, as I'm sure you know, a very admired and respected man," Olsen said, her hand still stroking the older woman's hand, waiting for her compose herself again.

"Dillon loved the men at work; he was always talking about them. And you, Miss Adams. He seemed quite proud of you and your work," Mrs. Archer said, a small smile coming to her lips as she spoke. "He never spoke of the cases, no, he was ever so careful about bringing his cases home. But the men, and his students, they were his very proudest achievements. Especially after our own boys ... well, they are settled and happy ... that's what's important."

Olsen nodded, continuing her silent comforting techniques. "And were there any cases over the years, Mrs. Archer, that the chief inspector had trouble leaving at work?"

"Ah no, not at all," Mrs. Archer replied and blew her nose. "He was a man ruled by routine. Very black-and-white, my Dillon was — in the very best of ways."

"Then I have to ask, Mrs. Archer," I put in, "why was he so distracted recently? He'd lost weight, he was preoccupied and forgetful at times — very out of character."

Mrs. Archer waved my analysis away. "That was his impending retirement. He was so worried about money..."

"Is that why he started gambling, Mrs. Archer?" I interrupted. "Because he was being retired from the police force?"

"Gambling?" Mrs. Archer bleated, half-rising out of her chair. "Ridiculous!"

I lifted up a pair of well-cared-for uniform boots that were hidden under an ottoman. "This fine silt around the edges here," I said, holding the boots with my left hand and pointing with my right, "it's common to racetracks, not to London streets."

She gaped at me, wordless, and Dr. Olsen rose to stand next to the older woman, her body language making it clear what she thought of my revelation.

"Miss Adams, that is quite enough," Dr. Olsen said, her arm firmly guiding the widow back down to the settee. "Mrs. Archer, pray forgive Miss Adams. She is ... unpracticed at interviewing..."

"Unpracticed at..." I repeated incredulously at the blonde woman. "Dr. Olsen, I believe..."

"And furthermore," she interrupted, "it seems patently obvious that Chief Inspector Archer was no more a gambler than I am."

She said the last firmly, her eyes angrily flashing at me. "Miss Adams, I think it would be best if you waited for me outside," she said over her shoulder, her eyes back on the widow Archer.

I had opened my mouth to angrily refuse when Mrs. Archer spoke up, two bright spots of color rising in her cheeks. "Yes, please leave, young lady. You are no longer welcome in my home, no matter how Dillon felt about you."

I took a deep breath, and giving the room one more quick inspection, I did as they bade, exiting the way I had come.

There was a sweet wrought-iron bench in the front yard, but I could not avail myself of its comfort, not the way I was feeling.

Steeling myself against the anger I could feel threatening to spill out of me, I instead focused on what I had learned in my short interview. This close to retirement, money would start to become tight, resulting in Archer's recent stressed demeanor. I paced back and forth, my arms cupped behind my back as I wore a small rut in the snow of the Archers' front yard.

So, the chief inspector needed money ... maybe he had taken to gambling, and maybe he had gotten himself into debt — the depth of which somehow had led to his death. That line of thinking unfortunately led back to suicide, a path I refused to travel, and I abruptly changed direction, stalking out the front gate to pace the sidewalk instead.

What if the men he was indebted to had killed him? I stopped suddenly. I would need to look at the family finances, I thought, as the front door opened and Dr. Olsen stepped out. She leaned back in to give Mrs. Archer a hug and then turned to walk in my direction.

Over Olsen's shoulder, Mrs. Archer threw a glare my way and then closed the door.

Olsen reached my side and to my astonishment gave me a grin. "Well done, Miss Adams — I couldn't have planned that better myself!"

Chapter Nine

I t was perfectly orchestrated, Jeryl, I mean, sir..." Dr. Olsen was explaining to Sergeant Michaels.

"It was perfectly mad," I put in, shaking my head at the excited blonde, still considering the new information I had about the woman's motivations. *Jeryl?* My chin came up as I looked at Sergeant Michaels and then back at Olsen — when did they start calling each other by their first names?

We were in Sergeant Michaels' office, having just returned from the Archers'. Olsen was barely sitting in her chair as she gave a report to the sergeant, and I was standing with my arms crossed, in the furthest corner away from her.

The sergeant raised his hands, palms out, at my contradictory words.

"Hang on, Adams, let the gel, I mean doctor, give her report in peace," he said, his eyes looking slightly less sleep-deprived than since last I saw him.

I leaned further into my corner.

"With Miss Adams so obviously playing the villain, Mrs. Archer turned to me as her ally," continued Olsen, tucking her hair behind her ear, drawing my attention to her face again so that I had to shake my head to stop seeing the resemblance I had earlier identified. "And she confided in me that yes, the chief inspector recently visited the Kempton Park Racetrack."

I leaned forward at this, nearly tripping myself in the process.

"But that he was there to drag their younger son back home," she explained, glancing at me with a smile. "It was brilliant the way you picked up on the soil, Miss Adams. We had not heard about the son's gambling problem prior to that."

"So the son is in debt?" I asked, happy to be gifted with a new clue, regardless of the source.

Dr. Olsen shook her head. "He was, but the debt has been paid off."

"When?" Michaels and I demanded in unison.

"Almost a month ago," she replied. "Weeks before the chief inspector's death."

"Did the son stand to inherit?" I asked, stepping forward to sit next to the doctor.

"That's a ghastly thought," Michaels said, scratching his chin but then nodding at Olsen. "But Adams is right. Any chance the son wanted to keep gambling? Without his dad's permission and funds he decided to kill him, make it look like a suicide and inherit the money to keep at it?"

Olsen tilted her head. "If so, then Mrs. Archer is completely in the dark as to her son's true nature. She believes him to be a lost soul, not an evil one."

Michaels scratched his chin again and then startled us both by bellowing out of his office: "Bonhomme! Oi! Get me that lawyer who made up the chief inspector's will!"

We stepped out into the main office area, and I turned to Olsen. "What about Archer's impending retirement?"

"It wasn't being enforced by the department — it was entirely Archer's idea," Olsen replied, receiving a nod from Michaels before she continued.

"Mrs. Archer believed it was the police forcing him to retire, but when I spoke to the sergeant and his superiors, they said Archer came to them with the idea. He gave no explanation, only that he wished to end his work both here and at the college and that he wanted to do it soon."

I looked at her, really looked at her then, probably for the first time since the day we had met. "You believe this all tracks back to a planned suicide, don't you, Doctor?"

She looked back at me evenly. "There was no one else on that roof. We both know. But I don't believe it was a normal suicide, no. Something drove him to jump off that building, Miss Adams, and whatever that was, it is not in any of the cases you've been looking at."

I nodded, agreeing with her, some of my guilt receding as a new idea came to mind. "He was wrapping things up neatly, paying off his son's debts, ending his tenure as professor and inspector, all toward a deadline..."

I paced back and forth, thinking about the weight loss, and that was when I spied Annie Coleson entering the large open bullpen outside Michaels' office.

"It's the weight loss," I said aloud, turning toward the doctor. "Dr. Olsen, do you think you could find out if the chief inspector was ill?"

She slowly nodded. "Yes, I think I could, with the sergeant's help."

"You think he was so ill he couldn't face it, Adams?" Michaels said.

"I think he might have been so ill that he wanted to make his death mean something," I said, my mind whirring now.

Annie's eyes were on Brian, who hadn't yet noticed her, so I stepped between the desks to arrive at her side, walking out of Michaels' office without a word.

"Annie, you didn't have to come down here to find me," I said, taking in the curious glances from the constabulary and glaring them away.

"I..." Annie finally tore her gaze away from her ex-boyfriend to look at me. "I wanted to tell you what I found out about..." She glanced over my shoulder to see Dr. Olsen regarding us intently from her chair, "about what you asked me to look into..."

"Ah, yes," I replied, thinking of my earlier realization. "I actually think I may have solved that mystery, but I'd be pleased to hear your findings nonetheless..."

"Miss Coleson," said the voice of Brian Dawes somewhere close behind me. "How are you?"

Annie smiled tremulously as he approached, and the sound in the room had dropped from a hum to near silence as she replied, "I am well, thank you. And your family?"

"Very well, thank you," he replied, shifting his weight. "My mother asked after you at dinner the other night. I will relay to her that you are well."

She nodded, her cheeks pale but her back ramrod-straight. "Thank you. I shall be sure to call on them soon. Right then, if you're caught up,

Portia, I should be off."

"Let me walk you out," I said, putting my arm on her back and walking her out past the room of staring men.

She let out her breath as soon as we passed through the doors. "There. That wasn't so bad. Like stepping into a cold bath."

"You didn't have to come down here to find me," I said.

"I did. I wanted to get it out of the way — my first time seeing Brian," she answered, obviously proud of herself. "And now it's done. So now when we see each other, as of course we must, given your working and living arrangements, it will be less awkward."

She gave me a peck on the cheek. "And I'd love to stay, but those brothers of mine are waiting for me at home. I only stopped in on my way from the office."

I watched her walk down the stairs with a smile. She was going to be fine. Especially if you counted the number of male heads that turned as she passed on the way to the tube stop.

The door opened behind me, and Brian joined me on the steps. "I am ready to leave when you are, Portia," he said. "We're already a half-hour late for supper."

CHAPTER TEN

I tried to broach the topic of Annie on our walk home, but Brian stubbornly refused to talk about her, citing a strict policy when it came to women.

"Annie is still very important to me, Portia," he offered as his only explanation on the matter. "And I hope someday to regain a friendship with her, but for now, best that she and I maintain our distance and that you and I avoid the subject."

I had come to a decision myself — that for Annie and me to continue to be friends, she deserved to know that not only were my feelings for Brian growing, but that he might someday reciprocate them. I could admit to myself now that I did hope for more with my handsome best friend, and I was unwilling to proceed down that path in secrecy. I glanced at his jaw, though, adamantly set against talking about Annie, and decided that I would handle her without him. I did not need his permission to deal with my best friend, even if she was his former love interest.

Seeking to regain a normal conversation, I pivoted to the cases being reviewed, looking for abnormalities.

"Most recently, we located some expensive cigars that Simmons had taken from evidence and given to his grandfather as a Christmas gift," Brian admitted, blowing out his breath in a long white stream. "That was a bloody depressing interview to conduct with a grieving family..."

"But still nothing on Gavin?" I prompted.

"Still nothing pointing directly to Dr. Whitaker," Brian bit out. "But trust me. I will find something."

I frowned at his vow. "Not for me, I hope, Brian. You know that I hold no ill will toward him."

"I don't understand how you can feel that way," he replied, shaking his head. "He lied to you, his closest ... friend ... for months!"

I knew that, but I also knew the depth of my feelings for the man, and while my ego was bruised by not having realized his criminal activity, my heart had never really been involved, and therefore had escaped unscathed.

Instead I said, "I just think it's more important that we help right the wrongs created by Simmons and Whitaker than actually bring the man to justice."

"I wonder if that has anything to do with your grandmother and the wrongs she has committed over the years," my partner said, his pace quickening as Baker Street came into sight. I wondered if we were going to drop our hands at the door, and almost as if in answer to my unspoken question, his grip tightened in mine. "Don't answer that. I don't think I want to know. What I want to know is what happened with you and the hyper-inquisitive Dr. Olsen," he said as we drew close to our shared front door. "When you came into the Yard, you looked livid, and you practically chased her into Michaels' office. But when you came back out..."

His words stopped as suddenly as his steps, and I nearly ran into his back.

"What?" I managed to ask before he leapt forward, wrenching open the front door and sprinting into the house. The smell of rotten eggs assaulted me immediately, and I fought down the feeling of nausea it caused. I turned away from the door, pulled up my scarf so it was firmly over my nose and mouth and then followed him in. I had just entered 221A through our shared hallway when two of the dogs pelted past me. I ignored them and as quickly as I could began opening windows on the main floor. Brian came back into sight, carrying his mother's prostrate body over his shoulder and running out the front door again. By the time he reentered, I had found Mr. Dawes and was laboriously dragging him by the arms through the living room. Brian quickly hoisted his father over his shoulder, pointing to the doorway as he wheezed.

I nodded, following him back out into the hallway, and ran up the stairs at top speed to my apartment door. It took two tries, and when I finally wedged it open, I could see why it had been so hard — Nerissa had passed out at the door and blocked it with her body. I squeezed in, wincing when I looked at the claw marks on the inside of my door, bundled her into my arms, and staggered out of 221 Baker Street into the blessedly fresh night air.

Chapter Eleven

Four hours later found me on my rooftop, my throat still burning, with Nerissa beside me, licking her paws from their recent bout with my door as she'd tried to escape the toxic environment.

A window in my apartment had been left propped open — a mistake I didn't remember making but which may have saved my bloodhound's life and those of my downstairs tenants.

In a cab, Brian and I had rushed his parents and my dog to the hospital. Both Dawes were recovering well, having only been subjected to the natural gas leak for moments, not hours, as Brian had dreaded. I had assured him of that fact, based on the escape of the Dawes' dogs moments before we got their masters out. The dogs were lower to the ground, with lower heart rates, and had managed to stay conscious, meaning the leak was not of a long duration.

Brian had nodded, his hand stroking his mother's hair, but it wasn't until his father coughed, just as we were pulling up to the hospital, that he actually believed me.

He was still at the hospital, but I had returned home to investigate and had found the severed pipe leading into my upstairs kitchen. Someone had pulled the pipe out of the wall, cut it with a very sharp saw and then inserted both ends back in, hiding their handiwork. Nerissa had therefore suffered the brunt of the gas leak, being on that floor, the gas spreading downstairs to assault my downstairs tenants second.

I considered ringing up Sergeant Michaels but decided to regroup with Brian before I took the case to the Yard.

The incident had to have something to do with a case, but which one? And why such a drastic effort to stop me or the constable from investigating something? On the ride to the hospital I had tried to broach the subject, but Brian had been terse in his answers.

Nerissa suddenly sat bolt upright, her head pointed directly to the metal stairway that led up to this rooftop. Moments later I could hear the sound of someone struggling up the stairway on high heels, and I relaxed, realizing who it was. I stroked Nerissa's ears, calming her down, as Dr. Heather Olsen swung her leg onto the roof.

"Careful, Doctor," I called out as she wavered and finally put both feet on gravel.

"Goodness, is this quite safe, Miss Adams?" she called back, making her way over to where Nerissa and I sat on a blanket.

"Safer than downstairs," I answered. "How did you know I was up here, though?"

She shrugged, daintily lowering herself onto the blanket, her eyes on Nerissa, who remained tense. "The note on your front door warned not to come in because of a gas leak, but your neighbor said he saw you less than twenty minutes ago behind the houses, looking into the kitchen window. He is quite nice, by the way. I went back behind the house to look for you and noticed this metal staircase leading up to the roof. It seemed a reasonable hideaway."

"Instinct?" I asked, smiling slightly as Nerissa finally gave up her watchful stance and dropped back down to lick at her paws.

"You prefer solitude to populous spots, so it made sense that you would retreat up here to think," she answered, looking at the bloodhound. "Whatever happened to your dog's paws?"

I quickly explained the events of the last few hours and offering Olsen a bottle of pop.

"Good God," she finally exclaimed, her hand extended to pat Nerissa sympathetically, but then hovering in the air over the dog's head. Nerissa looked up at the hand, at the doctor, and then she raised her snout to bump at Olsen's hand.

"That's encouragement — I'd take her up on it," I advised with a smile.

She did just that, stroking Nerissa's head. "Poor puppy," she crooned at the bloodhound, who responded by licking her hand and then returning to her paws again.

"Dr. Olsen," I said, drawing back her attention, "what's your instinct on the gas leak?"

She tilted her head. "What is yours?"

Becoming used to this line of questioning from her, I said, "I believe either Constable Dawes or I are being targeted, that our lives are in danger, and that whoever has targeted us is escalating in desperation ... which makes me think there is a deadline or a time limit on getting to us."

"Well, that is dire," she replied, considering my words, "but it reminds me of the conclusion I have come to with the chief inspector."

I shook my head, switching to that case. "You think the chief was being targeted as well?"

"It would explain the desperation that everyone, including yourself, saw in him in his last months of life," she replied, pushing her hair behind her ears as the wind blew around us. "And also the very uncharacteristic way he died. His suicide was one of desperation; I am convinced he talked himself into it, through his retirement, through his research with you... It makes me to think time had run out for him."

"He talked himself into it," I repeated. Then I said, "I think he threw his glasses off the roof of the college before he jumped."

Her eyes shifted to the side as she considered it. "An interesting idea. Throwing the glasses and then throwing himself. It sounds like a statement."

"Yes, a statement to someone else, though," I replied. "To whom was he sending a message?"

She wrapped her arms around herself. "Someone drove him up there to that roof, of that I am convinced."

I leaned back, pondering her supposition and feeling my stomach clench at the idea that that same person was now threatening Brian. "But who benefits from Archer's death? Or Brian's?" I said.

Olsen shook her head. "The two were on many cases from the past and present together, but so are others. No officer is assigned to a case alone, and there is no open case where only Archer and Dawes were assigned. I thought perhaps a case that you, Archer and Dawes were working on outside of the Yard?" she suggested, her eyes on me.

I was the one to shake my head this time. "I was working on the suicide paper with Archer, but no open cases, and that paper is wholly unrelated to the case Constable Dawes and I are looking into with Jenkins. In fact, Brian wasn't on the Jenkins case until Coby followed us home that night of the shooting."

"And what about the case you are trying to build against Gavin Whitaker?"

Instead of being annoyed that she knew about that, I found myself curiously comforted by her insight. "Archer wasn't really involved in that investigation. I barely am. Michaels has taken that one to heart, that a man under his command was taking money to obscure the path of justice. No, I don't think Gavin would strike out against me this way. I believe he wanted to protect me from his criminal activities."

That was when a third set of footsteps could be heard on my metal stairs, and Annie Coleson's bright red cap appeared as she climbed up. I stood, giving up on my vigil, and with Dr. Olsen's help folded up my blanket and walked toward Annie.

"My editor just told me what happened," she exclaimed, slipping all over the place as she quickly made her way to us and threw her arms around me.

"I'm fine," I said, hugging her and keeping my arm around her as she nodded at Dr. Olsen.

"What in the world happened? How are the Dawes?" she gulped as all three of us and Nerissa negotiated our way back to the staircase.

"Come, let's go back downstairs, and I can fill you in while I check on the Dawes' dogs. They seemed quite agitated to be dragged back into the house," I suggested, turning to the doctor. "You are, of course, welcome to join us, Heather."

Olsen, however, declined, and we said our goodbyes at the bottom of the metal stairs.

I waited until she had left our sight before turning to Annie, who said one word. "Heather?"

"If your findings on Dr. Heather Olsen match mine, Annie," I replied with a bemused smile, "it seems only fitting, no?"

Mr. and Mrs. Dawes were released from the hospital two days later, with a clean bill of health. When they arrived home, they found it filled with flowers and foodstuffs. They assumed it was from friends and neighbors, and a few items were, but I knew the majority had been delivered by Bruiser Jenkins.

He had stopped by the morning after the gas-leak event, filled with guilt at what had happened.

I had done my best to assure him that I held no ill will against him, and that I, in fact, thought this latest incident had nothing to do with his case. But then my grandmother had arrived on the scene.

Irene Adler by all accounts had been a force to be reckoned with when she was a young socialite and part-time criminal. Her activities on the wrong side of the law may have slowed as she aged, but her personality retained all its confident power.

When she saw to whom I was speaking, her eyes narrowed to dangerous slits, and, pointing her cane at her long-time friend, she said three words: "Leave London now."

He didn't argue but hung his head in response, and nothing I could say would keep him. He muttered that he would be gone before noon and then shuffled out of my flat, giving my grandmother a wide berth as he left.

It took nearly an hour to convince my grandmother that I had no intention of moving out of the Baker Street townhouse, and it was then that she admitted that she had found Coby and Ralston and was "dealing with them" herself.

"What does that mean?" I demanded, imagining all kinds of revenge an angry grandmother could exact upon men she thought responsible for harming me.

"It matters not," she declared, her nose in the air. "I alerted their intended mark, the man they were trying to gain access to through Jenkins. With his help, we will get to the bottom of this matter."

"I take it this 'mark' is the one actually doing your dirty work?" I asked, shaking my head. This was what Brian was referring to. I was developing a soft spot for the criminal element, namely my own grandmother. "Have they admitted to anything?"

She shrugged. "So far they claim innocence for both the shooting and the gas leak incident, but the full arsenal of persuasion has yet to be used on them."

"Grandmother, we don't even know that they were the ones who started the gas leak..." I started, but she raised her hand haughtily.

"Portia Constance Adams, if they wished to remain safe in their mothers' arms, they picked the wrong profession. They should not have taken on such a dangerous foe," she declared.

"Is that you or their original mark?" I asked, honestly feeling the woman in my house was the far more dangerous of the two, not even knowing her competition.

"Oh, do stop looking at me like that. They will be left at a convenient police station when they have admitted to their crimes," she said with another wave. "Surely you do not want me to interfere with a dangerous criminal's handling of two other even less intelligent criminals?"

The argument continued without resolution, and she was only slightly mollified when I told her that Sergeant Michaels had added two shifts to the patrol on Baker Street when he had gotten the full report from Brian and me hours earlier. I was in despair of escaping her debating tongue when Dr. Beanstine knocked on my door, saving me.

My grandmother still held out hope for a match between me and the young son of a duke and immediately turned from brooding and demanding to sweet and welcoming in his presence. She suggested I make a pot of tea while she made the young man comfortable, escorting him to the wing chairs, her voice sing-song for the first time today.

"And I couldn't believe it when I spoke to Brian," Beans was saying when I brought the tea tray to where they sat in front of my hearth. "I rushed right over to see how you were, Miss Adams."

"I am fine, Henry, thank you," I assured him.

"Thank goodness," he said, his eyes warm as he reached for a teacup. "I really couldn't bear the idea of you being injured."

My grandmother patted him on the knee.

I sat down on my small ottoman, well aware that Beans was madly in love with a certain duchess and saw me as I saw him: as a good friend. My grandmother, of course, knew of the relationship with the duchess but discounted it entirely, placing my looks far and above that of Beans' love interest and valuing them higher as well. I hadn't yet brought up my relationship with Brian, because it was so new, but knowing my grandmother, she was very soon sure to find out about it through her own means.

"I feel nothing is secure anymore," he admitted, putting down his teacup and rubbing his hands together. "First with Simmons and Whitaker and now with the chief inspector..."

"Oh, I know, dear, Portia has been distraught by the unfortunate incident," said my grandmother, looking my way and then dropping her voice conspiratorially. "She may seem like she is well, but she needs our support ... I do hope you will do your best to take care of each other..."

I was by now used to my grandmother's manipulative ways, but I had to say something at that.

"Now, you well know how busy poor Dr. Beanstine is now that he is covering for Dr. Whitaker's ... disappearance," I said, taking a sip of tea, swallowing hard as I thought of the added work Beans would now take on with Archer's death.

"True," Beans put in, "though that is a poor excuse for being a lesser friend. Your former charge has been most kind and comforting to me through this time." He put down his cup resolutely. "I promise you, even with this latest departure of Dr. Edwards, I will redouble my efforts as they apply to Miss Adams. She should not be alone at such a time, you are spot-on."

Not that I liked the man at all, but my curiosity got the best of me. "Where has Dr. Edwards gone off to, Henry?" I asked, secretly hoping the man had been transferred to a remote northern post for gross incompetence.

Beans shrugged his massive shoulders. "Not sure. The dean of the school is scrambling to fill the department in time for the winter session, but I think we will have to drop some classes or borrow some fourth-year medical students to cover the load. Edwards told the dean that the chief inspector's death bothered him more than he expected, and he asked for a few weeks' leave to visit his mum in Scotland."

"I'm shocked the man has a mother," I muttered under my breath, causing my grandmother to cough on her tea and requiring some claps to the back to restore her.

CHAPTER TWELVE

My overly social grandmother was back in London, and that meant being dragged to a seemingly endless line of parties. That, of course, required shopping for appropriate dresses, plus shopping for gifts. The truth was that I had missed her companionship, and with the added loss of Professor Archer, I really couldn't complain about the attention. I also realized that this was her way of keeping me out of Baker Street and in her sight, which was annoying but understandable from her point of view.

Brian was still kept busy with the Reed trial, but I stepped in to help him and Sergeant Michaels on a particularly tricky case involving missing food from a local soup kitchen. Items disappeared somewhere between the donations arriving from local restaurants and actually getting onto the tables of the growing number of impoverished Londoners. This was one of those cases where we couldn't get anyone to talk to us and where witnesses were virtually nonexistent. It was understandable, seeing as everyone (whether you were lucky enough to still have a job and money or not) was affected by the dramatic downturn in the economy.

Even the volunteers in the soup kitchen, who had filed the report and asked for help, hesitated to talk to us because they suspected the folks who were stealing the food were even more in need than the folks they were stealing from.

It was, therefore, a great relief when I brought forth evidence that the couple stealing the food was actually turning around and reselling it to another local soup kitchen. Michaels was thrilled with the result, which bolstered his standing in the community, resulting in a second-page story on the case in *The Sunday Times* and prompted a call from the Lord Mayor of London himself, commending him on the good work.

Annie and I also spent time together, shopping for her little brothers' upcoming birthday. My grandmother was instrumental in picking up on my friend's mood from her recent break-up, making sure that she, too, was invited to the society parties I was required to attend.

It was on one of these shopping expeditions that I caught sight of two people I did not expect to see: Doctors Edwards and Reed.

Annie and I were just exiting a children's toyshop, she having secured the 'perfect' wooden train set for her twin brothers. Her father had sent her the money for the purchase, and after several shops we found an appropriately priced locomotive.

"I cannot believe we got the last one, Portia," she exclaimed over the brightly wrapped box. "If only I could have gotten the wee conductor and engineer. Ah well, too expensive for the whole bunch. The boys'll be thrilled anyway!"

I patted my satchel, where the little wooden men sat, safely stowed, purchased while Annie was speaking to a clerk. I would give them to Annie's brothers as my own gift to them and a happy surprise for their sister.

That was when I saw the two men standing arguing in the alleyway.

"What is it, Portia?" Annie asked.

"Isn't that Dr. Reed, Annie?" I asked, sure I had recognized him from the newspapers.

She squinted through the cold rain. "Blimey, he's done up a bit, isn't he?" she said in surprise. "But yes, I do believe it is."

Without really waiting for her response, I stepped to the two men to hear Reed hiss, "... you best be careful of how you speak to me!"

But that was when Edwards recognized us, his eyes wide and worried.

"Dr. Edwards, I thought that was you," replied Annie, extending her gloved hand. "How are you?"

"And you are Dr. Reed, I believe?" I asked, extending my hand to the second man, who hesitated but then shook my hand briefly.

"Charmed, I'm sure," he replied, turning up his fine wool collar.

"Dr. Edwards, I had heard you were in Scotland," I remarked, realizing that his cheeks were slightly hollow and that that his usual look of condescension was missing. He was scared. That much was clear. But of what? This finely dressed man at his side?

He flinched slightly at my question and looked around worriedly. "Indeed, Miss Adams, I am leaving very soon to Scotland." He licked his lips and then repeated, "Very soon. As soon as I leave here, in fact."

Everything about his eyes and flexing of the muscles around his mouth told me that was a lie, but I also felt it wasn't a lie told for my benefit alone.

Reed, meanwhile, tipped his hat to us, promising to see us again soon (his eyes lingering on Annie at the last statement). He swaggered away, twirling his very ostentatious cane as he left, chest puffed and whistling.

Edwards shifted on his feet and with a mumbled "Good day" followed in the doctor's boot prints, though his exit was the complete opposite in attitude.

"Well, that was a bit odd, wasn't it?" Annie remarked, hugging the gift to her chest.

"You mean the fact that Edwards had been waiting outside the bank for the doctor for more than an hour, by the wetness of his coat?" I answered, my eyes following them as far as I could before the shadows of the cityscape obscured them. "Or that Reed associates with someone like Dr. Edwards? He travels in much richer circles. I wonder how they know each other."

"Dr. Edwards was supposed to be testifying at the Reed trial we've been covering, but the judge said he was unavailable," Annie explained, companionably sliding her arm into mine. "It's as you said, he was supposed to be in Scotland for the duration of the trial. I wonder if the judge knows they speak outside of court?"

"The duration of the trial," I repeated, allowing the small blonde to lead me back toward Brompton Road, as the rain slowed to a light drizzle.

"Edwards has lost weight," I said, pulling Annie to a halt.

She frowned up at me. "Not that it makes him any more attractive, but yes, I suppose he has."

"Yes," I answered, though not to her statement, as I sped up. "And I know why."

CHAPTER THIRTEEN

Annie and I wove our way through the desks of Scotland Yard, the majority of which were abandoned on the weekend.

As I had suspected, though, Sergeant Michaels was in his office, puffing away at a large cigar. What I didn't expect was that he would be speaking in low tones to Dr. Olsen. He glanced up, a look of guilt flashing across his ruddy features when he saw who it was.

"Ah ... Adams."

"Who else from this office is supposed to testify at the Reed trial, Sergeant?" I asked without preamble.

He blinked up at me and then turned his eyes toward Dr. Olsen.

"I was supposed to testify in January, Miss Adams," Dr. Olsen replied, turning to me curiously. "But as I was just telling the sergeant, I think the judge is days away from throwing out the Crown's charges."

"Aye, the lawyer for that there case is a complete tosser," Michaels growled before finally seeing who had come into the office with me, and sputtering, "Hey! That was off the ruddy record, Coleson!"

She rolled her eyes and put down the gift box she had been carrying. "Oh, calm yourself, Sergeant, we all know that your case is a hair's breadth away from being dismissed."

"Yes, Annie was just filling me in on the case against Dr. Reed and the diminishing witness list for the prosecution," I said with a speculative look toward the silvery blonde still seated in the office. "And I think with Doctor Olsen's help, I can connect not only this case and the attempts on Constable Dawes' life, but also the tragic loss of the chief inspector."

"The chief inspector wasn't assigned to the Reed case, Adams," Michaels breathed, but his eyes lit up with hope.

"No, Archer wasn't part of the criminal case. He knew Dr. Reed for a totally different reason," I agreed, watching as Dr. Olsen's eyes widened in realization and she began rapidly flipping through her clipboard. She found the line of notes she had been looking for and glanced up at me, a small smile starting in the corner of her mouth. I smiled back and proceeded to outline my plan.

"I don't like this plan," Brian whispered in my ear as we watched Annie and Dr. Olsen.

"Really, Dawes? Because we really didn't suspect that from the first three times you said it," hissed Sergeant Michaels from behind us both, lowering his binoculars just long enough to glare at his subordinate.

We were on the second-floor balcony of the courthouse, hidden behind some potted plants while Annie pretended to interview Dr. Olsen on the main floor. Annie was supposed to give credibility to Olsen's presence at the courthouse and was scheduled to wrap things up with the doctor very soon. The signal came in the form of a recess being called, and a steady stream of the curious public, the press, the prosecutor, the bailiffs and finally the defendant and his lawyer exited the courtroom.

Annie sprang up and thrust herself in front of the defendant. "Dr. Reed, sir! What do you think of the Crown's latest witness?"

A bailiff stepped forward at her sudden appearance but was waved back by Reed. Reed was a tall, slim man, with dark hair and features and the easy confidence of someone used to getting his own way. He smiled down at Annie. "Miss Coleson, again?"

"Yessir," Annie replied.

"Miss Coleson, I can't say I'm too worried about the testimony of a psychologist who had no involvement in this case until a few weeks ago," he said, his eyes flicking over to Dr. Olsen where she sat going over her notes only twenty feet away.

The rest of the small crowd had dispersed, leaving only one of the bailiffs, Annie and the two doctors.

· "Not from what she just told me, sir," said Annie, flipping nervously through her notebook. "It seems that Chief Inspector Archer had written some kind of note on the case."

Reed stiffened visibly but forced a smile. "Who? I am not sure I know that officer."

"Chief Inspector Archer," Annie repeated, her eyes on her notebook as her cheeks reddened, "recently passed away, poor man, but it seems his widow found a note he had written and brought it to Dr. Olsen's attention."

"And what was in this note?" asked Reed, stepping threateningly toward Annie.

Annie held her ground. "Not sure yet. Olsen says she'll give me an exclusive after she talks to the judge. But I thought you might like the opportunity to give me a comment first?"

"The thief was not involved in this case," Reed said smoothly, his eyes looking round and finding the bailiff still standing there. "And I cannot imagine that the judge will allow such last-minute evidence to be admitted. I know we will do everything in our power to dispute it."

"There," I said, pointing at the bailiff, who had moved closer to the conversation again. "Brian?"

"But what about your patients? Are you ready to answer to them about the charges against you?" demanded Annie, going off script and into full reporter mode.

"Ma'am, I'm going to have to ask you to leave the area now," the bailiff said to Annie, reaching to escort her out.

"That's the man who shot Coby," Brian affirmed, his voice cold and deliberate, watching as Annie was escorted out of the hallway, despite her protests.

"Now?" asked Sergeant Michaels.

"Yes, please, Sergeant," said I, watching tensely as Dr. Reed approached the still-seated Dr. Olsen.

CHAPTER FOURTEEN

B ack at the Yard, it took Sergeant Michaels less than a half hour to get a written confession from the bailiff, now identified as one Mark Thomas.

As soon as Annie made her way off the court steps, a full squadron of officers confronted Thomas. The man was shocked and actually pulled out his revolver, pointing it with shaking hands at the men sent to take him in. Realizing that he was vastly outnumbered, Thomas tried to turn the gun on himself but was denied even that, Bonhomme and Andrews wrestling him to the ground and disarming him.

His first words completely explained his suicidal actions. "The man holds my son's life in his very hands!" he managed to choke out as his hands were cuffed behind his back. "Please, do what you will with me, but what about my son?"

At the station house, he accepted a lit cigarette from Brian Dawes and then explained, "Reed said he wouldn't do the surgery on Aaron unless I got assigned to this case and helped him get it thrown out."

I was standing in the corner of the interrogation room, my arms crossed. "You were to bribe witnesses to change their testimony, and in return Dr. Reed would operate on your son?"

"He's the head of the surgical board. He decides if you get a surgery or not," Thomas answered, pulling a long drag from the cigarette to calm himself. He blew out smoke before continuing. "Your man Simmons was easy. Took the money without a second question. I made Edwards the same exact offer, and he turned me down."

I nodded, remembering how Dr. Edwards had been waiting for Reed outside the bank. Obviously, he knew of the schedule and decided to confront the doctor. My estimation of the disagreeable coroner went up as a result of that realization. He had tried to step in and stop this.

"But you didn't try to bribe me, did you, Thomas?" demanded Brian, leaning over the table. "You tried to kill me."

Thomas looked down at the table before answering. "I was sent to kill you — but I didn't have the heart ... so I fired a warning shot. I hit that man by mistake, I swear! My hands were shaking so badly." He demonstrated by raising his hands.

"And what about Miss Adams? And what about the gas leak that nearly killed my parents?" demanded Brian, clenching his fists so he wouldn't reach across the table.

"I opened the window upstairs," whispered Thomas, his eyes leaking tears. "And it was Reed who told me to involve the young miss — I swear. He said it would distract you."

"From the outside!" I declared, clapping my hands together, making Brian jump at the sound. "I knew I didn't leave it open! You climbed up my fire escape and opened my window. I was wondering how you got by Nerissa..."

"Distract you indeed, Dawes," Michaels said, switching back to the storyline. "Now, what happened with Edwards? Once he said no to the bribe, what did you do to him?"

Thomas took another drag but refused to meet our eyes. "Nothing. I told Reed that Edwards had said no to the bribe, and that Simmons didn't think your man here, Dawes, was even worth approaching with money. Then Simmons died, and I swear I had nothing to do with that! Reed told me I had to take care of you, kill you, sir, apologies. He said he'd take care of Edwards himself."

Michaels glanced at Brian. "We should get word to Edwards. He's in danger until we close this case down."

"No, I think Edwards has already been handled," I answered, looking to Dr. Olsen. "Don't you, Doc?"

"I do," she replied, her arms wrapped around herself. "Dr. Edwards' warning was Chief Inspector Archer's death."

Michaels' mouth dropped open, and Thomas's chin dropped to his chest in resignation.

"He tried the same thing on Archer that he did with you, didn't he, Thomas?" Olsen asked, the mixture of disgust and sympathy evident in her voice. "With Simmons gone, he needed Archer to make this case go away, and if he didn't, Reed would have refused to operate on him, poor man."

I shook my head, wishing my mentor had come to me with this impossible problem. Looking over at Michaels, I saw the same regret in his eyes and shook my head at him, trying to impart to him that I felt equally helpless.

"Archer had two deadlines — this case going through to court, and the time running out on his surgery," I explained, feeling the true grief over his choice wash over me, forcing me to swallow past the lump in my throat. "He couldn't break his commitment to the law, but he also knew that his chance of survival even with the surgery was tiny."

"He was black-and-white," said Olsen, repeating the widow's description. "He was not suicidal, but he committed suicide. The chief inspector saw no way out but to remove himself as a chess piece. If Reed couldn't use Archer, the surgery would have no reason not to proceed."

"Once you eliminate the impossible, whatever remains, no matter how improbable, must be the truth," I intoned, quoting my grandfather.

"That's why he threw the glasses before he jumped. He was declaring his choice. He jumped without fear or regret," Olsen said, nodding in agreement and recognition.

"Which Reed then used to strengthen his control over Thomas and threaten Dr. Edwards into silence," I said, my eyes back on Thomas.

Olsen's eyes softened as she turned her eyes back on Thomas, who by now was sobbing quietly. "No, Dr. Reed is a highly intelligent strategist who plays on the very basest human emotions. It's quite elementary, really — the man is a monster."

CHAPTER FIFTEEN

I had stayed long enough at the Yard to watch Dr. Reed be brought in and charged with attempted murder and several other crimes much more serious than the ones he had originally been in court for. The man's greed knew no bounds and ran the gamut of extortion to experimentation on patients, all in the name of amassing more money and more power for himself. If there was a way to manipulate the medical system, he had done it. He had become a monster who was unable to see himself as less than a god.

I took a long walk home, stopping once in a park to actually cry for the first time since being brought to the body of my friend and mentor a month ago. I wiped angrily at my eyes, glaring at the curious Londoners who stared at me, and then walked the rest of the way home.

On my front stoop, reminding me very much of the way I had found Annie Coleson last year, was Dr. Olsen.

"I came to say my goodbyes," she said, standing and shaking droplets of water off her coat and muff. "And to thank you for your work on this case, Miss Adams."

"Oh, I think at this point you should just call me Portia, don't you think, Cousin Heather?" I replied, opening the front door and inviting her in.

She stopped right on the threshold, and I continued to pull at my boots, allowing her time to compose herself.

I walked up the stairs, opening the door to Nerissa, who barked and jumped gleefully around me. The puddles of muddy water spoke of her earlier walk with the Dawes, and I made a mental note to thank them.

"Really, Heather, this house is as much yours as it is mine, so please do enter it," I called down the stairs without turning, patting Nerissa and refilling her food dish.

"You knew," said Dr. Olsen from my apartment doorway a moment later.

"Yes," I answered simply, giving Nerissa another scratch under her chin before hurling myself into my favorite chair with a satisfied, if tired, sigh.

When she said nothing more, I said, "Oh, do come in. The ghosts of our forefathers would approve."

"No, they wouldn't," she replied but stepped in.

"Yes, they would," I countered. "From what I've heard from the other Watsons, it was your father who was the black sheep of the family, not your mother and certainly not you."

She nodded slowly. "So you have ... talked to them about me?"

"I asked them about you, yes," I said. "The sons of Dr. John Watson who I have met are lovely and kind, much like their stepsister, my dear mother. I wish she could have known them. The Watsons are doctors, and each is happily married, with a gaggle of children; everything you would expect from such good stock as our grandfather."

She seemed to shrink at that. "And how did you know that I..." she started to say, finally taking a seat beside me.

"They know very little about you and your family, probably by your father's design," I replied, righting myself. "But they knew your father to be — forgive me — a lecherous, violent man who had driven away his wife and only daughter years ago."

She gulped audibly in response, and I stood to pour her a glass of water, which she accepted gratefully.

"It might interest you to know that they did try to find you and your mother, and that our grandfather spoke of you in his will," I said, "but your father did everything in his power to confuse their efforts, trying to get the money left to you for himself. And since your mother was trying to avoid your father, and he lived in London and you did not ... well, suffice to say, our uncles made sure your father did not get the money left to you."

She looked shocked but then sad with understanding. "He hated his brothers so much, and his father. Really anyone who succeeded and sought happiness."

I pointed at her cheek. "When I saw the bruise on your cheek, I made a petty remark about your husband, whom I have since learned you left a year ago. Just after your mother died."

She paled but nodded, her eyes downcast again.

"I assumed your husband had hit you, but it was your father again, wasn't it?" I asked, as gently as I could. "You came back to London upon separating from your husband and sought out your father. And at some point in your reunion he reverted to his normal state of rage and struck you?"

She nodded, her chin quivering, but pointed up. "He was drunk. As usual. And he hit me. Just like he used to hit Mum. I took my things and left. Moved into the hotel that same night and never looked back."

I nodded, watching Nerissa try to console the blonde doctor and loving my bloodhound for her sensitivity.

"So, it was the doctors Watson who told you who I was?" she asked, raising confused eyes.

"No, I haven't told them that I've actually met you," I answered, reaching for our grandfather's cane in the corner, the one she had been eyeing last time she was here. "I suspected something because you were reverential of the casebooks, but jealous of my connection to them."

I handed her the cane and leaned forward to my hearth, pulling at the secret handle that rotated the hidden shelf forward, and reached in to pull out a small diary.

"Our grandfather didn't just write about his exploits with Sherlock Holmes," I explained, pulling out a leaf I had inserted into the selected entry and handing the open diary to Olsen. "He also wrote about his first meeting with Mary, your grandmother."

She was scarcely breathing as I spoke.

"It turns out she had glorious silver blonde hair," I said with a smile. "I couldn't remember where I had seen hair like yours before till I met the newest member of the Watson family, who shares your freckles and hair color. It was Regulus, our uncle, who reminded me where those two inheritances come from."

She ran her finger over her grandfather's description of her grandmother, her smile widening.

"That's not all, you know," I said, drawing her eyes back to me. "Last time I was at the eldest Dr. Watson's house, I spent hours with his sons, my step-cousins, but your first cousins, I suppose. A fine brood to be sure. You have Scott's nose, and your eyes are very like little Samuel's."

"Really?" she whispered, clutching the cane and diary to her chest like a child.

I grinned. "Get your party shoes on, Cousin, we're going to the Watsons' for dinner tomorrow night. You're going to be quite the surprise!"

ACKNOWLEDGMENTS

I t's been an amazing year leading up to the publication of the third book in the Portia Adams series, and I am so grateful to all the fans and readers who have bought the books, reviewed them, and asked that they be stocked in their local libraries and so much more. I will never be able to thank you enough for your love and support. I only hope I can continue to be a part of your bookshelves, virtual and physical alike.

The Fierce Ink Books team continues to be fantastic to work with, and I am very lucky to be with them. Thank you so much Kat Kruger, Sarah Sawler, Allister Thompson, and Kim Hart Macneill.

Special thanks to my husband, Jason, and my son, Connor, for their love and support.

Keeping me on track on a daily basis is my friend Joyce Grant, who sits across from me working on her own fantastic books in the various cafes all over Toronto that host us. Joyce, you are the best!

There have been so many teachers and librarians who have supported my books since the first day of their publication, and I will never be able to repay them for that. This is especially true of Zelia Tavares and Kamla Rambaran, who worked with me this year on a mystery-writing workshop that their grade 6 classes knocked out of the ballpark. That workshop could not have happened without the Royal Ontario Museum's Kiron Mukherjee's brilliant help.

Beverly Wolov and Peter Blau are two brilliant Sherlockians who continue to help me in my research. Bev's knowledge of historical fashion and her willingness to read and correct my descriptions of the same have made this book an accurate representation of 1930s life.

The Bootmakers of Toronto and the Crime Writers of Canada have become dear friends in addition to being ardent supporters, and I am so pleased to have found them.

And just this year, Jael Richardson of the FOLD brought me into that fantastic group of creators, and I look forward to working with them for many years to come.

To all of my friends at the CBC, you serve as an inspiration to me each and every day — thank you.

The Canadian Children's Book Centre has seen fit to send me to Winnipeg this May for TD Book Week, so I am very grateful for that opportunity.

The Internets continue to be very kind to me in this process, so I am very thankful for my writers' groups (especially #write-o-rama on Facebook) and for all the folks who follow and comment on my blog and who invited me onto their websites for the blog tour.

Finally, thank you, dear reader, for buying *No Matter How Improbable!* If you get a chance, let me know what you think, on my blog, www.aportiaadamsadventure.com, and please do post a review on Amazon, Goodreads, or Chapters-Indigo.

Angela Misri is a Toronto journalist, writer and mom who has spent most of her working life making CBC Radio extraterrestrial through podcasts, live streams and websites. These days she's focusing on her writing but taking on freelance and digital projects along the side. Visit her blog at *www.aportiaadamsadventure.com*

Photo © Eugene Choi

Hair and makeup by Michelle Cho

PORTIA AS REVOLUTIONARY WOMAN

This is a fantastic moment in literary history when there are so many opportunities to read books with strong female protagonists, from Katniss Everdeen to Beatrice Prior to Cinder to my own Portia Adams.

In my head, I am forming a team of powerful women around Portia who will help her along at different parts of her ongoing story.

"Principessa" was born out of my love for the original Arthur Conan Doyle story, "An Illustrious Client," my favorite canon story for three reasons: it features Irene Adler, Sherlock Holmes is outsmarted by a woman who evades his capture and the complications of a client who is also royalty.

I set my story in Italy, where the rise of Fascism in the 1930s is slowly pushing the royal family out of power. The House of Savoy, which had ruled Italy since 1861, would be ousted by their people in a 1946 referendum. But in 1932, when my story is set, the tensions between the royal family, Mussolini and the pope were running high.

The main characters in "Principessa" are all women in different phases of life and power. Portia is the consulting detective from Baker Street who has become something of a curiosity to the people of London since the celebrity of her last case. Mrs. Elaine Ridley is a wealthy socialite who hires Portia to help her friend, the youngest princess of the House of Savoy, Maria Francesca, who is constrained by Nanny Pina.

It is through their experiences that you get a glimpse into what it was like to be a woman at that time. You see Portia, disguised as a maid for the purposes of investigation, and how she fits into the royal household. You see the independence of Elaine Ridley, a married woman with wealth who can travel the countryside with near impunity at this point. And you see a little of what it is like to be a princess, trapped within the boundaries of what is expected of a girl in the royal family.

When Portia comes back to London, she finds herself abandoned by her support system and struggles to find her footing. She reacts in the most Portia-like way, stubbornly marching through her daily work but feeling alone and hating that feeling. Women all around her were feeling the same way. With the economic woes of the Great Depression, more women were entering the workforce, putting off marriage and children and pushing the boundaries of their gender-enforced stereotypes.

Adler continues to be Adler, The Woman of such independence that she cares nothing for the social or legal constraints that would hold other women back — making her the best role model that Portia could have.

Portia and Annie are becoming sought-after in their fields, something that was reflected in the non-fiction world of the 1930s. This is the time of Dorothea Lange, American photographer of the Great Depression, and Maria Hagemeyer, who became a judge of the district court of Bonn in 1927.

In the final casebook, I introduce psychologist Heather Olsen, who is going to be a trusted member of team Portia in future stories. She brings an interesting element to Portia's casework that is both unappreciated and sorely needed.

The respect Sergeant Michaels shows to Dr. Olsen is important because, like most professions, it's not common to find women in psychology in the 1930s, even though the first woman to graduate with a PhD in psychology was Margaret Floy Washburn in 1894. I made sure that it was Portia who disdained Olsen's credentials and not a male character, to emphasize that she still needs to mature into her beliefs. Portia will be changed by this relationship, and in the best of ways.

I couldn't be more proud of Portia as she navigates the chilly waters of the male-dominated world of detective work and becomes part of the tide of revolutionary women rising in the 1930s.